Banshee

Hayden Thorne

Published by Hayden Thorne, 2019.

Also by Hayden Thorne

Arcana Europa
Guardian Angel
The Flowers of St. Aloysius
Hell-Knights
Children of Hyacinth
The Amaranth Maze
A Murder of Crows

Curiosities
Dollhouse
Automata
Eidolon

Dolores
Ambrose
Echoes in the Glass
A Dirge for St. Monica

Ghosts and Tea
The Ghosts of St. Grimald Priory
Agnes of Haywood Hall

A Most Unearthly Rival
The Haunted Inkwell
The House of Creeping Dolls

Grotesqueries
A Castle for Rowena
The Rusted Lily
Primavera

Masks
Masks: The Original Trilogy
Curse of Arachnaman
Mimi Attacks!
Dr. Morbid's Castle of Blood
The Porcelain Carnival

Standalone
Renfred's Masquerade
Rose and Spindle
Gold in the Clouds
Helleville
Icarus in Flight
Arabesque
Banshee
Wollstone
The Glass Minstrel
Henning
The Twilight Gods
The Book of Lost Princes
The Winter Garden and Other Stories

Desmond and Garrick
The Cecilian Blue-Collar Chronicles

Watch for more at https://haydenthorne.com.

Table of Contents

Chapter 1

I was six when the world shifted. It was 1838, the year of Her Majesty's coronation. A transition that—from all accounts—promised great changes, significant progress, perhaps a new era of prosperity for England.

Everyone I knew gave voice to their hopes. Yes, even in a tiny, insignificant village such as Gatcombe, nestled quietly in the rural detachedness of the Isle of Wight. People's expectations—already burdened by past wars and Bonaparte's threat only a few years before—had firmly fixed themselves on the slender, youthful shoulders of a new queen.

Lead us to a better place. Give us back our glory.

An adolescent monarch leading a new generation—folks in Gatcombe noted it and took great heart. Those of us who couldn't afford to go to London—that is, all of us—kept our eyes in the direction of the great city. Most drank to the queen's health, and most swore they could see a million explosions of fire lighting the night skies at the conclusion of that remarkable day. I myself saw nothing because it was all I could do to peer out of the window of the nursery, and all that met my gaze were shadows and darkness.

I'm much older now—nineteen years old, in fact—but I still look back to that year with great fondness and melancholy because it was also a year that marked a turning-point in my life. The effects might not be felt for several years afterward, but my sixth year of life was the time when my world expanded, and possibilities were suddenly allowed me. Not all of the effects were happy, but I've learned to welcome them—accept them—as an inextricable part of my youth.

Yes, even the darker, more frightening turns my adolescence had taken.

• • • •

WHEN MAMA FIRST ASKED Papa's permission to visit her brother and his family, I was surprised. I knew nothing about them, and being a mere child, I didn't really care to ask. I'd more pressing matters to attend to—my toys, books, and scattered local friends being the most important ones. Besides, Mama rarely talked about her family, and when she did, it was always with a distinct air of regret.

"It'll be good for Natty to widen his circle," she argued at the dinner-table. "Family should never be taken for granted, Frederick, especially with my brother's children being so nicely situated."

"Why—you haven't spoken with each other in years, Cecily."

Mama looked rueful. "I've written to them," she admitted, "and they wrote back, finally."

"Finally."

"Yes."

"How many times did you have to communicate with them before they decided it was worth their time to reply?" Papa prompted.

Mama shrugged, hesitated, but held his gaze. "Two. Maybe three. The point is, Frederick, they wrote back. I'm sorry I didn't tell you about my letters, but—"

"You waited till you heard from them."

"I'm sorry, my dear, but I really think it's time to mend things with Edward and Julia now that Papa's been gone for two years." Mama paused, coloring, and added, "Indeed, I waited till after he died. Taking a chance with my brother is far preferable to me. I know that Papa still wouldn't have welcomed me back after all these years. I'm sure you're convinced of that as well."

Papa at first looked doubtful and ate his soup in silence, frowning at his bowl and then at me as I held my breath and waited. Mama had said her piece and carried on with her meal, seemingly oblivious to the tension. The candles burnt their way down, forcing Mama to stop once and abandon her chair to search for her snuffers.

Papa never cared much for the way the wicks of tallow-candles curled into themselves as the flames consumed what they could, and Mama usually left those that illuminated the dining room alone. At that moment, however, she insisted on snuffing the wicks in the middle of a meal. I realized then she was nervous despite her calm front, and when Mama was anxious, it was difficult keeping her seated. The effects of her effort fascinated me, for they plunged the room into a dream-like state.

The candles' flames were brighter once Mama had done with them, but I'd always thought the dining room grew dimmer once she sat herself down again.

Our situation might be thought as modest, but Mama was an Ailesbury—the only daughter (albeit a disgraced one) of a baronet—and took it upon herself to ensure the vicarage's interior would never give visitors reason for derision or dismissive, patronizing praise. Our dining room, therefore, was refined in its decoration.

The walls were papered in red with colorful arabesques spreading, web-like, from end to end, top to bottom.

All the wood was dark, and the dramatic contrasts of wallpaper and chairs and table were further highlighted by the presence of the large sideboard against one wall, which Mama treasured above everything she owned.

China and silver—though humbler in design and value compared to those found in the great houses—lined every shelf with a rich assortment of shapes and decorations.

Mama had collected them since the day she eloped with Papa under threat of disinheritance, and she'd taken pride in displaying the triumphs of years past—triumphs in defiance of my grandfather's displeasure. All these she told me when I was older, and I recount them now with great fondness, considering the significance her past had given to something as simple as a collection of china. The middle cupboards held more dishes, and the bottom open shelves were lined with old books in faded leather.

During that moment of indecision, all these comfortable and familiar details appeared to melt into each other as the light softened—at least in my mind. I could swear the patterns in the wallpaper throbbed and slithered, wrapping around each other and moving as though they were swimming in thick red fluid. The dark wood of the table and chairs seemed to have turned black and death-like. Mama's delicately designed china appeared to glow, ghost-like, against the sideboard's shadowy form.

"Nathaniel, don't play with your soup. Eat it."

Her voice jolted me out of my temporary trance.

"I'm sorry, Mama," I said and quickly took in spoonful after spoonful of Dorcas' flavorful broth.

"Frederick, think of Natty and the opportunities," Mama insisted in her quiet way when the silence extended itself. "We can't have him spending every minute of his time with his nose in his books. The boy needs to be with children other than those in the village." She blushed when I frowned at her in my turn. What was wrong with my local friends, pray? "I think it'll be good for him to see more of the world outside Gatcombe and not be so timid toward those who are different from what he's used to. Why, the other day, I watched him playing by the road—"

"The road? Why was our son left to play by the road?" Papa interrupted. I'd never seen his eyes grow so big.

"—and Jack Burroughs drove by in his cart, laughing and whistling and calling out to Nathaniel, and the child ran away as though the very hounds of Hell were at his heels—"

"I'm not surprised. Jack Burroughs can send any sane creature running in terror from him."

"You understand my point, of course, Frederick."

Papa sighed and sank back down in his chair, his look of disapproval moving from Mama to me. "Why did you run from Mr. Burroughs, Natty?" he asked.

"He's loud and ugly, Papa," I replied, and he laughed. I grinned back and took in another spoonful of my soup.

Mama shook her head at us. Her eyes—large, expressive, brilliant—moved from Papa to me and back. "Do you see what I mean, my dear? That wasn't normal behavior."

"It's only one man, Cecily. That doesn't say much about Nathaniel save for the fact that he's an astute judge of character," Papa said in his most persuasive tone. "I'm familiar with Jack Burroughs' vices well enough to know I wouldn't wish my son to be too friendly with him."

Mama's face clouded. "The boy just complained about the man's loudness and ugliness. Since when did being loud and ugly turn a man into a villain? All they say about Mr. Burroughs is that he speaks in a most uncomfortable volume, and he's not handsome."

Papa waved his hand. "Stop being so literal," he said. "A child can only communicate so much. I daresay Natty knows a great deal more than that."

"One would assume being a vicar entitles you to exert a strong influence for good. Rather than judge the man, Frederick, perhaps you ought to fix your mind on saving him from himself."

"Cecily..."

"It was only a suggestion, of course."

"Indeed. I'll keep that in mind for my next sermon, my dear. Thank you." He sat back in his chair and sighed again. "Very well. I don't know how long you intend on staying with your brother—"

Mama's eyes lit up. "A month at most," she quickly replied. "Unless you prefer otherwise."

"A month will be fine for the boy. For both of you, really." Papa chuckled when Mama abandoned her chair and hurried to his side to embrace him and give him a kiss—a spontaneous, girlish display of affection that I'd never seen before. He patted her back awkwardly as she held him close, his grin broadening. "Now, now, you infant. It's not as though I just released you from prison."

Mama laughed. The meal continued in lighter conversation, with my parents engaging each other quite nicely.

I'd long finished with my meal, but I remained where I sat, enthralled by the cheerful and loving exchanges between them. When the meal was done and Papa stood up to lead us out of the dining room, I realized the candles' flames were flickering quite badly, and Mama didn't care to use her snuffers.

• • • •

MY COUSINS WERE CHILDREN of Mama's oldest brother, Edward Augustus Ailesbury—or Sir Edward Ailesbury, for he was a baronet who was hardly known hereabouts for his title and even less so for his accomplishments. It was a fact that offended him, from what I understood, perhaps because he felt quite cut off from the rest of England's gentry by suffering the indignity of owning impressive property in a small island.

His family lived in relative splendor in Havenstreet, compared to our cloistered and limited existence in Gatcombe. The afternoon of our arrival at Northwode Hall, I was left in the drawing room with my cousins. Meanwhile, Mama, my uncle, and my aunt shut themselves away for a longish conversation.

I must confess to being nearly struck dumb by the vastness of the room and its remarkable ornamentation. The drawing room in the vicarage was only half the size of my uncle's, and it couldn't boast anything close to half the amount of furnishings and miscellaneous objects that my uncle's drawing room contained.

The walls were covered from floor to ceiling with red paper decorated with a darker red webbing of iris-shaped patterns. The carpet underfoot filled my vision with a field of dark green roses, leaves, and vines. The large mantelpiece gleamed in all its heavy, mahogany glory, an equally large mirror sitting atop it, framed in intricately carved and gilded wood.

An old ancestral portrait that hung on the opposite wall was captured in the glass. I couldn't help but feel as though I were being watched from both sides by a silent and disapproving aunt under a hideous white wig from a century ago.

Thankfully the drawing room was blessed with several tall windows that drew in light from outside, helping break up such oppressive grandeur.

On a stiffly cushioned chair I sat, half-puzzled, half-dizzy, and rendered speechless by my companions' imposing (so I then thought) presence. Edward, Marianne, and Vincent circled me like carrion at first, staring me up and down and exchanging whispered remarks about what they saw before giggling softly.

Edward, who was the oldest at thirteen and therefore the unchallenged leader, marched confidently toward my chair and began to stick his finger at me—my chest, my forehead, my stomach, my arm, and my knee—declaring with every thrust, "You're a fine thing, aren't you? Do you like to sleep with your father's Bible? Do you let your mother dress you like a baby? You probably cry like a baby, I reckon! Will you cry now if I do this? Or this?"

I took everything he did to be nothing more than a stupid joke, though I remained puzzled as to how I was expected to laugh at his silly bullying. All the same, I thought to play the meek, subservient outcast to his masterful dominance.

"Yes, sir," I replied. When I raised a hand in a reflexive move to ward off a particularly hard stab against my chest, my cousin slapped it away.

"Here, stop!" he cried. "You baby! I knew you're too soft."

I crossed my arms on my chest. "Might I go to my room, please?"

"Might? May! You may if you give us..." Edward paused, frowned deeply, and then turned to Marianne.

"How much should it be?"

"A thousand pounds!"

"A thousand pounds," my cousin said, once again looking down at me with a broad grin. "Can you manage that?"

"I don't think Mama brought that much with her," I said.

Edward threw his hands up in mock resignation. "Then I'm sorry for you." He continued his assault on my person to the delight of his brother and sister, reshaping his taunts into a tuneless nonsensical song.

"Hey do! How do! Ponies on a string! Hee now! How now! Natty's gone to sing!"

"Pinch his cheeks, Edward!" Marianne cried, clapping her hands.

When Edward reached forward to torment my left cheek, I turned and bit his hand. He cried out in pain and snatched his hand away, nearly tearing my head off my shoulders because I dug my teeth firmly into his skin.

"Oh! You filthy brute!" he exclaimed, staring in horror at his wet hand, now exhibiting small, reddish teeth marks. Flushing, he glared at me and gave me a box on the ear before running out of the room with threats of getting me flogged by my uncle.

Vincent and Marianne remained behind, looking stunned. They were silent for a moment before Marianne followed her brother out in a rush of silk and ribbon and a high squeal of "Edward! Can we ride our horses now?"

Vincent lingered for a bit, scratching the back of his head as he stared at the door.

Then he turned to me and laughed. "Capital! Capital! You savage little puppy!" he cried, taking one of my hands and shaking it vigorously. Still laughing, he followed his brother and sister out, his hands in his pockets, his pace idle.

"May I ride with you? Can you show me how to ride? I promise I won't be a nuisance!" I called out, but all I heard back were Vincent's receding footsteps.

I shook my head and sighed once I was alone. "Blockheads," I grumbled. Thank heaven my parents weren't there to hear me. That was one of those unfortunate words I'd learned while playing with some of our neighbors' children in Gatcombe. I leapt off the chair and ran in the direction of my uncle's gardens, delighting in the prospect of so much space and solitude.

• • • •

UNCLE EDWARD NEVER flogged me. Indeed, he found the incident rather humorous and even said so over dinner that same day.

"What a sprightly little imp you are!" He laughed, his voice shaking the walls around us. I thought I saw some of the portraits lining the expansive dining room tremble in their elaborate frames. I discovered later on he was quite drunk that evening; in fact, he was a remarkable drinker. "Oh, ho! I daresay you're suitably defended against Satan's forces, eh, Nathaniel? You've learned much from the Bible, I see!"

"Edward, please!" Aunt Julia hissed from her end of the table. She turned a dark, disapproving gaze from her husband to me. Had she been given a chance, perhaps she'd have flogged me, herself.

I glanced at Mama, who sat beside me. She looked sufficiently mortified. I tapped her arm, muttering, "I'm sorry, Mama."

"Oh, Natty," she whispered back, shaking her head at me and looking so despondent that I nearly sank to my knees beside her and begged for forgiveness. "What were you thinking? Your papa and I aren't raising a savage. I expect you to apologize to your cousin after dinner."

I apologized again, and she sighed and turned her attention back to her dinner.

My cousin Edward sulked as much as my aunt. I knew then I was meant to suffer at his hands from that moment on. To be sure, Vincent warned me about that before dinner.

"You offended a gentleman," he'd said with a sly little grin, "and a gentleman never takes an insult so lightly."

Chapter 2

Vengeance was, indeed, Edward's, and it came quickly. Precisely a day and a half after my arrival, in fact. I was in my uncle's library when Edward and Vincent decided to include me in their game.

"There you are!" Vincent cried as he peered through the door. I lay on the floor near the window, stretched out on my stomach. A monstrous atlas had caught my attention, and I'd lost myself utterly within its massive and discolored pages. "Come, cousin, we need you! Come along!"

I stared at him and hesitated. "What for?"

Vincent's head vanished for a few seconds, and I heard a low hum of voices beyond the door. I suppose at this point logic should have intervened and warned me to unlatch one of the windows and remove myself from the library as quickly as I could, but I was a slave to curiosity.

"Here," Edward declared with much authority as he pushed his way through the door, a white dress—or a dress that had been white once upon a time—draped over his arm, the rest of its bulk dragging across the floor. Behind him Vincent marched, his hands clasped behind his back.

"What's that?" I asked.

"Take that book away," he ordered, and Vincent walked over to me and confiscated the atlas and threw it down on the floor, kicking it away. "Now come here."

"Go on. We haven't got all day," Vincent urged with a sharp tug on my coat.

I scrambled to my feet and reluctantly approached Edward. My gaze was fixed in vague fascination on the dress, which was of a filthy yellow hue that reminded me of disease. A few spots of brown here and there looked ominous though I wouldn't have been able to guess their possible origins.

I stood before my cousin, who dusted off the dress with sharp sweeps of his hand, his face pinched in concentration.

"Here!" The horrid thing was flung over me, and I was suddenly engulfed in a sea of rotting silk and lace.

The weight of the dress muffled my cries of disgust and horror. I swung my arms about, grabbing and punching and tearing.

"Stop that! Fool!" Edward retorted from somewhere outside. "You'll ruin this thing!"

I felt the dress tugged here and there till my head somehow managed to slip through the neck hole, and I was dizzily staring at my cousins once again. The dress hung loose around me, stained silk spilling onto the floor and flowing outward and around me like a tiny pond of decay and time.

Edward and Vincent walked in a thoughtful circle like a pair of scientists closely observing a strange artifact. They hardly spoke above a whisper, touching and pointing at details here and there, nodding and looking quite intelligent as they carried on.

At length they stopped.

"We found this dress upstairs," Edward said, looking at me. "And we wanted to see if the rumors were true."

"What rumors?" I pressed, shifting from one foot to another and listening to the heavy rustling of old silk when I moved.

"This dress was worn by a great-aunt. She died a long time ago—threw herself out the window when she was tossed aside for another woman. Those brown stains? Her blood, cousin. She was wearing this dress when she died from what I hear." Edward grinned and leaned closer. "And you're in it now."

How I managed to tear the ghastly thing off me, I couldn't recall. I was free of it in a moment, however, amid my cousins' loud whoops of laughter. Parts of the dress were torn, and I stood on that dreadful pile of discolored silk, stamping my feet in a mad effort to obliterate its existence under my weight.

Then I lunged at my cousins and struck Edward quite hard with a tightly balled fist. He walked about with a faint bruise under his left eye for a day or two, I think.

Mama was furious and refused to speak with me while I served my punishment: three days of isolation in my assigned room.

I dreamt of her, however. Every night for three nights, I dreamt that she crept into my room under the cover of darkness, knelt on the floor beside my bed, and watched me for a moment. She said nothing, made no other sound but the soft rustling of her skirts against the floor.

Perhaps the most curious thing about these recurring dreams was the palpable air of sadness that marked her presence, and somehow, I was convinced it had nothing to do with my behavior and its embarrassing consequence.

The sadness, I believed then, was one that wasn't fixed in the present, but in another point in time entirely. It was an odd conclusion, brought about by an odd sensation and a quiet voice in my mind.

• • • •

HETTY WAS THE GIRL into whose care I was deposited.

She was, I believe, no more than seventeen then. A typical country lass, admirably robust and vigorous, her freckled complexion frozen in a perpetual flush. She became my dearest friend for the remaining time I spent at my uncle's. After my fit of hysterics in the library (the purported bloody wedding-dress being whisked away and hidden in some secret room in the house), Hetty was there to raise my spirits since Aunt Julia had ordered my cousins to keep their distance from me lest I tear them all to pieces before the month's end.

Hetty scolded me for giving vent to my fury and comforted me with kind words and a tray of tea and cakes. I was to have my tea in my room alone, according to Aunt Julia—less risk of my emptying a bottle of poison into my cousins' cups, I suppose. Hetty demonstrated a familial sort of fondness for me, something which I'd never before expected.

"You remind me of my littlest nephew," she said one quiet afternoon as she watched me put up a gallant front gnawing through a piece of dry and tasteless cake. She sat on a chair next to my bed, one that was uncomfortably far too small for her. It was a miracle that she didn't fall off.

I looked at her in some surprise. That was the first time she'd made any reference to her family, but I suppose my guilt was that I never thought to ask.

"Do you see him often?"

Hetty smiled impishly. "I really don't want to see him at all, to be sure, Master Natty."

"Why not? Is he very disagreeable?" I frowned. If I reminded her of her nephew, did it mean I was hopelessly disagreeable as well?

"No, no! Indeed, poor Jack was as far from being disagreeable then as he is now! My brother's little boy lies in the churchyard of St. Margaret's."

"Oh. Dead, Hetty?"

She nodded, her smile softening as she turned her gaze to her hands. "Been four years now, I reckon. Very sensitive boy, Jack was. Very sickly."

I hesitated, dismayed by the comparison. "I'm like him?"

"When he lived, of course! You silly thing!" She laughed heartily. "Jack had a good deal of fire in him, like you, but his poor little body was too weak for his spirit."

"I don't think I like fire. It gives me nothing but trouble."

Hetty regarded me with a thoughtful tilt of her head. "But it's your nature, Master Natty."

"No one likes my nature." I hesitated. "I make Mama too sad."

"Ah, but I do! And so does your papa, and I'm sure your mama does, too." She pointed at my little plate. "Now, come. You need to finish your cake and to stop sulking. If you go on like this, I can't take you out to the garden for a quick walk."

"Can I go riding sometime?"

Hetty laughed again. "All you need to do is ask your uncle. To be sure, Master Vincent's been talking about showing you Ares—his pony. Master Edward might not like you, but his brother does." Giggling softly, she leaned forward and whispered, "He said that you're a damned fine soldier."

"You really shouldn't use bad words, Hetty. If you don't get flogged for it now, you'll have your tongue buried in hot coals after you die."

"My stars, where did you get such an idea? Your papa?"

I shrugged and picked at another piece of cake. "No one. I just made it up."

Unfortunately, any schemes of riding were quickly dashed because Vincent fell out of a tree and sprained his ankle badly. I'd nothing to do with his accident and made sure my aunt knew it. She said nothing, but I could tell she still disapproved of me, regardless, though she took care not to show it in Mama's company.

Hetty and I began our daily walks in the garden, taking care to avoid my cousins. To do this we confined our time outside to a small area that was the least frequented as its location in my uncle's estate offered no promising prospects. That is, it faced low hills sparsely dotted with sad-looking trees, the only indication of human existence being the rotting shell of a burnt farmhouse to the east.

Little by little, Hetty coaxed me out of my boredom with teasing references to stories her grandparents had shared with her.

"If you do this for me, I'll tell you about this" and its thousand and one variations, depending on the situation at hand, was her magic spell. I was hungry enough for friendlier exchanges with anyone in that household to encourage her schemes.

I was far too young to care for idle stories about my uncle's family—my nurse proved to be an insatiable gossip—so Hetty regaled me with a host of unusual stories her grandparents told her when she was about my age.

The fascination I felt was childish at best because these tales were macabre, filled with some of the most dreadful situations involving supernatural forces that most rational adults would easily have dismissed. Ghosts, demons, goblins, creatures that stalked homes, forests, lonely roads, all hungry for revenge, salvation, or simple human contact, peopled these tales.

"They're not real!" I argued once.

"Oh, but they are! My grandfather saw spirits wandering through an old churchyard when he was younger."

"What for?"

"Why, they never knew that they were dead, of course! They moved around at night as they did when they were still alive!"

"But why wouldn't they know?"

Hetty pressed a finger against her lips to caution me.

"Because," she replied, her voice dropping, "there are those who simply can't let go. They're attached too closely to something or someone, and they can't move on to the other side even after they die."

"Someone?" I echoed, horrified. "People are haunted, too?"

"They can be, yes. Sometimes there are specters that appear before people actually die."

I shuddered. "No, there aren't! That's silly!"

"Oh, but there are! I'm not talking about a banshee, either, which is the spirit of a woman—a fairy woman, really—haunting a family to warn them of someone's death."

"That's not possible. You can't haunt anyone unless you're dead. Where else can the ghost come from?"

Hetty merely shook her head, smiling indulgently. "To be sure, Master Natty, I can't say where the specter comes from. Does it appear as a warning? Does it appear because the person marked for death wishes to die so badly? Or does it appear because whoever sees it wishes for someone else to die so badly? Sometimes desperation—if you feel it so deeply like it's tightly wrapped around your core—turns into something quite unexpected."

I swallowed. "Have you seen something that's like a banshee but isn't?"

"No."

I sighed and waved her away, grumbling at her silly attempt at trickery, while she laughed, an odd sparkle in her eyes.

By the time daylight waned and evening crept into my room, I'd be walking around in a strange daze, half-terrified and half-excited by all kinds of dark possibilities. The shadows that slithered soundlessly from behind the furniture or from the corners of the room suddenly dragged me into their world.

I watched them flit across the floor or raise themselves up along the walls. I wondered where they fled in the day, how their dark world carried on with every passing minute. I wondered if they watched me sleep or read my books by the window.

Hetty didn't have many stories about them, so I made up my own as I lay in bed, waiting for sleep to claim me.

They became the heroes of my crude nursery tales and led me into one grand adventure after another. With black, shapeless fingers they tugged at my nightshirt and pointed me in one direction or another, unknown journeys apparently lying in wait.

In all those adventures, I was the fortunate traveler who dogged their steps with awed fascination, watching them conquer my uncle's massive, elaborate garden on black steeds. Or, with their drawn swords, drive the hellish forces of my cousins back indoors and the cowardly warmth of a thousand candles.

Or, with silent gallantry, shield a pair of servants with a handsome black cloak as they spent brief, stolen minutes in the garden together.

Those were my little games, and for a time, I enjoyed them. Every so often I even thought to entertain my nurse with my creations, and I became a storyteller of dubious skill but of impressive imagination. I provided crude illustrations for my stories, which she happily accepted.

"There!" I said with a proud smile as I held up a torn sheet of paper with a drawing of a fiery horse.

"You're as good as Master Edward!" she cried, but I doubted it, not having seen anything from my cousin that vaguely resembled a drawing. "I like it!"

I frowned. "You aren't supposed to like it. It's the Devil's steed, galloping through the moors."

"Ah! And what's it supposed to do?"

"I don't know," I replied with a bewildered shrug. "Eat things? What do demon horses do when they're not in the fiery pit?"

"Run around, I reckon—cause all sorts of trouble. I'm sure, Master Natty, that your demon horse can gallop up walls and over roofs."

I blinked. "Are you certain?"

"Why, of course! Anything that belongs to the Devil can do all sorts of horrible things. Surely your papa would agree."

I stared doubtfully at my drawing, shocked that I just managed to illustrate something quite horrific. I was ready for some hair-raising tales, but imagining a black horse cloaked with fire that galloped up walls and over roofs conquered my will, and I quickly reshaped the drawing into something less terrible. In the end, it turned into a horned snake with a tail tipped with fire.

When I felt lively enough, I'd put on a little production by throwing a blanket over my head and crawling all over the floor, moaning and sighing and doing what I could to become a convincing shadow character.

Hetty, bless her, understood my aim well enough to play along, pretending surprise or terror when required and, in the end, becoming a significant part of my little world of make-believe.

By taking chilling fireside themes and shaping them with my own vision, I'd managed to overcome my initial fears of the unknown and the supernatural—or at the very least learned to minimize their effects. I continued to jump at sudden movements or feel my skin crawl at certain nocturnal sounds. Or I'd hide, suffocating, under my blankets when my imagination overreached itself, but I also found recovery to be quicker.

The gradual shift in my behavior encouraged Hetty, and she rewarded me with more cake and supernatural tales. For all her efforts, though, I'd grown to prefer my own little tales of shadow adventures.

• • • •

THE MONTH CAME TO AN end, and I regretted leaving Northwode Hall. Though I hardly spent time with my cousins as Mama had at first hoped, I still felt buoyed and refreshed, my imagination burning. I asked her if we could take Hetty back with us.

"Natty," she said, sighing, as my uncle's carriage took us back to Gatcombe, "I hope that you'll understand the importance of this visit someday and how your remarkable behavior nearly affected all my hopes."

"Oh—is it very important, Mama?"

"More so than you think, dearest, but I won't talk any more about it."

She smiled at me then—a familiar, comforting smile.

The day was brilliant, warm, and cheerful, but I suddenly felt a wave of coldness sweep over me. My skin prickled, and my spirits sagged under an odd sense of desolation. I slid down my seat and climbed next to Mama. With a sigh, she pulled onto her lap and embraced me, pressing my head against her while she quietly sang a lullaby.

I held her tightly all the way home, falling asleep against her breast while feeling her arms around me, securing me with warmth.

• • • •

MAMA AND I VISITED Northwode Hall thrice more afterward—a surprise to me, given my wild behavior the first time around. In fact, I expected to be forbidden to step within the borders of Havenstreet, but I'd been forgiven, for the most part, that is, and welcomed back.

Uncle Edward had taken to me well enough, I suppose, but Aunt Julia kept her distance. Edward, being several years older than I, had gone on to mingle with the larger, more fashionable world around them before he vanished within university walls. He didn't have time for me, and he didn't seem to care much for the loss.

Vincent, who was two years younger than his brother, had a friendlier disposition, though he knew my place well enough to enjoy a good joke or two at my expense.

As for Marianne, who was a year younger than Vincent, she simply ignored me, all her attention bent on her coming-out and all the preparations that, I suppose, were required of her. Her governess, Aunt Julia, and another lady from their circle—one who traveled often to Paris, bringing back all kinds of fashion trends for Marianne—became her world. Marianne happily lost herself in the attention and all the fussing over her appearance and deportment.

I was pleased to see Hetty again, though she was no longer charged to be my temporary nurse. I was on my own, having shown myself to be much improved in temper and no longer in need of a guardian. I missed our stories, I must confess, and when she left Northwode Hall for Suffolk and a new employer, I was so despondent that I didn't care to remain with my cousins.

I was eight, ten, and thirteen during those visits. When Edward first and then Vincent left for Oxford, my visits stopped, but Mama's didn't. She continued to see Uncle Edward and Aunt Julia though for only a weekend or half a week at most.

All her visits, in fact, coincided with lavish dinner-parties or balls that my aunt and uncle occasionally held. Papa was invited, but he always refused, giving his parish duties for his excuse. He allowed Mama to go, however, having seen how much pleasure her visits to Havenstreet gave her, and Aunt Julia became her constant companion in Papa's absence.

Her visits delighted me. When she returned home, Mama was always refreshed, almost as though she'd shed several years and had gone back to the height of her youth. In fact, at times I could barely recognize her. Her complexion glowed, her eyes sparkled with a bright light, and her humor was utterly infectious. She recounted her adventures at the dinner-table with so much spirit and energy that Papa and I were always reduced to amused and awed listeners.

"Do you remember Lady So-and-So and Lord This-and-That?" she'd ask Papa.

"Yes, I believe I do," he'd answer, and from there a steady litany of accounts would come flying out of Mama's lips.

"Sir Joseph Wellham was there, Frederick. Can you believe that he still visits Havenstreet? He's so altered now, though—I never would've recognized him had Julia not presented him to me."

"An old rival of mine, eh?" Papa laughed. "What a pity it is, then, that Natty didn't come with you, Cecily. You'd have presented the boy, boasted about your family, and declared yourself the happiest woman on earth."

Mama laughed with him. "I did! I did! Sir Joseph wasn't pleased, I think."

Past acquaintances and friends, some of them being former suitors of Mama, would come alive in the course of conversation. Papa indulged her, listening with a smile and laughing in turn, at times giving a clever or sly observation regarding a defeated rival of his, for which Mama would blush and scold him playfully.

You had so many gentlemen pursuing you, and yet you chose me, Papa seemed to say, and even though I was quite young then, I still felt a surge of pleasure and comfort in his triumph over his wealthier rivals.

"I've made peace with my brother at last," she once told me when I was around twelve, I believe, her features all aglow as she set her sewing-basket on her lap.

"Were they very angry with you, Mama?" I prodded from where I sat on the floor, close to her chair, a small pile of books before me.

She nodded. Her eyes twinkled in the candlelight as she smiled at me, her manner surprisingly open and relaxed.

Papa was away visiting a sick neighbor and wasn't expected back till after dinner. I suspected his absence contributed to her almost childish ease in the way she communicated with me.

"They were, I'm afraid, dearest, but I'll tell you my story in time. Not now."

"Are they angry with Papa?"

"A little less so, but don't worry about that. I'm happy, and so is he."

"Is he forgiven now, too?"

She hesitated for a fraction of a second, but I sensed it as though it were an hour. "Of course, he is!"

"What did you do to upset Grandpapa?"

Mama drew her shoulders back and regarded me with a faint smile. "I loved prudently, Nathaniel. I hope to see you do the same someday."

The candlelight flickered, and Mama set her basket aside, stood up, and swept across the room with her beloved snuffers. She appeared so content and pleased with herself doing something as simple as trimming a candle's wick that I simply couldn't imagine her in any capacity other than a modest vicar's wife, who worried about proper illumination.

Chapter 3

---

atcombe, Isle of Wight, 1849

G   I was seventeen when an opportunity for travel asserted itself through a letter from Vincent, of all people.

All my friends (save for perhaps three) have taken up that vile yoke called marriage, and I'm left to my own devices. Papa and Mama have joined the damnable chorus of 'for better or for worse,' and I'm determined to keep my independence for as long as I can. Besides, I've yet to meet a lady who's tolerable enough in beauty at the very least.

That said, I'm about to embark on a new adventure up north, and I've marked Somerset for my conquest—Exmoor, to be more specific. I daresay you'll be a good traveling-companion, Nathaniel, considering the tame beauty of that countryside. I thought of you, in fact, when I made my plans, given your childishly pensive nature, and I expect a visit to the pretty cottages and picturesque moors will draw out the poet in you and reshape your character into something more colorful and less sulky.

I've one friend from university who'll be traveling with us. It was he who helped me settle on a destination, for his family owns some property in Liscombe, and we're to be his guests there. Whether or not you're able to get along with him is no concern of mine, of course, for two companions on such a long journey are far better than one, and I, at least, am guaranteed conversation from either of you should the third fellow grow tedious.

We leave in five days.

"Pensive?" I echoed as I reread the missive. "How was I pensive?" An obsession with my uncle's old atlas made for a sober, thoughtful bent, I suppose.

I showed my parents the letter, and it was unanimously well-received, though Papa objected to Vincent's tone. "Arrogant pup," he muttered, shaking his head and scowling. Then he sighed. "But I suppose it would do you much good to get out there in the world and experience the best alongside the worst, Natty."

"Vincent's a good fellow, Papa."

"I suppose he is. University conceit shows itself in the worst possible way. I sometimes fear for you, Nathaniel, if you choose to take that road. Young aristocrats—they make the worst students imaginable and are more than capable of corrupting the saintliest of the lot."

I suppressed a grin. "Have you any advice before my cousin ruins my dreams of adventure forever?"

"Nothing more than this—keep your head, no matter what." Papa managed a weak smile in return. "But somehow I feel that I shouldn't worry about you despite your present protection. I sense it here." He pressed a hand against his stomach.

"I exasperated you when I played outdoors."

"As a child, you did. I won't deny that. You're a young man now, though. I suppose it would do me a world of good to let you fly on your own and trust your Mama's and my efforts at raising a good man."

I noted that he didn't say "good Christian" as he used to do, when I was much younger. It took me some time to understand Papa's complexity. I wrote back to Vincent and spent the next few days preparing for my journey.

• • • •

WE KEPT TWO SERVANTS then—Dorcas and Stephen, two of the most loyal helpers an employer could ever hope to have. They'd been with us since Mama was big with me, and not once did they falter in their duties, but I cared nothing for that. They were far more than servants to me, and in my youth, I sometimes feared the possibility of their abandoning us the way Hetty had abandoned Northwode Hall. Their behavior was reassurance enough of their devotion, but I couldn't help myself all the same.

Loss was a most repugnant idea to me. I could endure the loss of friends to marriage or work or, sadly, illness, but I could never reconcile myself to the loss of anyone in our household. I suppose losing Hetty was the closest I'd come to losing someone I loved the most.

It was rather odd, really, that I grew so attached to her in such a short time. Perhaps, in my own childish way, I'd fallen in love with the girl—or perhaps fancied that I had.

Unlike Hetty, Dorcas in her youth was thin and almost delicate-looking. No color touched her complexion, and no shadow darkened her hair, which was of a pale yellow hue.

Even her eyes were a light blue and were fringed with lashes that one had to strain to see. Her movements were a perfect match as she seemed to flit from one room to another, barely making a sound—yes, even when she was engaged in heavy work.

Dorcas, bless her, grew more doting with every passing year. She alternately coddled and reprimanded me, at times perhaps risking her position when I proved to be too much trouble.

"You'll not wander away from your companions. You won't sample any of those disgusting pleasures that promise you nothing more than a life of vice. Better to avoid being placed in a situation where you can be tempted, Natty! Good heavens, but young people nowadays can be so reckless!"

She chattered on and on as she busied herself in the kitchen, preparing things for me to eat while on the road.

In truth, though, I'd only asked for an almond cake, and she kindly obliged, turning one thing into a virtual banquet by cutting the cake into smaller and more manageable pieces for consumption. I couldn't help but think of the miracle of the two bread loaves and jokingly referred to them when she "miraculously" turned one cake into several.

"I swear to return no less virtuous than I am now, Dorcas," I replied as I sampled a piece, earning myself a sharp crack of a spoon against my hand.

"If thieving like this is what you call virtuous, I'd hate to see you come back altered for the worse," she said, her round face (she'd grown plump in her older years) creasing in a frown.

I laughed as I gingerly rubbed my hand.

"I think being with Vincent hour after hour will cure me of any desire I might have of sampling danger."

"You shouldn't have any desire in the first place, you saucy boy."

"No, I suppose you're right." I stood up, still laughing, and gave her a grand bow. "I promise not to stray. I'll remain as meek and innocent as you now see me and return with nothing but stories to share."

Dorcas snorted as she carefully wrapped the pieces of cake for me. "God save the world from young rascals like you."

• • • •

I WAS EXCITED—A GREAT deal more than I cared to confess, even to myself. Though I was quite calm and settled throughout my preparations, I couldn't ignore the wild hammering of my heart as I fixed my mind on Somerset and the road that would take me there. I'd long been aware of its great literary heritage.

Our little library served as sanctuary to a few volumes of Wordsworth's poetry, and I often lost myself between their pages and poetic images of rustic idylls long gone. True, my youth and inexperience in complex reading left me quite bewildered as to Wordsworth's more beguiling and cryptic passages. But I took what I could, anyway, and seared in my mind all those charming pictures of simple country life.

With Papa's guidance, I'd taken to "The Ruined Cottage" and "Michael" with an appetite that must have been rare in a boy my age. The poems entranced me with their elegiac imagery and language. I spent the evening before my departure copying both poems in my little pocket-journal, destroying my wrist, my back, and my eyesight in hopes of referring to them when the right moment came.

I'd convinced myself I'd be spending quite a bit of time sitting on the hillside, lost in contemplation as Wordsworth perhaps used to do. Those were to be the most ideal times to reread those beloved verses and reflect upon them.

I left the following morning, my spirits bursting with anxiety, excitement, and even sadness at leaving my family behind. I fought to keep myself from looking out the window once my uncle's carriage—thoughtfully sent to the vicarage at Vincent's orders—lurched into movement, knowing the sight of my parents standing at the doorstep with Dorcas and Stephen would only cause my resolve to waver.

A voice in my mind took to whispering something about some fear I might have of blessing my family with a final glimpse of me in my youthful naïveté because the person I'd surely become on my return would fall far short of their expectations and hope.

"Better not to let them see you as a child," the voice said. "What remembrances they might have ought to suffice—safe in the haven of the vicarage, not of you smiling and waving at them as you ride off to be devoured by the world."

I consoled myself with Dorcas' cakes, grateful for the privacy of being the carriage's only occupant and wondering how many of these vehicles my uncle owned. I later learned he owned two.

By the time I arrived at Northwode Hall, I'd consumed nearly half of the cut-up pieces. I was certain it wouldn't please Dorcas because she'd expressly forbidden me from eating more than three at a time. To my credit, I didn't become ill from my gluttony and was in very cheerful spirits when I stood before the great house.

My aunt and uncle were away visiting friends, and they'd taken Edward and Marianne with them. They were expected back at Northwode Hall that evening, which made Vincent's desire to leave all the greater.

"We ought to leave after lunch, cousin," he said almost breathlessly as he linked arms with me, nearly dragging me along with his long and hurried stride. "Nothing could be worse than to be caught by the family. I'd already put up with all sorts of damnable sermons last night and this morning. For sanity's sake, I'd like to ride off in the early afternoon."

"As you wish." I replied, panting. "Where are we going?"

"Right now, to the drawing room. You need to meet the third of our party." I glanced at Vincent and caught him looking at me from the corner of his eyes, his brows raised. "Surely you remember that bit about my friend coming with us?"

"Yes, of course."

In truth, I'd nearly forgotten about him, so caught up was I with the thought of Exmoor and its untamed beauties. As I struggled to keep up with my cousin's pace, my heart sank. This third member of our party was a university friend. He was, therefore, most likely no less troublesome than my cousin.

In a mild state of panic, I began to entertain all sorts of scenes involving endless debauches—wine, women, perhaps even gambling—with me caught and made useless by my age and, yes, dependence on my cousin's knowledge of the world.

I winced when we finally reached the drawing room door, and Vincent quickly knocked and flung the door open, sweeping across the threshold with me on his arm.

How would I manage two drunken men if the situation were to arise? What would I do if both of them were to be embroiled in some sort of difficulty of an amorous nature?

I was seventeen. They were both twenty-two, my cousin's friend perhaps older, perhaps a little younger, than Vincent. I could see them easily sidestepping one sordid situation after another, given their experience, while I'd be knocked about in my own stupid way.

"God help me," I whispered, closing my eyes from the possibilities.

"Come, come. Nathaniel, this is my friend, Miles Lovell. He's been my guest for the past fortnight, and I'm about to be his."

I blinked my eyes open and rested my gaze on a gentleman standing a few feet away, regarding me with unmistakable confusion. He stood a little taller than Vincent.

His figure was lean, his movements and mannerisms refined and exquisitely controlled. There was a certain graceful negligence in the way he carried himself—an aristocratic ease that was haughty, and yet not.

I couldn't help but stare, puzzled by the way he so easily captured and held my attention without trying. His dark eyes moved between me and Vincent and then back, and I saw the faintest crease forming between his brows. It was gone in a moment, and he stepped forward to offer his hand.

"A pleasure, Nathaniel," he said, his voice still betraying his bewilderment. He suddenly paused and blushed. "Forgive the impropriety of using your Christian name, but I was never told of your surname."

"Nathaniel Frederick Wakeman, sir," I said, grasping his hand and shaking it tentatively. His manner proved to be infectious, and I found myself glancing at Vincent in growing confusion as well. Was something wrong? Had I done something wrong?

Mr. Lovell appeared to have read my thoughts, for he kept staring at me as though studying an unusual specimen. He shook his head and laughed lightly. "Forgive me, Master Wakeman, if I disconcerted you. I was just surprised. I knew that you were coming, but I never expected you to be so young."

It was my turn to frown. Vincent had walked away with a chuckle. "I'm seventeen, sir. Wouldn't that be old enough?"

Mr. Lovell's expression shifted to one of mild amusement. His eyes sparkled as a small smile lit his face.

"Of course," he said lightly. "You've crumbs all over your clothes."

He walked off to join my cousin when I glanced down to find bits of almond cake clinging to my coat and trousers. The two of them were soon lost in conversation while I brushed myself clean, muttering under my breath and completely ignored.

Chapter 4

I braced myself for an endless ordeal on the road. I expected embarrassments and humiliation, with Vincent bringing up every sordid account regarding my earlier years with my cousins and enjoying himself at my expense. Imagine my astonishment (and guarded relief) at his dismissing my existence entirely with nothing more than a "Natty here's yet to see the world. I daresay he'll be a bit shocked with us, but the boy needs to grow up sometime."

To my fellow travelers' credit, they'd decided to break up our journey between two days. Mr. Lovell's father had generously sent one of the family carriages to collect us after we crossed the water, and concern for the poor horses' welfare was foremost in Mr. Lovell's mind. I believe we stopped for rest every eight miles at most.

We traveled by ferry from Yarmouth to Lymington, for it offered us the shortest route to Somerset. It was a tiny blessing, to be sure, given our disadvantage of no convenient railway service from the port to Somerset.

The long, uncomfortable coach ride was therefore spent with my attention divided between the glorious scenery outside and the cryptic but vivacious exchanges between my cousin and his friend. Most of the conversation delved into university things (with a good deal of Latin and Greek being thrown in for variety) as well as family life.

Mr. Lovell sat beside me and faced Vincent. I thought it an odd thing since I was a guest and ought to be sitting next to my cousin, but Vincent needed more room for rest, and he was apparently known to require—no, demand—sleep despite the rough roads.

I must say, Vincent had grown up to be quite handsome and dissipated. Once done with university, he'd gone on to travel a great deal, with no real purpose in mind other than to postpone the inevitable—that is, secure a profession of some kind.

While in Oxford, he'd come home for a scant few days in between terms and then flee in the company of a few good friends for God knew what corners of the world. He was always at odds with my uncle—how he complained about it in the course of our travels!—and they quarreled many times when he was at home. As the case always is where spoiled and indulged children are concerned, my cousin was still allowed to live freely, amassing debts here and there as though he were in perpetual competition with Edward.

Mr. Lovell leaned forward and rested his elbows on his knees as he sought to bridge the gap between them. He didn't seem to be aware of my existence except for those moments when the coach's jostling caused him to bump against me. He'd turn to look at me for two seconds and a hastily muttered "Oh—begging your pardon," before sliding a few inches away and returning to the conversation.

The rough roads and harsh bouncing of the coach, though, would push him back to a closer proximity, and once our shoulders or arms touched, he'd come back to the present, mutter another apology, and move away.

I grew quite tired of responding with a polite "It's quite all right, thank you," and simply allowed myself to be bumped, diverting my full attention to the countryside once I was convinced I could never keep up with my companions and all their high scholarly talk.

In the course of half-listening to them at first, I could only learn so much about Mr. Lovell. He was the third son of a baron who was a notorious misanthrope. He was known to lock himself away in his study and grudgingly communicate with the world through letters and a very rare private meeting with anyone who didn't displease him.

His wife and his children—all five of them, I learned with much surprise—had full run of the house, so to speak, and dinner-parties, dances, and card games were very much the norm, so long as the master of the house wasn't going to be bothered by the frivolities.

I couldn't understand how a gentleman in such standing would allow his household to run mad and not concern himself with the family's reputation or his, given his disinclination to participate and be a proper host.

Things seemed to work themselves out well enough, however. According to Mr. Lovell, friends and acquaintances of the family didn't seem to mind at all. I could only guess, had Lord Lovell braved the waters and emerged from his hiding-place for a moment of conversation and companionship, everyone would have great cause to be concerned.

As for Miles Lovell, he was the third son, the third university graduate, and one of two who were presently being harangued with regard to his future. His oldest brother was married. His older sister was married, and the younger one was lately engaged. Only he and an older brother had yet to be matched, but they both seemed to have schemed to keep themselves single till they reached thirty.

"I've only just left university," Mr. Lovell once said in a tone that revealed much of his frustration. "I've far too many things to do and see before sacrificing myself to domesticity."

"Yes—try telling my parents that," Vincent replied, snorting.

"It horrifies me when people speak as though such things are so easy to—" Mr. Lovell stopped abruptly as though catching himself at a precipice. Then he shook his head and sighed, terminating it with a low chuckle.

"What?"

"Nothing. Never mind."

I could sympathize with him in some way, I suppose, but I regarded myself as fortunate then, because Papa and Mama never forced similar expectations on me. Mama had told me to love prudently a few years before, and I kept her words to heart. Papa simply kept me educated and well-versed on as many subjects as he could find the time for; otherwise, I explored knowledge on my own.

I often begged him for a trip to Newport or Ryde, where I could find new books for my tiny library, and he always obliged me. We hadn't talked about university yet, but I was sure that the time would come soon enough.

For the most part, my life at the vicarage was perfectly quiet and idyllic, even with my occasional duties around the parish that subjected me to the unhappiness of those less fortunate than I—assisting Papa in caring for the sick and the dying, offering comfort to grieving children, bringing baskets of bread or pots of soup to the hungry with Stephen's help.

I welcomed our frequent stops for rest and refreshments. I was quite keen on restoring my energy with a quick walk before our meal, and no one kept me back.

Twice or thrice I followed Mr. Lovell, curious to see how he managed his equipage, for he traveled (I thought) in grand style. His valet and the coachman appeared to be in good terms, unlike Vincent's servant, who always seemed miserable and sullen. My cousin didn't care to take his valet with him because he found the fellow to be more of a hindrance than help in his travels.

"I ought to dismiss the fellow," he complained. "But every time I so much as hint at terminating him, the ridiculous creature cries like a girl, wringing his hands and making a damned theatrical show of things. I'm waiting till some-one recommends a good replacement. In the meantime, I'm not too inclined on taking him with me everywhere I go."

Mr. Lovell's servant was a tall, well-built and smartly uniformed man with a thin, bird-like voice and dark, narrow eyes. Hosler—that was the fellow's name—harbored a clear disdain toward me and my plain, shabby traveling-suit. When I tried to engage him in a quick conversation, he appeared to find it a te-dious and unnecessary task and simply answered my questions with a word or two at most and a contemptuous raking of his eyes over my person.

Once he turned away from me with an unflattering curl of his lip. He was quick and efficient, however, and went about his tasks without much prompt-ing from his master.

That he greatly esteemed Mr. Lovell was evident in the remarkable amount of care with which he dispensed his duties.

Mr. Lovell impressed me by seeing to things in a manner I didn't expect from one in his station. He ordered the driver to feed the horses well before himself. He was, I'd later learn, excessively fond of animals and was known to bully those who were unfortunate enough to be caught raising an abusive hand at a horse, a dog, a cat, or any farm animal.

For all that, however, I also discovered he was never allowed to keep a pet, for half the family couldn't bear to be within ten feet of a dog or cat without being reduced to a miserable state of sneezing.

When Vincent and I settled ourselves down for a proper meal, in fact, Mr. Lovell always joined us several minutes afterward having looked after the horses first.

"All's well, all's well," he'd say with a broad though tired grin, and he'd slide onto the bench and take his place beside me, with Vincent once again comman-deering his attention, while I kept to myself. Exhaustion held my tongue and bent all my thoughts on my food. My cousin could have gone on and on with a litany of abuses heaped upon my head, and I wouldn't have noticed anything.

"Dear heaven, this is a thousand times better than Dorcas' cooking," I'd say, but my words were always drowned out by the potatoes and the meat I was de-termined to choke myself with.

In the course of repeating the soul-draining exertions of rough ride-hot meal-rough ride, the final distance—all covered in the waning light and deepening shadows of the second day—found me slumping in my seat, finally succumbing to fatigue.

Sustaining rest proved to be difficult at first because of the coach's jarring rumble, and I kept bumping my head against the side. It would startle me awake and cause a bit of a headache to set in till I was forced to shift and find a more accommodating position. This only led to my sliding back against the side of the coach and giving my sore skull another dull thump.

Eventually—and by some miracle—I fell asleep.

I awoke later not because of my head suffering yet another undignified rattling, but rather because of a low voice speaking close to my ear. I reluctantly emerged from sleep, blinking in confusion at first and eventually realizing I wasn't positioned quite right. The world had tilted a little, I thought through the heavy, dissipating fog, and within moments I realized I was resting on something warm and much softer than the coach seat.

"We're here, Master Wakeman," Mr. Lovell's voice broke through my consciousness.

I strained my eyes in the dimness around me and discovered I was leaning heavily on Mr. Lovell's shoulder. The gentleman had sought to accommodate my need for rest by pulling me down and offering himself for my cushion—or did I, myself, move?

In fact, I'd apparently slipped while unconscious till my downward progress was halted with my head cradled against Mr. Lovell's neck. It was a good thing, too. Heaven forbid that I'd awaken to find myself lying shamelessly on his lap.

Across the way, Vincent had also fallen asleep, but he had the entire seat to himself and lay comfortably situated, or so it seemed, with his coat shed and carefully folded and used for his head.

"Oh," I stammered, raising myself up, mortified and disheveled. "I'm so sorry. I didn't mean to sleep on you that way."

"There's no need to apologize," Mr. Lovell replied with a hint of humor in his voice. "I didn't think you'd be comfortable enough getting your head banged up against the walls."

"It wouldn't have been a problem at all, sir."

"It would have been. I've seen you more than once get jarred awake, and believe me, I know how it feels." He rubbed the side of his head and offered me a half-smile. "When I travel with my family, I always terminate my rides with a sore lump on my skull."

I quickly combed my hair back with my hands, only to make a greater mess of things. My hair seemed to have fixed itself into a permanent tousle that, I was sure, gave my head a comically imbalanced shape. Mr. Lovell merely watched me with growing amusement as he sat up and straightened his clothes.

"Thank you. I'm terribly sorry you weren't able to rest. Oh, dear—" I leaned down and retrieved his hat, which had tumbled down to rest near my feet. My face burning, I fumbled around my pockets, pulled out my handkerchief, and brushed dirt off Mr. Lovell's hat before giving it back to him. "I don't think it's ruined, sir."

"It's only a hat, Master Wakeman," he replied, chuckling, as he took it from me. "I dropped it, but I didn't want to disturb your sleep and retrieve it."

"I'm very sorry."

He grinned and shook his head, his gaze drifting from me to my cousin, who'd begun to stir. "Nothing to apologize for. I'd sooner keep myself awake till we reach the end of the road. That's always a promise of a better restful evening ahead of me."

I nodded, my face still feverish from embarrassment. "I'll be happy to return the favor," I replied lamely, and he laughed.

"I'll hold you to your promise," he said and then leaned over to give Vincent a sharp slap on the knee.

"Come, come, Ailesbury, wake up! Damned lazy beast!"

Vincent laughed in turn as he groggily sat up, knuckling sleep from his eyes. "Go hang yourself, Lovell," he said. "This confounded vehicle is dreadful. I swear the seats are made of marble."

"You're always welcome to walk the rest of the way, you know."

"I might have to consider that, thank you. Ah, I see that little Natty's awake as well."

"I'm quite rested," I said.

Vincent's good humor turned sly. "I'm sure it was delightful."

"Why, yes, it was."

He laughed in that loud, braying way that was always his hallmark, and Mr. Lovell followed suit, his mirth periodically broken up with insults leveled against my cousin.

"Insolent monkey" and "foul barbarian" being the only ones I managed to catch. I watched my companions with growing confusion. What was so humorous? Sleeping on Mr. Lovell's shoulder was comfortable, and I wasn't going to deny it. Impropriety aside, what reason did I have to lie?

Now my cousin was once again awake, the remaining distance was covered with the two of them chattering on in their usual indolent way, and I stared out the window in sullen silence. I wished I could look at Mr. Lovell again, but I'd been caught off my guard one too many times already. I daresay my pride wouldn't be able to withstand another assault.

Chapter 5

The Lovell family owned Shepley Abbey in Liscombe. Even in the darkness, I saw it was beautiful—a dignified pile of weathered rock with the church lying in ruins beside the priory, the chapter house flanked—and dwarfed—by the two magnificent structures and the more imposing presence of history.

Northwode Hall could never compare to the solemn grandeur of such a place. Vincent whistled as the coach came to a stop. The night had arrived, but the sky was clear, and the moon allowed us a tolerable view of the area. I expected the daytime to bless us with something more remarkable, and despite my exhaustion, I could feel my body thrum with excitement at the prospects.

"My God," Vincent breathed, leaning forward and staring out the window. "How on earth does your family manage to keep this place? I can't imagine anything less than a damned village working to maintain every inch of this monster!"

Mr. Lovell laughed while Hosler, having descended from his perch, opened the door for his master. Our host alighted with remarkable grace for someone who'd been in cramped quarters for such a long time. Indeed, I believe Mr. Lovell lightly hopped out of the vehicle, while Vincent and I nearly tumbled out on weak legs.

"The secret is a set of well-trained servants, Ailesbury, and nothing more. Come along."

"Ruins! Look there, Natty, something for you, I'm sure!"

"What am I supposed to do with a ruined church?" I asked, stumbling after my companions and sparing a brief glance at the church's crumbling silhouette. "It's no use to anyone, destroyed like that." Suddenly aware of offending our host, I quickly added, "I quite like its appearance, though. I believe I can spend hours exploring and admiring it."

"You like its appearance—in the dark?" Mr. Lovell said with a grin. I was sure I blushed. "I admire your eyesight."

"I despair for you, cousin. I now see we've got quite a challenge on our hands," Vincent observed cheerfully. "Perhaps I ought to have waited till after you left university before inviting you like this. Then again, I suppose it also depends on whether or not you'd actually go to university."

"Papa encourages me to take my time," I said. It was something close to the truth, at least.

"What, and be ignorant for God knows how long? Damned irregular!"

We reached the door, which the butler had flung wide open in welcome to us. A warm glow of light spilled out onto the ground and the surrounding night, melting by degrees as it penetrated the darkness. Footmen hurried out to gather our things, and Mr. Lovell exchanged brief words with his valet and the butler. Then we were all led inside.

I was too much in awe of Shepley Abbey's interior to pay my cousin much heed, though he continued his teasing as we followed our host through the time-rich and time-ravaged corridors. My uncle's great house had been my only experience with homes for the wealthy, and until that moment, I was convinced I'd surely never see anything that would surpass it.

Everything in Shepley Abbey seemed to overwhelm in factors of ten. The corridors appeared to be ten times longer, ten times wider. Ten times more ancestral portraits that reached back to heaven knew when bloomed on the walls.

Pale, serene faces peered out at me. Ponderous wigs, stiff ruffs, and exquisitely embroidered silk served to balance their frail, spectral aspects with heavy grandeur. The dark wood paneling that looked like rich earth against a sky of flowery paper in deep blue with small, elegant gold edgings and columns—everything looking ten times richer, deeper, and more elegant. Odds and ends of china and flowers in all sorts of containers strategically scattered up and down every room—again, ten times more of this and that and the other.

Wealth of the older kind, that which linked me back to ageless courts and monarchs, bore down on me in a heavy gilded cloud. One would think he was suddenly in a child's storybook, fumbling his way through a strange house whose walls, floors, and doors would recede with every step closer, and he'd be tumbling into space soaked in old, old money.

By the time we reached the drawing room to meet Lord Lovell, my head felt as though it had swelled to about twenty times its size with the dull thudding of pain that had claimed it.

"Mama, Richard, and Camilla are away," Mr. Lovell said as we walked up to the door. "They've been invited to stay at Jane and Horace's and aren't expected back for another week, I believe."

"Your sister?" Vincent asked almost breathlessly as he straightened his coat and tugged at its sleeves.

"Oldest sister, yes. She and Horace live in Bedford—all the better to protect their privacy, you know. Dear Jane's always had a bit of Papa's misanthropic streak in her, though it took marriage to draw some of it out. I fear for her when the children come. My oldest brother, David, and his family prefer London. You'll be fortunate if you see them once, really." Mr. Lovell paused as he knocked on the library door.

"Is that you, Miles?" a man's voice boomed from somewhere behind the thick wood.

"Yes, Papa."

"Are you alone?"

"No, sir. My friends are here like I told you."

I thought I heard what seemed to be a loud harrumph, at which Mr. Lovell exchanged amused glances with Vincent, who sniggered quietly. "Very well then, come on in."

Mr. Lovell swung the doors open and strode inside.

Shepley Abbey's drawing room was easily grander than Northwode Hall's and quite effectively put our small, modest one in the vicarage to shame. The vastness of space was enhanced—indeed, aided—by the lightness that soaked the general environment.

Ceiling, walls, and carpet were in a soft white, any manner of decoration, such as floral motifs and elegant arabesques, being limited to very pale, complementary hues of pink, green, yellow, and blue. The only dark tones to be seen were in some of the chairs (rich, dark green—very masculine, indeed) and the few scattered exotic pieces that I couldn't identify, odd things that the family had purchased during their travels, I was told later.

Unlike the drawing room in Northwode Hall, which had a heavy, ponderous elegance about it with its deep, rich hues, this one raised my spirits with its cheerful refinement. It was almost comical, really, to find such a gruff and scowling creature for its master.

Vincent and I followed Mr. Lovell in a very short line and were about to march right up to where Lord Lovell sat when I was forced to stop.

"You—yes, the boy at the end—good lord, how old were you when you went to university? Ten?" A large, broad-shouldered and broad-faced man with a thick, gray mustache and beard beckoned to me from where he sat, in an easy chair that was large enough to devour anyone who dared set his backside upon it.

I regarded him in confusion and instinctively glanced over my shoulder to see if it was I he'd spoken to. Seeing no one behind me, I mutely raised my eyebrows and pointed at myself, completely unaware at that moment of how ridiculous I must have looked.

"Yes, yes, you—how—well, never mind. Do shut the door behind you, sir! I won't have my privacy violated because of some child's carelessness."

I turned around and hurried over to the door and shut it, while Mr. Lovell chided his father. "If you insist on treating my friends so shabbily, I'll have to take them elsewhere. I won't keep them from spreading all kinds of horrid complaints about your welcome, either."

"Oh, pah!" the old gentleman snorted with a sharp wave of a thick hand, his glower shifting from his son to me as I took my place beside Vincent. "What, should a man my age and position be punished for saying aloud what others most likely keep unspoken? You, sir!"

"Yes, my lord?" I asked, no less confounded than before.

"How old are you, by God?"

"Seventeen, my lord."

"There!" Lord Lovell grunted with what appeared to be a grin of triumph as he sat back with a shrug of his wide shoulders. He nodded at Mr. Lovell. "A mere child, you see?"

"He was never at university, Papa. He's Vincent's cousin, if you'd only allow me to explain." He raised a hand just as Lord Lovell opened his mouth to speak, and I was quite amazed he was able to tear a moment of silence from the old gentleman. "Papa, this is Mr. Vincent Ailesbury, my good friend from Oxford. And this is Mr. Nathaniel Wakeman, his cousin. Gentlemen, my father, Lord Lovell."

My surprise at watching the son master his father if only for a brief moment might have remained unsurpassed were it not for Mr. Lovell's conduct during the introductions. What carelessness, negligence, youthful self-indulgence and frivolity that I'd witnessed before had quickly given way to a manner so restrained, so dignified, so somber, and yet so charming.

I was nearly left wondering if the gentleman with whom I rode to Somerset was the same one who stood tall and straight beside me, maneuvering the conversation deftly from what could be an embarrassing situation to one of slightly formal civility.

Even the great baron seemed to have been taken by that remarkable turn. He sat back, regarding his son with a smile whose humor shifted from crudeness to pride. Then, as though manipulated by someone else's puppet-strings, he rose to greet Vincent and me with a slight bow and a firm handshake. He even apologized for his behavior, which I accepted with an embarrassed protest.

"We'll have a bit of a light meal, Papa, and then we're off to bed," Mr. Lovell said. "There's no need to ring for anyone. I've given orders to Mrs. Flanders."

"Very well, very well. Off with you then. I hope, gentlemen, you'll join me sometime for some fishing. There's a lake a mile north, and it can easily be reached on foot if you're inclined to such exercise. With the rest of the family gone, I've been diverting myself there. It's quite calming, you know—helps one think."

"Thank you, my lord. We look forward to it," Vincent replied in his most polite tones.

The three of us withdrew silently, Mr. Lovell leading the way. With me trailing behind, I took care to shut the door quietly, and I glanced up just as the gap shrank in time to catch Lord Lovell's gaze fixed upon me. He nodded with an approving grunt.

"Do forgive Papa, Master Wakeman," Mr. Lovell said as we walked toward the dining room. He'd slowed his pace to match mine till we were both walking side-by-side, with Vincent ambling before us, turning corners as Mr. Lovell instructed. "He's—a bit of an eccentric fellow, I must confess—doesn't take to company very well, I'm afraid."

"It's quite all right, sir," I replied hastily, catching his eye with a little smile. "I never felt threatened in his presence, to be sure, though he did startle me at first."

"So you wouldn't mind it so much if he were to hurl all kinds of abuses at you." His voice was light and playful. I couldn't help but smile under its influence.

"Indeed, no," I said, meeting his gaze boldly as he inclined his head to better look at me from where he walked. "I'm actually intrigued. I hope to be better acquainted with his lordship if it pleases him—and if it pleases you as well, sir."

The golden warmth of the light softened and enhanced edges and color. What shadows were there were lightened, and Mr. Lovell's dark features seemed edged with a faint mist. I tried to read his gaze, but found myself staring rudely instead, most likely with a look of profound bewilderment on my face. He didn't seem put out by my outrageous behavior; indeed, he appeared even more amused.

"There's no need to call me 'sir.'"

"Oh—very well—Mr. Lovell, si—Mr. Lovell," I laughed. "I'm sorry, but I can't, sir."

He merely watched me, a faint crease appearing between his brows though he laughed along. He opened his mouth as if to speak again, but he hesitated, appeared to think twice, and then resigned himself to simply looking away, a thoughtful smile lingering.

When I retired that night, I kept seeing him in my mind even as I slowly faded away into sleep.

I awoke the following morning very much refreshed and in unusually cheerful spirits. That is, until I looked into the mirror.

I'd seen my reflection countless times in the past, and there was never anything remarkable in what met my gaze. That morning, however, I was suddenly struck by the mortifying degree of rusticity in my appearance. My hair was short and neat enough, having been recently cut, but it still looked like an unmanageable dark mop resting atop my skull.

"Oh, lord," I breathed as I combed it several times till my scalp throbbed in dull pain. A few freckles dotted my face, which were inherited from Papa. Until that morning, the freckles had always been faint—indeed, completely unnoticeable. Now they seemed like a sea of horrid, discolored spots brought on by some dreadful disease. I stared at them, my reflection registering dismay. It was too late to turn around and retrace my steps back to Gatcombe, however.

My gaze dropped to the slightly wrinkled and dismally unremarkable suit that covered my figure. A very respectable blending of black and brown, with my white shirt, which Mama herself made—the very thought of their working their awful rustic power with my too-evident freckles made my stomach tighten in faint panic.

"Vicar's son from The Isle of Wight!" my reflection seemed to scream.

Before black clouds fully devoured me, I managed to shake off my mortification with a deep breath, a muttered "Ridiculous vanity and utter nonsense!" and a squaring of my shoulders. I knew Mr. Lovell, being a real gentleman, would ignore my plain clothes. From what I'd observed the last two days, he was clearly a man who valued good conversation far above mere fripperies.

All the same, I took care to appear as clean and as tidy as I possibly could so as not to embarrass myself at the breakfast-table.

Vincent was standing by one of the windows in the dining room when I made my entrance, red-faced with embarrassment. I'd lost my way and had to solicit assistance from a bemused servant for instructions on finding the dining room. Mr. Lovell had yet to appear.

I quickly walked up to my cousin, startling him from his reverie. "Do you notice anything unusual or different about me? Since—since yesterday, I mean," I whispered, my gaze darting back to the door.

Vincent blinked. "What?"

"Do I look any differently from yesterday? Do you see anything strange? Anything at all?"

"Um—no. Should I?"

"Thank heaven for that," I said in relief. Vincent stared at me in bewildered silence. I gave his shoulder a cheerful pat as I moved off. "Carry on, cousin."

Mr. Lovell appeared just as I stepped away from my cousin. "I come empty-handed. Papa's run off as I feared. He vanished with a servant to only God knows where—maybe fishing, maybe the moors. I don't know."

He laughed as he showed us to our respective seats. "He won't be joining us for breakfast, gentlemen. Are you interested in horses, sir? Exmoor boasts a lovely wild breed, and I'll be happy to show them to you sometime."

"Thank you, sir," I replied as I took my seat, pleased with his attention. "I've never heard of horses on the moors, but I'd love to see a few."

"Good! We'll have plenty of time to explore the countryside hereabouts." Mr. Lovell paused, his eyes fixed on me. "I say, how did you sleep last night?"

"Very well, thank you. Is there anything wrong?"

"No, no—it's just that—there seems to be something different about you this morning."

My belly tightened. "I think it's the air, sir," I stammered, waving a hand in a vague gesture. "It's different from what I'm used to on The Isle of Wight. Quite fresh, I might add." I was fast sinking. "This is lovely china, Mr. Lovell."

Across the table from where I sat, Vincent rolled his eyes. Mr. Lovell merely smiled as he poured himself some coffee. "Mama will be pleased to hear that."

Unfortunately I conducted myself far too well over breakfast, thought of every word and every movement too much and too carefully. Nothing I did felt natural, but I was determined to impress my host—and in doing so, stiffly, and like a machine, brought my cup to my lips and spilled my coffee all over my trousers.

I retreated to my bedroom, red-faced, my thighs hot and wet, and defeated by an overuse of logic. I rejoined my companions in another pair of old trousers—a great deal more like my plain, unremarkable self. That is, I hardly spoke a word.

Chapter 6

It didn't surprise me at all to see my cousin, within three days of our arrival, attach himself suddenly and completely to a lady of questionable merit. Mr. Lovell's younger sister was still away, but even if she weren't, she was happily engaged and was therefore ineligible for Vincent's brand of passion. For that Miss Camilla was surely blessed.

It was on the evening of our second day when Mr. Lovell took us to a ball in Winsford—"A glamorous night of waltzes, drink, and beautiful rich people," my cousin slyly whispered to me before emptying his glass of brandy as we waited for the carriage.

The festivities were held in Huntley House, tucked away in the southern borders of Dulverton. The house was the Lovell family's nearest neighbor of considerable wealth, and even then, the current resident was a tenant, not the owner, and he held no title but that of a gentleman of great income.

A vast, sprawling lawn ringed with ancient oaks cradled its lonely occupant—an old house whose chalk-colored stone walls were choked with ivy as it stood proud in its indeterminate pedigree.

I'd never been to a ball. I didn't know what to expect other than to ensure that I didn't get crushed to death by a swirl of giddy dancers. Avoiding injury was no mean feat, to be sure. Either the ballroom was too small for such a great company, or there were simply far too many guests present even for such a large house. It took me some time, but I eventually found a section of the ballroom's periphery that held the least number of observers.

There were also a few ornamental potted plants there, which offered me a safe haven.

I wove my blandly clothed self among more fashionable figures without trouble. Not only was my suit too plain to vie for attention amid the endless sea of lace and colored silk, feathers and brilliant baubles, but my figure was thin enough to be safely enveloped by the immense yardage of ladies' skirts and the elegant darkness of gentlemen's tailcoats—even as I walked among them.

I stopped behind one of the ornamental plants and half-hid myself behind its leaves. A part of myself wished miserably that I were back in the vicarage, lost in the calm of my bedroom or Papa's library, my favorite book lying open before me. Another part, however, marveled at the scene, so vastly removed from the rural simplicity of Gatcombe.

A small orchestra stood against the wall directly opposite mine, separated from the rest of the ballroom by pretty shrubbery set in two pots that flanked them. I stood at a point where I could catch a satisfactory glimpse of two ends of the ballroom, both with great doors that opened to the library in one and a sitting room in another.

I found the door leading to the library to be a favorite vanishing point for older guests. I later learned it was in the library where they passed the time in sober and more dignified card-games while the younger guests swept through the other door in order to rest and refresh themselves in the sitting room between dances.

It was a good scheme all in all because the waltz was an infinite dance from what I could see. I could scarcely guess how the ladies and gentlemen present could move around and around the ballroom without a single pause for breath—or, indeed, their conscience. I caught myself more than once frowning at the intimacy of each couple as they swirled past me.

All I knew about dances were limited to Mama's descriptions of quadrilles and Stephen's nostalgic accounts of country-dancing in his youth. I'd heard of waltzes, but nothing in my limited knowledge prepared me for the remarkable audacity of what I witnessed that evening. Ladies and their partners held each other in a manner that inspired a confusing mix of embarrassment and wonder in me.

It was every bit a miracle that I was practically invisible to the company present because I now shudder at the thought of the drop-jawed and wide-eyed look that surely had fixed itself on my face.

Looking around, I found some of the spectators standing along the ballroom's periphery looking mortified as they watched the dancers. They were mostly older, many of them flanking young ladies who looked utterly miserable as they were kept from dancing by their chaperones.

A friendly greeting from an acquaintance did nothing to assuage the older guests' shock and outrage, and they held their ground, watching the impropriety of the scene before them and yet appearing enthralled. With the passage of time, however, I found myself growing more and more comfortable with the scandalous nature of the ball and enjoying the music's curious beauty.

I was also quite glad—at first, that is—for the occasional distraction offered by Vincent and his drunken attempts at teaching me the essentials of courtship.

The Hon. Elizabeth Riddell, known within Somerset's fashionable circles to be an insufferable flirt, had aimed and shot her arrows with stunning accuracy. Vincent, struck in the heart, obligingly collapsed at her feet, quite dazed and speaking in tongues. Surely, I thought, there wasn't a love more fascinating to watch than what I was being subjected to between Vincent and Miss Riddell.

"Watch, cousin," Vincent gurgled as he staggered over to me, clapping a damp hand against my shoulder and grasping me tightly as he struggled to keep himself upright. It was a wonder he found me hiding behind foliage despite his drunkenness. "Let this be your first lesson in gallantry, romance, and the pursuit of all that's beautiful and perfect. I daresay you've not much experience in this sort of thing, if at all."

"Well—Mama owns a few novels, but I never read them," I began, fighting off a grimace as Vincent leaned close, belching clouds of champagne, Madeira, sherry, port, or what on earth it was he'd been imbibing. "And I've never courted a lady before."

I tried to shake off his hand with a few shrugs, but he kept his hold despite his intoxication.

"I feel sorry for you, then, but never fear. You'll enjoy the benefit of practical instruction—instruction by example, I mean." He turned and gestured with his other hand, which held his glass, spilling some of his drink when he did. "See there, across the room—that charmer in red with the shapeliest, whitest neck that could ever be had by a woman?"

Across the ballroom and past the waltzing couples, the lady stood with a few friends—laughing, conversing, blushing, and ensuring that her shapeliest, whitest neck was never in want of admirers. She threw her head back so many times, which made me wonder if she'd ever awoken on any given morning with a bad ache in the much-celebrated part of her body.

"Yes, I see her."

"I'm in love, you see, and I hope to secure her hand before we return home." He raised his glass in the lady's direction, perhaps toasting her health.

I looked askance at him. "And I'm to learn from you?"

"Naturally. We're family. You're younger and require guidance in delicate matters. God forbid that you go about courting women like an insipid puppy and forming embarrassing connections."

"Very well then."

Vincent smiled foggily, clapped my back one more time, and then stumbled off for more drink—reinforcements, I suppose, for all the violent lovemaking he was set to do. I sighed and watched my cousin vanish in the crowd, immediately turning my attention to the dancers.

At that point, I'd already grown quite intoxicated in my own way, the music and the endless dancing sweeping me up with their strange, luxurious charm.

Scandalous intimacy aside, I suppose it was the heady mix of music, light, movement, and color that kept me entranced—mesmerized, almost, watching people move around a golden, misty ballroom as though they were colorful fairies flying in perpetual circles and near-embraces with each other.

One dream-like scene followed another. Inevitably, my attention was wholly fixed on Mr. Lovell, who was (unsurprisingly) never in want of a partner. I sought to study him—his manners, his conversation—because he certainly rose well above my cousin in my estimation without exerting much effort.

Though as confident and vivacious as Vincent, Mr. Lovell still embodied what I believed to be a real gentleman's qualities, his friendliness being more refined and dignified than my cousin's.

Vincent's manners—though he might be born to and shaped within the bounds of privilege like Mr. Lovell—were marred by coarseness so unbecoming to him, one that even someone in my position could easily see and not avoid censuring.

That evening, I tried to compare both of them, shifting my attention from the drunken flirtation that took place across the ballroom and the easy, charming enticement that went on in time with the orchestra.

Mr. Lovell must have changed partners half a dozen times, though I'd seen him vanish into the sitting room around four times in the course of his dancing, before he finally withdrew in exhaustion. I couldn't blame him at all.

With every lady he honored with his attention, he behaved without the mortifying exaggerations that a gentleman could easily resort to when caught up in a wild spiral of excitement. I might have caught sight of him in brief flashes, but I was convinced of his behavior, his embodiment of all that was admirable in a gentleman.

His attention was wholly fixed on the lady, and he smiled without faltering, that quiet display of pleasure broken on occasion whenever he spoke or laughed at something his partner said. I was amazed that they could even converse, with all their exertions. The way he carried himself, the way he held his partners—I studied everything, even felt a mild stab of jealousy and yearning.

"If I could only be like him," I muttered, convinced I understood the true nature of my jealousy. Now I laugh at myself. Lord Lovell was correct. I was a mere child then.

I'd completely given up on Vincent and his questionable courtship. Having caught Miss Riddell encouraging another gentleman's attentions while my cousin momentarily vanished from her side, very likely to find more drink, I merely shook my head and shrugged it all away.

It was perhaps a bold turning up of my nose at romance, but I felt I'd seen quite enough for one night and sought the quiet of the garden.

I slipped out of the ballroom and eventually found my way outside, where several guests strolled or simply spent the time in conversation.

The evening was quite warm and comfortable, and I luxuriated in the openness and the fresh air as I walked down a path, discreetly avoiding stray couples here and there. My thoughts threatened to take a darker turn as I whiled away my time in the garden. There were too many figures—cloaked by the night, ensured their privacy by the trees and the perfectly groomed shrubbery—that stirred a certain uncomfortable yearning in me.

There was certainly something mocking about the scene. The perfection of a moonlit garden, the muffled sounds of a romantic waltz from within doors, nipped away at the edges of my mind and roused a few doubts about my own chances at happiness.

It was a strange turn. I'd always been fond of solitude because it offered me a certain familiar comfort—that of my own thoughts and the calm of Nature around me. That evening, however, no comfort awaited me in the moonlit gardens. Only loneliness.

"Let me love prudently," I whispered again and again, my steps seemingly guided by my words. I realized afterward I'd been walking in wide, thoughtless circles around the garden. A repetitious movement, not unlike that prayer—I'd call it a prayer—in four anxious words.

When we returned to Shepley Abbey, I made good my promise to my host. Mr. Lovell, utterly spent, fell asleep on my shoulder, while Vincent once again lay across his seat, quite unconscious.

· · · ·

MY COUSIN REMAINED in bed the following day, suffering from all the ill effects of his debauchery, and I was grateful Lord Lovell had plenty of servants who could look after Vincent. I certainly wasn't willing to put up with his complaints.

"Give him time," Mr. Lovell said over breakfast. "Your cousin's quite resilient. He's been through this sort of thing before."

"Several times, I'd imagine," I replied dryly as I bit into my toast.

"Yes, several—but you can't expect much else from university."

"You've turned out quite well."

He laughed and thanked me, but I couldn't help but wonder if he truly appreciated what I said because I meant every word and hoped he would see that. As it happened, he rewarded me with an invitation to an exploration of the countryside by way of his favorite footpaths.

"I think a bit of an adventure would suit you," he said. "There are a few churches along the way that offer travelers pretty enough views that break up the monotony of trees and hills."

"Thank you," I replied.

"Good! We can go after breakfast."

I stared at him in a mixture of surprise, relief, and jubilation. He wished to show me his world, and Vincent wasn't expected to join us. I welcomed my host's invitation with a silent cheer but took care to express my appreciation and gratitude in a more dignified manner.

Energy and interest flared, I finished my meal and excused myself. I needed to change into a more proper walking costume—which, really, didn't mean much. I merely threw on the same jacket I wore in my journey to Liscombe and combed my hair.

I was ready in minutes and hurried downstairs to the sitting room, where Mr. Lovell instructed me to go. When I opened the door, however, I found my host in the company of two ladies and a gentleman—unexpected guests, I assumed, judging from the startled yet pleased expression on Mr. Lovell's face as he conversed with them in his usual warm, cheerful way. I hesitated at the door, deciding what to do next, when I caught Mr. Lovell's attention.

He stopped the conversation and beckoned to me with a nod and a wave.

"A moment, if you please," he said to his companions.

The three guests turned to look in my direction just as I stepped in, and Mr. Lovell quitted their company to meet me halfway. I recognized none of them. The gentleman looked older than Mr. Lovell, but he carried himself no differently, perhaps with even greater dignity, which made me assume that he was a man of some stature.

Even the two ladies with him—one who appeared to be in her forties and was perhaps a relation of some kind, the other quite a bit younger, very likely a year or two older than I—regarded me with the same air of haughty curiosity. They acknowledged me with the slightest nod, the older lady raising a brow.

A man of no consequence could easily be dismissed, and they turned away once I was properly, thoroughly appraised. Mr. Lovell took me gently by my elbow and led me back to the door.

"I'm afraid I can't join you this morning," he said in low tones. "Do forgive me for abandoning you like this, but Lord Thornber and his family—"

"It's quite all right," I interrupted with a faint smile. "I'm keen on exploring the countryside hereabouts. I don't mind doing it alone for now."

Mr. Lovell looked relieved, and he released my arm.

"Thank you, Master Wakeman—Nathaniel. I promise to spend some time in your company another day as I've yet to enjoy your conversation without the world intruding."

I stammered my thanks, barely able to absorb the directions to the footpaths he proceeded to give me. His brief mention of my Christian name lingered, and I was entranced not so much by his unusual usage but by the gentle manner with which he said it.

Chapter 7

I must confess, my expectations regarding footpaths in and around Liscombe were at first quite low, my defense being almost seventeen years of wandering through an intricate network of trails dissecting the Isle of Wight. I was, in brief, terribly spoiled and quite unforgiving of anything outside my beloved childhood haunts.

Mr. Lovell had given me a good deal of information—though perhaps not complete—regarding the natural splendor of his Exmoor home. While I accepted his fond and enthusiastic descriptions, I secretly believed the West Somerset area to be insignificant in so many ways compared to the contained—and, therefore, wonderfully preserved—beauties of the Isle of Wight's ageless landscape.

I arrived at Liscombe without much understanding of, and appreciation for, endless moors and only associated them with old romantic tales of very little importance.

These tales seemed to be peopled with characters who brooded and pined and allowed themselves to be overruled by base passions, qualities which always left me huffing in impatience as I listened to Mama recount their stories.

Once I stepped onto a footpath and surrendered myself to Nature and to chance, however, I was completely transported within minutes. My initial prejudices and doubts dissolved quickly and easily with every step I took away from Shepley Abbey.

Trails crisscrossed here and there, and though I was more than once sorely tempted to stray onto those not recommended by my host, fear of losing my way easily overrode curiosity. I kept to specific paths and was never disappointed.

Mr. Lovell's instructions led me down a pretty trail that meandered alongside the River Barle, taking me through wooded areas and bluebell forests that forced me to slow my steps or to stop completely, while I gazed around with my breath held.

Those vividly colored flowers took on the quality of an indulged infant, with lush greenery cradling it below and long, arching branches of trees shadowing it above. Just like an elaborate baby carriage it all appeared, occasional birdsong not unlike a mother's gentle humming. And with the river a few feet away, my solitary walk took on a wonderfully meditative feel, and my mind and spirits experienced a renewal.

I reached the Tarr Steps and enjoyed a slow and appreciative walk across those ancient stones. Several times along the way, though the bridge itself wasn't very long, I took care to stop and gaze up and down the river, absorbing what I could of the clear and gently flowing water that passed under me.

In that one moment crossing that bridge, I could feel history bearing down heavily on me. Immeasurable time flowing between rocks and grass, branches and leaves, flowers and drops of water, and an unknown point in history during which heavy slabs of stone were set upon each other by unknown men, bridging one side of the river Barle to another.

Once I reached the other side of the river, I began to entertain hopes of walking through these same paths again in the company of Mr. Lovell. He'd have much to say about the area, I was sure, and listening to him recount local legends would certainly make my appreciation of Exmoor a great deal more profound.

Well past the river, somewhere before Hawkridge, I believe, stood an old church that had suffered a great decline in preceding years, according to Mr. Lovell. As this unfortunate detail was given to me quickly and almost thoughtlessly—because Mr. Lovell needed to return to his guests—I never discovered the reason why.

All I knew was that less than a dozen worshippers crossed the church's threshold, a far, far cry from its better days, when its stone walls thrummed with the meditative voices of its flock.

I wondered how Papa would take to such a sad affair. I doubted if he were to see his own church suffer a similar indignity, being well-liked by everyone in the village. There was still that chance, I thought, however remote.

The languishing church was called St. Bertram. I followed the path till I found a smaller trail—one nearly obscured by an overgrowth of grass and weeds, clearly indicating lack of use—that branched out in a northwest direction.

It was that small path that I was instructed to follow, and I found myself wandering through a rather dense wood that seemed to bury me alive in thick shadows and plunging temperatures. It wasn't a large area, however, and within moments I emerged and was once again walking in sunlight, the trees around me suddenly scattered over a vast area and allowing me an unimpeded view of the countryside once again.

A low stone wall on one side of the path alerted me to St. Bertram's location, which was several yards further, up a very low slope. An old iron gate, about the same height as the wall, marked the churchyard's entrance. It had no lock of any kind, and I pushed past it, wincing at the sharp, grating noise it made, and walked up the path.

It gently turned to the right. The old church peered over its collection of decaying gravestones at me—quite pitiful in its isolation and worsening neglect, I thought. It was intact on the outside; indeed, as I studied it from the path, I found it unremarkable—no different from all the other country churches I'd seen. Against a brilliant blue sky, its weathered stones and narrow arched and pointed windows looked quaint enough and nothing more.

"The church is left open," Mr. Lovell had told me, "quite likely because of its abandonment. In the two visits I've made, I found the interior exceptionally clean and well-tended though no footsteps must have marked its floors for several days. It's a pity, really."

I found this to be true. The door was unlocked, and on closer examination, I found that whatever used to secure it in the past had been taken out. As to whether it was removed on purpose or it simply was too old and damaged to be any use, I could only guess.

The interior was just as Mr. Lovell described—clean and well-tended. The walls were mirrors of the church's exterior, weathered stone exposed and smoothed by centuries protected from the elements.

Old and nearly faded stone plaques marked the walls, memorials alternating with the narrow windows and an occasional sacred painting. Dark, heavy timber formed the ceiling, with beams stretching from one wall to another in a somber, repetitious pattern of lines.

A pointed arch marked the chancel, with a fairly elaborate altar, looking as though it had been cut from the same tree from which the beams had originated, carefully tucked away a little behind this arch. With the pulpit on the left side and the pews that filled the nave, St. Bertram was, indeed, a beautiful church, but in a vaguely unsettling manner.

It was the strangeness that one often felt when surrounded by something so old and so remote as to be untouchable in many ways. There was no connection there—no sense of familiarity because everything that could legitimately lay claim on it had long vanished, and I was nothing more than a witness to the remnants of the past.

The only thing that connected me to the moment was the presence of a woman. A widow, to be exact, because she was dressed in mournful black from head to toe, and she'd taken her place near the front of the church, where she lost herself in prayer.

I quietly made my way to one of the rear pews and remained there, lost in thought. It was comforting, really, to have company in such a desolate place despite the nature of her visit.

I reflected for a while, my thoughts wandering aimlessly down so many paths till I felt more and more comfortable inside that church, and it seemed as though I was no longer detached from my surroundings. History might have caught up with me, or I might have been transported back to the distant past, I couldn't say.

The woman eventually finished, and she abandoned her place in a rustle of heavy silk. Her mind must have been completely occupied by something—perhaps mournful recollections—because she appeared not to notice me.

Her head held high, she stared straight ahead, the picture of serene and melancholy strength. Her stride was slow and measured, almost idle, and I must confess to being strangely mesmerized as I watched her approach the door. A quick and quiet step past the open door, and she was gone, her spell finally broken.

"Mama?" I murmured.

The word just came out because the widow, I thought, bore Mama's resemblance. And uncannily so. I shook my head and chided myself, chuckling sheepishly.

"Don't be stupid, Nathaniel."

I allowed myself a few bewildered minutes before making my way toward the altar because I was interested in one of the paintings that hung on the wall directly before me.

As I passed the pew where the widow prayed, I caught sight of an object on the floor. It was a miniature, on closer inspection, of a golden-haired young lady in old-fashioned dress, whose features had faded or perhaps scratched out. I couldn't say with any accuracy. What I did know was that it must have been dropped by accident.

Forgetting the painting, I hurried out of the church with the miniature in hand, but I saw no signs of the widow anywhere. I made my way past the gate and looked up and down the path, with no success. She could have gone anywhere, given the nature of the trails that cut through the area in endless, random patterns.

All the same, I decided to follow the path that led further north, but after several minutes of walking, I could see nothing but more trees and more paths, and once again, fear of losing my way halted my progress. I turned around and retraced my steps, returning to St. Bertram's church in hopes of finding the widow there, looking for her lost treasure. I was once again disappointed.

"I suppose it would be best to leave this here," I muttered, idly fingering the miniature as I walked toward the front of the church. "If she discovers the loss, she can come back here and find it without trouble."

It was definitely a young lady's portrait I held, someone who lived sometime in the early part of the century, judging from her dress. Her hair reminded me of all those old portraits I'd seen both in my uncle's house and in Shepley Abbey—all swept up in an elegant collection of curls that ladies in Bonaparte's days highly favored.

The matter of her face puzzled me, however.

She must have been pretty, judging from the delicate lines used in capturing her likeness, but her face was completely gone. In the sunlight, I could see her features didn't fade in time as I at first suspected. There were scratch marks, most definitely, and when I touched the surface with my fingers, I felt faint grooves caused by something sharp repeatedly scraping against the ivory.

It was unsettling, to be sure, looking at that little portrait. The purposeful obliteration of the sitter's features was certainly one thing, but what troubled me more was the end result. The lady seemed to regard me with, literally, a blank face that conveyed a sense of someone who was neither alive nor dead but was unarguably real.

I set the miniature on the pew where I assumed the widow prayed. Then I went about my idle business of inspecting church artifacts, making my slow, scholarly way around St. Bertram's interior.

When I reached the door, I felt relief and a surge of energy. The calm and the isolation had invigorated my spirit, and I looked forward to returning to Shepley Abbey and engaging Mr. Lovell in conversation about my adventures in his beloved countryside.

It was with a lazy, indulgent pace that I walked past the dense area of trees and back to the Tarr Steps, past bluebell forests and the Barle river. I saw no signs of the widow anywhere, but at that point, she'd vanished from my mind and left none of her unusual traces behind.

I stopped once I reached the end of the footpath and was once again within the shadows of Shepley Abbey's ruins, the daylight warming me. I was about halfway closer when a pair of horses and riders appeared from another direction and approached me in a light canter. One of the riders was Lord Lovell. I assumed that the pale, proud gentleman on the other horse was the manservant.

"Ah, youth amid the ruins!" Lord Lovell cried as he neared me. "Damned fine day to be out and about, eh?"

"It is, my lord," I replied, barely containing a smile. "Did you have a good ride?"

He alighted from his horse while his servant, already on his feet, took the reins from him. "I did, yes. Along with you now, Sebastian," he said, nodding at his servant.

Sebastian bowed his head and led the horses away without a word. Lord Lovell paused to take a deep breath, turning his face to the sun. Then he grinned at me and lightly thumped his chest with his open palms.

"I see my son let you loose on our deserted footpaths like a lost little imp," he continued as he led the way to the house.

"Lord Thornber and his family arrived just as we were preparing for a walk. Mr. Lovell was obliged to remain behind."

"Ah. That's damned inconvenient. Miles would have shown you much out there. The boy's just as fond of rambling adventures as I am."

I found it a little difficult to keep pace with him because he had a long, manly stride that never faltered in energy.

For his age and his reputation for hiding within doors, his exertions came as a surprise to me. "It was no trouble at all, my lord," I said, slightly panting. "Mr. Lovell gave me excellent instructions, and I didn't get lost finding St. Bertram's."

"What—St. Bertram's, did you say? What the deuce was Miles thinking, sending you there?"

"It's a beautiful church."

I glanced at him and caught him staring at me from the corner of his eyes. "Beautiful, eh? I'm sure the dead would be flattered to know."

"Dead?"

We'd reached the door then, and Lord Lovell swept through, with me close behind. Even within doors, he continued his remarkable stride as he negotiated his way through the hallways in the direction of the drawing room. Even his voice remained loud as though the sense of being enclosed by his house had yet to touch him.

"Why, naturally, boy! Aren't ghosts shades of the dead?" Here he burst out laughing, his voice echoing up and down the hallway. "Haunted church, indeed—absurd superstitions, I say! The only thing haunting St. Bertram's is its hopeless site. Who in his right mind would go to that godforsaken patch of earth for a word with God, I ask you?"

"I saw a widow there, my lord, praying."

We'd reached the drawing room by then, with Lord Lovell beckoning me inside.

"I suppose it's a proper enough church to run and hide to if one were bereaved. Haunted—pah! You see what ignorance does? It makes one's mind fertile ground for superstitious claptrap. Take a minute to converse with any of the villagers around here, and you'll know what I mean."

He shook a finger at me. "If you wish to do good, young man, get yourself a proper education. A head half-filled with facts is far preferable to one packed to bursting with ghouls and talking cats. Now then."

He grinned and observed me with his head back and his eyes peering over his nose, his thick beard sticking out like a withering shrub that had been frozen stiff by winter. "Have you a taste for burgundy? Sauterne?"

"N—No." I dared not tell him that I'd sampled—illicitly—some of Papa's port before, but the taste wasn't to my liking.

"Capital! You're not a man until you set your throat aflame with a man's drink, I say," he said, his eyes gleaming.

He made a move toward one side of the room, where a low, handsome cabinet in gleaming mahogany stood—a very visible piece of furniture against a light, elegant backdrop. I understood its purpose soon enough, when a key appeared in Lord Lovell's hand, and he unlocked the carved doors to expose the cabinet's interior.

Bottles and decanters of all shapes and sizes filled the dark space within. My host had just begun to look through his treasure when a cough from the direction of the drawing room door interrupted him.

"Papa, I'm amazed at you," Mr. Lovell said. He crossed his arms over his chest as he leaned against the doorway, frowning at his father.

"It's only a glass, for God's sake," Lord Lovell retorted. When he saw his son wasn't bent on negotiation, he shrugged and turned to me. "I send Miles off to university, and he returns more virtuous than a confounded clergyman. Damned waste of my money."

Chapter 8

For the remainder of our visit, I managed to spend time alone in Mr. Lovell's company no more than twice—one time on horseback as he took me to Withypool, or somewhere thereabouts, to see the free-roaming ponies so unique to Exmoor.

It was a captivating sight, to be sure, and I could have stood for an eternity where I'd dismounted, my mouth hanging open as I watched those magnificent creatures go about their business completely at ease in such a wild area and lending it a certain majesty with their presence.

"They're a gentle breed for all their wildness—indeed, they're quite shy of people," Mr. Lovell remarked. "I've always thought them to be living metaphors of some kind."

"As well as they ought to be," I breathed, entranced.

The ponies—there were probably ten of them in the little herd I was watching—moved idly among themselves, their long, wide heads bobbing gently up and down, almost like thoughtful scholars in the midst of a particularly involved lesson.

Seize the world, their bulging eyes seemed to say, and I imagined their gazes being thorough in the way they swept over their surroundings, absorbing what they could with so much eagerness. Their broad backs appeared to gleam in the sun, but perhaps that was nothing more than enthusiastic fancy on my part as I admired their robust, bay forms.

The other time spent in Mr. Lovell's company wasn't a retracing of those footpaths I took some days before.

It was, rather, an afternoon moving about the ruins of Shepley Abbey's church. He busied himself with a longish history of his father's property, while I barely listened, my attention being largely divided between the poetic beauty of weathered rocks, half-formed walls, and crumbling windows, and Mr. Lovell himself.

I followed his hands when he gestured, indicating long-gone places within the church, with my mind struggling hard to conjure up what puny little images it could of naves, altars, and magnificent stone columns that must have soared heavenward. I listened to his voice and its light, cheerful tone, a quiet burst of laughter occasionally breaking up his words.

Like those moor ponies I watched before, Mr. Lovell—though perhaps he might take exception to being compared to a horse—fascinated me in ways I simply couldn't explain in adequate terms. I followed him about without any thought as to how I must have appeared either to him or to anyone else.

My youth and the new world that spread itself so invitingly before me kept me in a wide-eyed and yet blind state all that time, and any thoughts of impropriety never once crossed my mind.

I couldn't recall how long we spent there, picking our way through scattered rocks or gingerly stepping over low, broken walls. In time, we were sitting amid the wreckage of the western wall, our faces turned outward.

The scenery before us echoed the turn of our conversation—rolling for the most part, at times bare, at times thickly textured, but everything wide and infinite. We'd been blessed with fine weather since our arrival, and even the moors into which we'd ridden were cloaked with brilliant sunlight and cloudless skies.

"Perhaps I ought to bring you here more often," Mr. Lovell once joked, pausing in his tracks and gazing up with a smile. "The sun seems to follow your steps, Master Wakeman. God knows, we need as much of that here as anywhere."

"It's nothing more than pure luck, sir," I replied.

Mr. Lovell turned to me, still smiling. "Allow me my romantic ideas. It's quite rare that I indulge in them, you know."

I could only rub the back of my neck and shrug, turning away with my face burning but feeling very pleased.

It was, I believe, during a moment of silence when I happened to glance to my right with a sigh of contentment, my gaze moving over an area sparsely lined with trees some distance from the ruins.

"Someone seems to have lost her way," I observed, nodding in the direction of the trees.

A woman stood among the trees, but her figure was still quite visible. She appeared to be standing still and gazing at us from where she was sheltered—or at least in our direction, for I couldn't see her eyes, given the distance.

She must be tall, I thought, when I compared her height to that of the trees that flanked her. She was also quite slender, judging from the width of her shoulders. She must have been wearing a cloak of some kind, for her hair looked to be covered by dark cloth, which also hung down from her narrow shoulders, obscuring her form and keeping me from properly discerning her appearance.

Her dress was a stark contrast to her cloak—made of light stuff, clearly, but as to whether or not it was white or simply a pale shade of something, I couldn't tell. I could, however, distinguish her bodice and her skirts though with some difficulty.

Mr. Lovell's attention was fixed on something else.

When I first looked to my right, he'd just turned his gaze elsewhere and had inclined his head accordingly. Perhaps he'd lost himself so thoroughly in his thoughts or what it was he was observing during that long quiet moment, but he didn't appear to hear me at first.

I turned to find him staring off in the distance as though in a trance, and I gently touched his arm. He blinked and looked at me.

"I beg your pardon?"

"A lady," I replied. "Over there. I think she knows you."

"Oh? Is it Miss Thornber? Where is she?"

"In the trees over there," I replied. We both turned to look and found the area deserted.

"Where?" he insisted.

"She was there a moment ago," I replied, now embarrassed. "She must have hurried off when I caught her staring at you."

"Was it Miss Thornber? Ah, never mind. Of course it wasn't. She's gone off to Bath with her family."

I frowned as I cudgeled my brain for memories of this Miss Thornber. I saw a vague image of that young lady who had appeared with two other people some days earlier, preventing Mr. Lovell from joining me for a walk. "No," I at length said. "I don't think it was her."

"She knows me?"

"It appeared so. She was looking at you when I saw her—must have been watching you for some time before I turned around, but she did nothing—just stood there."

Mr. Lovell shrugged and smiled at me. "She could very well be a stranger," he said. "People wander around this area all the time, what with all those paths around us. I can't even count the number of those who appeared at our doorstep because they'd lost their way."

I nodded and returned his smile. Miss Thornber—the name fixed itself in my mind, to my consternation. I certainly remembered her as well as Lord Thornber and Lady Graham, who was, I learned afterward, the young lady's aunt.

The thought didn't at all sit well with me, for I'd long learned Miss Thornber was regarded by everyone as Mr. Lovell's intended match though the gentleman had said nothing more on the matter other than a vague acknowledgement of those expectations.

I suppose I was resentful for being made to remember such a point at a moment when an escape from everything—or, rather, a selfish assurance of being the only person in Mr. Lovell's company—was granted me, regardless of its duration. We were no longer alone.

In my own way, I was resentful of the lady's intrusion even if it was nothing more than memory, but what could I do? I wasn't a good friend, I wasn't a lady, and above all, I wasn't a lady who was intended for him. I'd no claims over Mr. Lovell in any way, save perhaps for an odd moment or so spent in idle conversation, but I still agonized in a childish desire to be accorded attention despite all the facts that certainly disqualified me from that privilege.

I glanced back at the trees and found them still deserted.

The conversation picked up once again, meandering, directionless, for the rest of our time together. My spirits were a little lower than they had been at the beginning, and I didn't contribute as much as I ought to, but I thought I sustained a cheerful enough tone and manner. As long as Mr. Lovell noticed nothing amiss, I was happy to pretend.

• • • •

I BELIEVE I SPENT ALL of six hours in Lord Lovell's company. Vincent and I joined him for fishing one morning, nearly a week after our arrival. Then, not including meal times, we also had the pleasure of crossing paths with his lordship here and there, in various rooms at various times.

During those moments, moreover, our conversations went no further than the usual pleasantries and perhaps an odd admonition or two.

Those would be placed mostly at my feet because, as he once said, "You're too young and too impressionable from what I can see, Master Wakeman. While that might be an admirable quality for someone who lives out his life in a novel, it's quite impractical in the real world. It's for your own good that everyone older than you gives you a damned thorough verbal thrashing when needed, and, by God, you'd do well not to ignore them."

Yes, my lord. Indeed, my lord. Thank you, my lord. If I could only count the number of times I'd said these and the variations in which they came...

The grumpy gentleman was otherwise quite civil to me, and for that I was grateful. He was far too brittle for me to enjoy his company more often, however, and he spent most of his time shut away, communicating only through Sebastian. Not even Mr. Lovell could change his mind, though the son might exert his influence over his father very effectively in some ways.

I never was able to experience Lord Lovell's method of initiating one into manhood. Burgundy and sauterne remained elusive indulgences to me, and I contented myself with tea and coffee instead.

"Perhaps it's just as well we didn't spend a lot of time in his company, Natty," Vincent said once, his eyes following Lord Lovell's broad figure as it shuffled out of the parlor, where my cousin and I were enjoying an afternoon of cards. "He's too cantankerous for my taste, and while I appreciate a lecture or two, a little goes a long way."

I tried not to roll my eyes. Vincent was never fond of lectures, and he knew I knew it. "I like him, actually," I said instead. "His gruffness is something I associate with a grandfatherly kind of affection."

"Lord, you really are a bit of a baby."

"Is it safe to assume then that his lordship took you to task over something?"

"He did, yes. Miss Elizabeth Riddell, as a matter of fact."

"Oh."

"I assured him, though, things didn't go as far as he feared." Vincent snorted, his brows creasing deeply as he cast black looks at his cards. "Thank God I saw her for what she truly was."

"There'll be someone else, I'm sure."

"Now you sound like Mama. I like my independence the way it is, thank you. Indeed, if anyone ought to be married, it would be Lovell, but the damned fellow continues to hold us all off. Everyone can see how fond he is of Miss Thornber, and he even told me one reason for his inviting me here was support."

I regarded my cousin. "How so?"

"Silly fellow wanted me to be his crutch. He told me he planned to propose to Miss Thornber, but needed a bit of support from a friend, but for all my efforts at advising him, nothing's happened. Ridiculous fellow changed his mind all of a sudden." Vincent shook his head and sighed. "Well, at the very least we still managed an enjoyable holiday of sorts, haven't we, cousin?"

"Indeed." I grinned triumphantly and threw down my cards. "You lose."

Chapter 9

M r. Lovell rode with us to Bridgwater, where Vincent and I began our torturous journey back to Hampshire. We stopped for refreshments and rest twice along the way. I was grateful, certainly, that Mr. Lovell was there for at least a small part of our journey, enduring the discomfort as well as dwindling humor.

"I believe I owe you a visit, Master Wakeman," he said as we shook hands outside the last inn.

"Thank you, sir. I enjoyed my stay."

"As did I. I'm only sorry your stay wasn't long and that I wasn't able to spend as much time as I'd first hoped with you."

Vincent snorted. "Now, now, Lovell. You're beginning to sound like a heartbroken suitor."

Mr. Lovell purposefully ignored my cousin as he leaned a little closer and said in a mock whisper, "Next time, sir, we ought to make sure your cousin won't be in our company."

"Of course," I replied with equal solemnity.

Vincent merely flung a few well-chosen insults our way, which Mr. Lovell rendered innocuous with a chuckle and a touch of his hat, his gaze still fixed on me.

It was with battered dignity that Vincent agreed to take the less private coaches, given the distance we needed to cover.

"This is intolerable," he ground out as he stared miserably at our intended vehicle while passengers' trunks and bags were secured atop the coach. "I've never once set foot inside one of these—these—monstrosities! Just look at it! Never have I dreamt of stooping to these depths just to go home."

"But surely it's all the same," I protested foolishly. "As long as it takes you from one point to the next, it shouldn't be too dreadful, should it?" What did I know then? I'd only been familiar with my uncle's private carriage and the pony and trap, which my family owned.

Vincent eyed me with a great deal of scorn. "Considering who Papa is, cousin, one ought not to be surprised if I raised a few objections, don't you think? Oh, never mind. You don't think at all."

Within moments I was uncomfortably situated in a giant, lumbering coach, painfully cramped as I sat wedged between my cousin and a huge, bearded man in coarse clothes who, by some miracle, managed to sleep most of the way. I realized before long the fellow was quite drunk, and his loud, grating snoring filled the coach's interior with the awful scent of wine and his last meal.

Vincent and I snarled at each other—much to the amusement of the small and slightly ragged family sitting across from us—as we fought for a tolerable position. Riding such a long distance in such an uncomfortable vehicle, one among a few we boarded, at that, our minds were driven to distraction by a fellow passenger's horrible snoring and reeking exhalations.

My cousin and I quarreled over every little thing when we were outside each coach. We quarreled over every little thing while we were inside each coach. We quarreled over every little thing while resting and fortifying ourselves with refreshments.

In a final act of desperation, Vincent thought to pay for a higher fare, bullying me into giving up what was left of my own money to add to his own, and we boarded the mail coach somewhere near Dorset's western borders.

"Thank God," he sighed as we stumbled inside the vehicle, encouraged by the privacy that an expensive fare assured us.

I only wished that our newfound privacy also allowed us better rest and a more enjoyable ride. The mail coach was—though impressively fast on the road—no less uncomfortable than the stagecoaches we'd just ridden.

Our mood remained sour, however. We quarreled over every little thing once we reached Lymington and had boarded a ferry for Yarmouth. By the time we reached my uncle's house (after one more miserable coach ride), we were near murdering each other.

Thank heaven we were both so exhausted to do much more than to throw on clean, comfortable clothes and crawl into bed after a most welcome, warm bath.

I rested at my uncle's for one more evening and was ready to leave for the vicarage the following morning.

I was appropriately quizzed over my adventures, and I did what I could to satisfy my cousins' curiosity despite the fact that I wasn't too keen on sharing much. Edward didn't care for my sojourn. He listened as long as he could tolerate my rambling account before pointedly turning away and engaging his parents to a livelier—far livelier—conversation about some very promising property somewhere in Brighton.

Edward had grown up into the very fellow novels often mocked and brought low in vindictive ink and paper—the heir of his father's property, a fine specimen of dissolute and disarming humanity, always at the mercy of his lust for pleasure and excitement.

He wasn't what one would call classically handsome, but he was tolerable to look upon. He wasn't quite as tall as my uncle, but he was just as broad and thick-limbed, his straw-colored hair an amusing match for his brother and sister, his blue eyes deep-set and quite close to each other, giving him an impression of being cross-eyed from a distance.

He walked with long and lazy strides, and he smirked more often than he smiled. I'm sure his charm would have risen some more had he no propensity toward foul language.

I was told he'd learned such speech at university—a surprising revelation, to be sure, as I'd always expected scholars to pepper their conversations with ostentatious displays of Greek and Latin, not profanity that would make the crudest sailor blush.

As for Marianne—she grew up as well as a young lady should, I suppose, given her connections. She was pretty—exceedingly so, I might add, for she'd inherited her mother's best features, with curves and soft lines from head to toe, gentle hues of pink suffusing her cheeks.

Her taste in fashionable things enjoyed a refinement through her adolescence, and on her coming-out, she'd become the most sought-after young lady on the Isle of Wight. Or so I was told.

She was also, for good or ill, known to be a prodigious flirt. She enjoyed pitting hopeful suitors against each other. Vincent claimed Marianne would often stand back with a delighted smile, her eyes narrowing and darting back and forth between her young men as they fought to out-gallant each other.

"You'll have ample opportunities of seeing that for yourself, cousin," he'd appended, smirking behind his glass of brandy.

I didn't need to be convinced of it that evening.

"I suppose the dances were rather quaint," Marianne said with a coy smile that felt calculated. Her eyes narrowed slightly as she regarded me from where she sat across the table.

"I saw nothing unusual about them," I replied.

"Ah, I was thinking about the effects of the moors on such gatherings," she quickly amended with a nod.

"The moors did nothing, I'm sure."

"Those places are so desolate and bleak—quite wild and not in a good way. I tend to regard anything associated with those landscapes to be primitive. Were the people in attendance very coarse and savage?"

I stared at her for a moment, a rebuke poised on my lips, but caught the subtle gleam of humor in her eyes. "You're teasing me again, cousin."

Marianne laughed. "I can't help it. You make it far too difficult to resist, Natty. But come—I meant nothing bad. Pray don't be so sensitive and let this ruin your mood."

She exchanged glances with Vincent, who merely grinned as he finished his meal, his gaze moving between me and his sister.

Marianne wasn't finished with me. "Now tell me, my dear, why didn't you dance?"

"I don't know how," I said, my cheeks warming, and immediately turned my attention to searching for the butter.

"Oh, what a pity. And there I was, hoping to hear you confess something more tragically romantic. Then again, perhaps that would be expecting too much from you, you poor, simple thing." Marianne shook her head, looking both pretty and sad, even managing to thrust her lower lip very slightly out, while Vincent sniggered.

"I'll promise you this, cousin," she continued. "When we host a ball next, be sure to come, and I can persuade a friend to teach you. Sarah Jessop will be the perfect tutor for you."

"Well—"

"Oh, come now! Stop being so shy! She's a dear friend, and she'll look at you as a younger brother. With all that time she spends in the ballrooms of London and Bath, I daresay you can't find a better tutor." Marianne paused and leaned forward, her eyes narrowing in emphasis.

"She's quite popular in Paris as well, you know. There! I'll write to her directly!"

Around us, the rest of the family continued to speak among themselves, completely oblivious to our conversation. I finished my meal in haste, eager to leave as soon as I could and place a good distance between me and my cousins. My uncle was kind enough to offer his carriage despite a none-too-subtle look of disapproval from Aunt Julia and from Edward.

When I left for the vicarage, my uncle not only offered his carriage but also presented me with two new books.

"I saw these when I was in London a month ago," he said, nodding at the books as I held them close. "They didn't seem to be the sorts of books your cousins would fancy, and your mother once told me how fond you are of these things, so I bought them for you. For my part, I care little for insipid verse and silly, sentimental adventures. I suppose young people today will have their own curious diversions."

"Thank you, Uncle," I said, abashed. "I'll make good use of them."

"Very well, very well. Away with you, then." He waved me off and turned around just as the carriage rumbled away, carrying me with it.

I leaned out the window to wave at Marianne and my aunt and uncle—Edward and Vincent thought to remain indoors—calling out my thanks one final time.

As I withdrew back inside the coach, my gaze swept past the trees that lined the driveway, and I caught sight of something that, at first, didn't quite settle into my mind. It was such a fleeting glimpse that nothing truly fixed itself in my mind's eye in anything more than fragments, but those same fragments dealt me with such a blow as to nearly knock me off my seat in my shock.

I must have stared at the empty seat before me, blinking in confusion, for a few seconds before leaning out the carriage window once again, this time craning my neck as I sought to catch sight of what had just startled me.

I didn't expect to see it again because I was convinced it was nothing more than a trick of the mind caused by exhaustion or even the carriage's forward motion and the resulting shadows cast by the trees.

I'd hoped to see nothing back there.

I was wrong, however.

A woman stood by the side of the road, her figure unmoving as it dwindled in the distance. I could see no fluttering of her skirts or her cloak, which meant she wasn't walking. She stood, however, facing forward, following the road's direction.

I recognized her immediately as the woman I'd seen lurking among the trees behind Shepley Abbey, for she was dressed the same way, her figure not at all varying from the tall and slender shape I'd seen a few days earlier.

"No, I must be mistaken," I muttered, my gaze still on her. "Her dress appears to be common enough."

I couldn't convince myself, however, no matter what I tried to say, no matter how many times I said it. The woman was still visible to me—though considerably reduced by the growing distance between us—when I pulled myself back inside the carriage.

I must have stared at nothing for several moments afterward, my mind working hard to understand what had just happened. All efforts were easily negated when I became aware of an uncomfortable tingling up and down my arms—an unsettling crawling of the skin that made me shiver involuntarily.

I couldn't be sure of certain details, only the more general impression of the woman and her appearance, but somehow something nagged at me for a while. It was an insistent fragment of my memory, one that had taken a hold of me and refused to let go because of its fantastic, awful nature.

The woman was cloaked in dark material—perhaps black. Her dress was light, quite likely plain white. The only part of her body that showed was her face, for I saw no arms, no hands, no shoes, no hair. Her face was white—not pale like Marianne's complexion, but white.

Bloodless, almost. Her mouth was tiny, perhaps as pale as her skin. And her eyes—I shiver even now to think about them—her eyes were closed. She seemed to be asleep on her feet, if I were to find a more appropriate description.

And yet I sensed, indeed I knew, she was looking at me. There was something about that slumbering face that told me I was being watched.

"Impossible," I said aloud, seeking comfort in the sound of my voice. "I caught her in the midst of blinking. That's all it is. Or she simply closed her eyes for a moment or turned her gaze down. There's nothing unusual about that. No, nothing at all."

I didn't know how long I sat there, absorbing these recollected bits and feeling a vague fear press down upon me. A sudden bump on the road startled me out of my strange fancies, and when I realized that I had my new books on my lap, I immediately turned to them for my diversion.

Little by little, the cold fear that lingered inside the carriage dissipated. The memory of that strange woman melted under the onslaught of Smollett's satirical prose, and I was chuckling at poor Matthew Bramble's cantankerous letters to his long-suffering doctor.

The other book my uncle gave me was a collection of Keats' poetry, and I eagerly sampled some of the verses, grateful beyond words for this sudden bounty. My thoughts drifted here and there, eventually settling on one of the recent conversations I'd had with Papa regarding the course I wished to take for my future.

Reading those two books allowed me an opportunity for quick reflection. No, I might not have the talent to write comical adventures or beautiful poetry, but I felt I had passion enough to share such treasures to those who wished to benefit from them.

By the time the gabled roof of the vicarage broke through the trees, I'd settled on employment that was something in which I could happily strive to excel. In brief, I'd decided to become a schoolmaster. Surely, I thought, my parents would welcome such a noble enterprise, given their passion for good education.

Chapter 10

"What possessed you into thinking that you're meant to be a school-master?" Mama asked over dinner that evening. "Who planted those absurd ideas in your head?" She then turned to Papa. "Frederick? Do you know anything about this?"

Papa shook his head, looking equally perplexed.

"Come now, Cecily. Whatever choices Nathaniel makes, he does on his own. It's all we can do to advise him, not bully him down one path or another."

"You spoke with the boy, though, before he left."

"I did, yes. I offered him something my father never gave me: a choice."

"But, surely, we ought to encourage him to aim higher than this!" Mama turned back to me with a look of clear dismay. "Oh, Natty. You really need to consider things more carefully. Why else do you think I sought out my brother, with no assurance he'd take me back? It wasn't for my sake I risked more rejection from the only other family that's left to me. It was all for you, you ridiculous boy. Think of the connections your uncle has—the advantages his position can give you."

I watched Papa, not Mama, the entire time.

He ate his meal as he always did, with careful precision and a solemn air—or so it appeared to me at first. The longer I watched him, however, the more I noticed the way his hands trembled slightly whenever he used his knife and fork. He held his glass with both hands as well as though to steady it while he drank its contents. Little by little, I began to sense distress in him—the strong man of God, who always kept me in awe with his mere presence.

"What happened while I was gone?" I asked.

"Natty," Mama began, "your father and I sat down with your uncle while you were away, and we've all decided—"

"Indeed," Papa muttered behind his glass.

"—that you're to be properly taught—"

"As if I never taught my own son enough."

Mama glanced at him, blushing. "Frederick, please. Everything's been settled, and we've agreed on the terms according to your demands." She hesitated.

"Might I remind you, my dear, that I've already stopped my visits to my brother? I promised you, did I not, in return for this?"

Papa took a deep breath and ran a tired hand across his brows. "Your visits to Havenstreet were interfering with your duties around here. The balls—the dinner-parties—the people your brother surrounds himself with—I wouldn't have asked you to stop them, otherwise."

I stared at him, bewildered. There was something in the tone of his voice that didn't convince me of his purpose, but I shook off the doubts. It was difficult reading him when he was unusually emotional like this.

Mama, for her part, looked pained. Papa's words stung her, and the resentment that rippled out of her could be felt from where I sat between them. "I'm not arguing against your prohibitions, Frederick," she said with forced calm. "Now, please. We've made a bargain, and I expect you to keep your end."

"I will *not* have my son brought up by that man!" Papa exclaimed, pounding a fist against the table and rattling all the dishes. "What agreement we made among ourselves was forced on me, Cecily, and you know that too well!"

I sat, frozen in shock. Never had I heard my father raise his voice to my mother like this. Arguments between them in the past were always quiet and fairly civil.

"Your son isn't about to be taken away from you, Frederick. Please be reasonable. What would you have Nathaniel do? Be another man of God, completely dependent on someone's patronage with very little else to his name? You're unhappy where you are now! Do you wish the same for your only son?"

I stared in horror at Papa. How had that come about? I'd never heard a word of complaint from him for as long as I could remember. He seemed devoted enough to his profession, and he dispensed his duties around the parish with consistent energy.

When he spoke of the sick, the newly deceased, or the newly wed among his parishioners, he'd always done so without a hint of resentment or malice in his tone. Even when he criticized those whom he considered to be beyond his reach, he'd always done so with dry levity in his manner—as though he were left with nothing but good humor in the face of hopeless sinning.

Papa finished his drink and pushed his chair back, nearly upsetting it in his agitation. His face was deeply flushed. Even in the soft glow of candlelight, I could see every line and every shadow that marked his face. He seemed to age before me.

"Nathaniel," Papa said in a quiet yet tremulous voice, "your uncle has generously offered to—help us—with your education. The university was his idea—as was it your mother's." He glanced at Mama when he spoke, but I could read nothing in his gaze. He blinked and looked back at me, and the tired resignation was once again there. "I accepted on the condition that the choice of school—and profession—would lie completely on your shoulders and no one else's."

"It's a very generous offer, Nathaniel," Mama said, her voice much quieter now and no less sad than Papa's. "Your father can only afford so much, as you know. We might not be poor, but you grew up in a far more modest situation than your cousins, and you've done extremely well. Now you're offered a chance to rise above this—"

"Without the curse of idleness that's a gentleman's birthright," Papa cut in with some emphasis.

Mama nodded and held my gaze. "If you rise above your situation, Natty, it's because of hard work, and you've always proven yourself to be a good, dutiful boy. Your uncle's connections will help you reach your goals far more easily than ours ever can. We're sure of it." It was now her turn to appear as though she were withering in front of me. "Think of it—what if something were to happen to either of us? Perhaps even both, God forbid? What's left for my poor boy?"

I finally looked down at my half-eaten food, my appetite now gone. "Am I expected to live with my cousins? I'd rather not."

"It's your choice—yours alone," Papa replied, again with emphasis. "Neither of us will force you to go down a road that doesn't suit you, regarding your future profession. If you wish to be reassured, however, no—the subject of living with your cousins was never discussed. Then again, Natty, I wouldn't have allowed it."

"However, your father and I would be—much obliged—if you were to take up your uncle's offer for assistance," Mama added. She spoke slowly as though choosing her words with great care. "You can see how difficult it is for your father to take, but he understands the necessity, and opportunities like this don't happen along every day."

I moved my gaze from one parent to another. I was shocked, to be sure, though perhaps I shouldn't have been, given my uncle's earlier display of generosity. I was grateful, yes, but I was mostly grieving for Papa as I watched him walk out of the dining room, his figure bent under a weight I couldn't see.

I could only imagine the conversation between him, Mama, and my aunt and uncle to be a painful one. His pride—indeed, what was left of it—was quite likely pounded to dust in the presence of the man who'd long despised him for taking Mama away. I couldn't hold myself back any longer.

"You're killing him!" I cried, turning to my mother. "You and my uncle!"

"Do you want to be miserable like your father?" she asked, her tone matching mine. "What I—we—chose to do, Nathaniel, we've done so for your sake, not ours, and your father understands it. Regardless of your consent or our private opinions, your future happiness is what drives us to humble ourselves like this before your uncle. I won't have my son pay us back with impertinence!"

"Why do you insist on saying that Papa's miserable?"

She hesitated, averting her gaze and taking a calming sip of her drink. "Your father never wished to be in the church, Natty," she said in a softer voice. "He'd set his heart on America, where he'd hoped to work his way to great wealth. But his family exerted their influence on him, and he agreed. He called himself a coward when he spoke of it—told me all this once and no more. He's too bitter—regrets too much—though he never shows it."

"Does he regret you—or me?" I asked, feeling a little sickened by the thought.

"No, he doesn't," she quickly replied with an earnest and intense look in my direction. "Don't ever think that. Your father loves us both, be assured. I ask you, though, never to mention this to him. I'm telling you this once, and that's all. He's determined to look forward, not back, but sometimes he simply can't run away from his past, and I want you to understand why he reacts the way he does to—to your uncle. Wealth and control are like poison to him, Natty."

I nodded. "I swear I won't mention anything to him."

I learned so much about my father that evening, all of it a great surprise. Mama claimed Papa's history had been kept from me for good reason—my youth, which he was determined not to taint with knowledge of his past failings—and now was the right moment for revelations.

His family was a distant branch of a great, ancient line, and they owned a living—a small, humble one in the Isle of Wight, from where they originally came. They were eager to give it to the youngest son, preferring to see him on English soil.

My grandparents decided to move off the island once the living was filled. They claimed the isolation depressed their spirits enough to affect their health, which was, I suppose, somewhat true. I now understand my grandmother was especially delicate and prone to all kinds of respiratory and gastric distresses.

So they moved, the property—already quite run-down from years of aristocratic pauperism—sold to a gentleman of no consequence but plenty of money, who, in turn, leased it to anyone who could afford it. The heir to the property, my father's older brother, cared nothing for it. He'd exerted his influence on his parents successfully enough to be able to escape to London, where he was determined to remain for the rest of his life.

So they all moved away, and they left Papa behind. Any references to them in conversation were limited to a quick and vague word or two and nothing more when I was much younger. I remembered not being encouraged at all to inquire after them.

As a child, I didn't care much about the mystery of Papa's past. I was far too content with my situation to bother. At seventeen, I finally understood the reasons for my parents' silence. Papa had completely cut his family off without regrets. Till today, I truly don't know what had become of my paternal grandparents and my uncle. Perhaps things are better this way.

To what extent Papa's disappointments had shaped his overbearing protectiveness toward me could only be guessed. By the time Mama ended her narrative, my spirits were no longer depressed—only defiant on my parents' behalf.

Papa was abandoned. Mama, disinherited. He remained cut off. She had to humble herself and beg forgiveness from her brother for my sake. For a brief, shining moment, I took pride in being the child of outcasts, and a boy's wild, untested idealism buoyed me.

Silence pervaded for what felt like an eternity. Mama remained at the table with me while I thought things over.

I could be anything I wanted—a barrister, a banker, perhaps even a statesman if I were to aim for loftier goals.

My uncle had opened his purse-strings and offered me the world, one in which a religious calling seemed to have no place. Papa might have been offended and hurt by Mama's earlier bluntness, but I knew that what she said was the truth despite its ugliness.

I took a deep breath and looked up to find Mama still watching me closely, her features a pale mask. "I'd very much like to go to a teaching college," I said, taking note of the gradual melting of ice before me, the look of melancholy hope giving way to one of horror. "I do believe I'm capable of being a very good schoolmaster someday. However, I'll keep my choices open if it pleases you."

There are no words, even now, to describe the general dismay that met my declaration. For several days afterward, Mama argued and pled incessantly with me, and Papa shook his head and visibly checked himself.

Their dreams were much higher than mine. Even Papa, despite his promises never to hold me back as his own father did him, was confused by my resolution though he might appear to deny it.

"I'd expected something more," he once muttered. I was sure he didn't intend me to hear, but I did.

"We'll talk about this on another day," Mama promised every time, her voice firm. "For now, I want you to think—really think—of where you're headed with this—this ridiculous scheme of yours, Natty."

I weathered the storm by turning to my books, especially those which my uncle gave me. When I could, I ventured out to see my friends and help Papa dispense his Christian duties, visiting poorer neighbors and offering them comfort and assistance. When I crossed their worn thresholds, my resolution strengthened.

The sight of the children—poorly dressed, thin, pale, already deprived of so much even before they reached their fifth year—ate steadily into me, and at night, when I was supposed to be asleep, I'd be reading and writing in my journal. I was one of the fortunate ones, I kept reminding myself. What was the point of all the glamour of the more prestigious professions, when they didn't directly benefit the poorest in England?

No. I believed myself at a great advantage, being the son of a vicar. I'd seen the best and the worst in the parish, at my uncle's estate, and on Exmoor. I was convinced my eyes had been opened in better ways than my peers could say about their own experiences.

I was young, and I was an idealist. My world was shaped in ways that were painfully incompatible with my parents', and I was reconciled to it. Perhaps they didn't understand then, but I always hoped—no, expected—they would understand and even gladly welcome my decision someday.

My friends in my youth, already a few, had gone off their own ways. Three remained on the island, but they were all older and married and too immersed in their families and duties to spend time with me. One left for London, and I never heard from him again.

Advice and companionship, comfort and conversation—I had none, but I'd long grown used to being on my own regarding so many things. While it disturbed me a little to know I did rather badly in establishing good friendships, I didn't find it too difficult turning inward for what I needed.

. . . .

IT WAS ABOUT A WEEK after my return from Exmoor when I received a letter from Mr. Lovell. A surprise, yes, for I never gave him my address, so I could only assume that he'd asked Vincent for it.

I took to one of my favorite haunts in order to read his letter. The island was laced—intricately, I might add—with an impressive network of footpaths, which offered me some much-needed diversion and exercise.

I often wandered aimlessly from one path to another, my nose buried between the pages of a book, wholly unaware of where I was headed but still confident enough to know, regardless of where I found myself in the end, it would be very easy to retrace my steps and emerge from the trees, stepping confidently onto the grass that surrounded the vicarage.

Those footpaths were in my blood, one would say, and I was their supreme master.

Mr. Lovell's letter was a very genial one, and I believed I smiled all the way through reading its contents.

I don't think there's any need to remind you that you're owed a visit, he wrote. Things in Shepley Abbey have taken a very quiet and, indeed, painfully domestic turn.

With my family once again together (with the exception of Jane and David), normality has set in, and with it, an ever-growing restlessness that's always been my failing. I do believe the cloistered beauty of your little island beckons.

I chuckled quietly as I read on, my spirits rising with every word. "Yes, you're more than welcome here," I murmured. I refolded the letter and pocketed it as I walked on, determined to use up my time properly and not give in to the temptation of hurrying back to the vicarage and writing a prompt response.

A minute or so afterward I realized the air around me seemed to have thickened and turned strangely oppressive, forcing me to breathe more deeply. Though the sun continued to shine and the sky remained clear, the asphyxiating sensation lingered. I gave up on my walk and returned home, a bit disappointed.

I noticed Mama when I walked past the open door to the parlor. She stood just a few feet past the door, her back to me and her head bent.

"I'm back," I called out.

She spun around, startled, a small gasp escaping her. I saw then that she'd been reading a letter, which she nearly dropped.

"Nathaniel! Oh!"

"I'm sorry if I surprised you."

The color crept back to her face. Where she turned horribly pale but a moment ago, she now blushed deeply. She fumbled for a few scattered seconds. Her hands shook as she folded her letter and slipped it between the pages of a book she carried.

"It's quite all right, Natty," she said with a deep breath. "I—I was just reading a letter from a friend. I haven't heard from her in a long while, and I'm afraid I got too absorbed in what I was doing."

"She's well, I hope."

"She's quite ill, I'm afraid." Mama pressed pale fingers against her temple. The tremor finally left her voice, and she spoke calmly. "I didn't see you come in. Is there anything you need, dearest?"

"No, I'm about to wash up for tea."

"Ah. Very good. After reading my poor friend's letter, I'm in dreadful need of light conversation." She smiled at me, and I realized then how tired she looked—aged, almost.

"Are you well?"

"Me? Why, of course! What makes you ask such a thing?" she visibly brightened with amusement, but the exhaustion was still there.

I wiped my hands against my trousers. "I'm sorry for distressing you with our arguments about the work I'd like to do," I said. "I don't mean to cause you so much grief, but I'm only trying to show you that I can think for myself, and—"

"Natty, please. This isn't the time for a discussion."

I held my tongue and bowed, frowning at my shoes. I wished my parents would listen to me—respect me enough to treat my opinions as those of an adult, not a child.

Mama sighed. "You're just as willful as your mother. Now come. Give me a kiss and show me you're not angry. Pray, let's not start another quarrel."

I walked to her and kissed a pale cheek. She smiled, her eyes misty as I pulled away. She reached out to graze a hand against my face as though to prove to herself I was flesh and blood. When she spoke, however, her voice was firm and cheerful.

"I asked Dorcas to make us some of your favorite almond cakes."

I hurried upstairs to clean up, my spirits soaring, my mind filled with Mr. Lovell's letter and the promise of his company.

Chapter 11

When Mr. Lovell arrived, he stayed at Northwode Hall. I didn't begrudge them the honor of his company; on the contrary, I was rather hoping he'd stay with them, for I didn't think the vicarage to be a proper place for him despite its spiritual but humble allure. Occasional dinners or tea at the vicarage would have to suffice. All other times, I feared I'd no other choice but to keep him elsewhere completely.

Feared...

I feared, yes.

Perhaps I ought to say I wished to keep him diverted somewhere else, preferably some place far and within doors. Those promised walks through familiar and beloved footpaths had grown questionable during that time between his final letter to me and his arrival. I truly couldn't say why or how, but something seemed to have changed—something in the air.

Whether at leisure or in the course of helping Papa around the parish, my frequent walks had taken a strange turn. Regardless of the weather and the time of the day, the paths—once I'd wandered far enough through them—or at least the general environment, would undergo an alteration. The change was always slight, but it was still noticeable, and it was always enough to make me slow my pace or stop altogether, looking around me in some confusion.

The alteration was one that affected the senses at a level that seemed just slightly below the surface, in a manner of speaking. I knew, without knowing completely, that something was wrong. I felt it without completely feeling it. I saw it, smelled it, heard it, tasted it—without fully experiencing its concreteness. It was a vague, wordless voice that called out to me—an airy hand touching my shoulder and urging me to turn around, startled.

Indeed, there was nothing wrong with the environment. Trees, shrubbery, a variety of plant life—winding paths that converged and diverged at varying points—birds breaking the calm with their chirping or the fluttering of their wings—everything appeared and behaved as it ought to. I could find no fault in the sky above me, though at times it would hang in a heavy gray canopy, rain often breaking through if I lingered too long. There was still nothing abnormal in its shifts in weather.

For all those, however, I walked down familiar paths with a growing sense of unease. My gaze would sweep from side to side, and occasionally I'd glance over my shoulder with my breath held, for I could swear I wasn't alone.

If I were to ignore those feelings of disquiet, I'd continue my walk, but the skin on the back of my neck would prickle as though cold, invisible fingers felt their way up and down my spine. Anxiety, faintly simmering then, would steadily grow into a vague, gnawing fear. My steps would quicken till the sensation eventually dissipated, and I'd hurried down several paths, nearly breathless from my exertions.

For some time I believed myself unwell, and perhaps my walks had exacerbated my condition without my knowing it. I stopped my walks altogether for a brief period, hoping more time spent resting within doors would help me.

I'd even asked for Dr. Sharpton, the physician, who kindly—and with a clear air of bewilderment—examined me and declared me a healthy boy. I'd also turned to my usual source of comfort and spent a good deal of time reading my books, and after a while, I'd cleared my mind of all dark suppositions and fantastic flights.

"Such rubbish," I chided myself again and again. To demonstrate my improved condition, I took to walking as soon as the rains stopped, and as expected, I felt nothing, sensed nothing amiss.

Until the week of Mr. Lovell's visit, that is. For three days straight I carried on as before, and for three days straight I felt another presence along those paths—felt the weight of someone's eyes fixed upon me, but from which direction, I could never tell because I failed to discover it.

All my efforts at exploring the area—moving outside the path and into the trees, swinging my stick as I went, calling out to whoever was hiding in the shadows—all my efforts came to nothing. Rooks that I'd frightened out of their nests or their perches answered me with their frantic cawing. Sometimes it would be the breeze calling back to me between the branches.

My exploration would stoke the fires, and I'd conclude my failed search with greater confidence and a surer step. Once the sensation crept up to me again, however (and that came very quickly), how easily did that burst of courage melt under that nagging reminder of being in the presence of someone unseen. Within moments, I was once again a nervous adventurer, my gaze always restless, my head turning on occasion as I looked behind me.

I stopped my walks two days before Mr. Lovell arrived and simply dedicated myself to my books and helping around the vicarage. It was a much-needed respite, to be sure, and my shaken spirits, influenced by the anticipation of seeing Mr. Lovell again, quieted down to a more pleasurable anxiety.

I received a note from him upon his arrival at Northwode Hall. The following day, a carriage drew up to the front door, and I met him there with a hearty welcome and a vigorous shaking of his hand.

"I'm very pleased to see your home, finally," he said with a brilliant grin.

"It's not as grand as what you're used to, I'm sure."

"Master Wakeman, it's a delightful home all the same. The grandest mansion would be no better than the tiniest, most wretched hovel if its occupants were worthless, unsalvageable scoundrels."

"Well, I suppose nothing can be safer than a vicarage." I laughed. "We've God's protection, as you know, as well as His careful eye. Scandalous behavior is not a threat in our household."

His eyes sparkled. "How disappointing," he remarked, his voice dropping as he regarded me.

"I can always invite Vincent for dinner—"

"Mmm—there's really no need to threaten me," he cut in, and I laughed as I led him indoors.

My parents took to him extremely well, which was a great relief to me, I must confess. Over lunch, he entertained us with accounts of his family. Mama, especially, listened to him in rapt attention. She barely touched her food, with her attention so decidedly fixed. Papa appeared to be no less fascinated though at first he greeted our guest with a degree of caution, his eyes narrowing as he boldly took in Mr. Lovell's figure and manners.

Over lunch, he engaged our guest in lively conversation, withdrawing a little if only to allow Mr. Lovell plenty of room to speak and to satisfy our curiosity.

Indeed, the general atmosphere in the dining room that day was remarkable. I dared not interrupt the exchange and only spoke when required. I was so entranced with the strangely wonderful atmosphere that pervaded our meal and was happy enough sitting back in the shadows and listening to everything that was said.

We took a walk afterward because Mr. Lovell wished to explore the famed footpaths on the island, and I'd boasted endlessly of their superiority over those that crisscrossed the greater part of England.

"Besides," he said, "I abandoned you back in Liscombe. I now hope to do penance."

I welcomed the suggestion. Still in high spirits after a very successful lunch with my parents, I cared nothing for any strange occurrences along the paths. Besides, I told myself, Mr. Lovell was with me, and I daresay that was enough to fight off all feelings of disquiet that might arise.

Indeed, nothing happened for some time. We merely followed one footpath after another, with Mr. Lovell choosing the course we were to take, and we spent the time mostly lost in idle conversation. Time was never a factor to me, and neither was the weather. It could very well turn dark and stormy for all I cared, as long as I was able to enjoy his company uninterrupted.

"I must thank you," he said after a brief pause in our conversation.

"What for?"

"The diversion."

I glanced at him, my eyebrows raised. "Oh? Do you mean to say that balls, hunting parties, the theatre, and private concerts aren't as grand—" I paused to wave at the footpath before us. "—as walks past old trees and shrubbery?"

"My dear Nathaniel, have you any idea how tiring all those 'grand diversions' can be? They've their virtues, yes, but it takes a certain temperament to withstand an endless stream of them year in and year out with grace and cheerfulness. I'm afraid it isn't mine."

"But you seemed to be quite comfortable with them," I replied, my thoughts straying to the ball we'd attended at Huntley House. "I watched you dance with so many ladies without faltering. And your spirits remained high through the evening."

"My position has taught me much. I daresay I'd have gone on and on like that without understanding my limits had it not been..." Mr. Lovell broke off and left the sentence hanging.

"Had it not been for me, you mean?" I said, and he met my gaze with a sheepish little smile.

"It's a compliment, sir, not an insult," he hastily amended. "Even as a child, I was safely entrenched in certain circles. I've grown so comfortable in them, not knowing much about what lies beyond. No, that's not true. I suppose I've always known, but I was never given the incentive to explore it."

"Had it not been for me," I cut in with a burst of laughter. "God help me if your family and friends were to discover my part in your corruption."

He sighed and shook his head though he remained cheerful. "Laugh all you want, sir, but I think of this as a blessing."

I must confess I believed him to be momentarily charmed by the novelty of simple, rustic company. Once back in that familiar glittering world of his, he was sure to forget everything that might have raised his interest while conversing with me. I said nothing, of course.

We must have walked for about two miles all in all when the feeling of disquiet crept back, unwanted and unexpected. I felt the weight of unseen, watchful eyes upon me, sending chills through my spine. I chattered on, however, determined not to be overcome by that familiar, creeping fear.

"I've only recently learned about Papa's family," I said. "Mama told me my paternal grandparents once lived in Everleigh, just outside Gatcombe. I'd yet to see it as I'd—" I shivered. Cursing inwardly, I shook off my growing nervousness and pushed on. "With my grandparents long gone away, the property is now on lease. It has been for years, Mama said, but not consistently. I—I think tenants came and went, and at the moment—" I paused to take a calming breath. My heart hammered in my chest despite my efforts. "It's—it's currently empty, I understand."

"Ah, what a shame. Let's hope a new tenant will be found. The thought of a great house being left empty distresses me." He glanced at me. "We can go there now if you wish. How far is it from here? Perhaps we ought to ride there."

I swallowed. "Not too far, I think," I replied, pointing to the north. "I understand it's past Gatcombe's borders in the direction of Carisbrooke Castle." My voice faltered, but I kept the conversation alive. "I've been down that road before, but I never gave the area much thought until—until now. I expect it will—it will feel like a treasure hunt, searching for Everleigh. I understand it's fairly hid—hidden away."

Mr. Lovell glanced at me again with a look of concern.

"Are you well? Do you wish to go back home?"

"I'm well, yes, thank you," I replied with a small, forced laugh. "I think I ate a little too quickly, that's all. Oh, I should tell you about Mr. Burroughs. He was a brick-maker who used to frighten me when I was a child..."

The chill deepened. It took me everything I had to avoid looking behind me because if the thought of being followed unnerved me, the possibility of being regarded as mad by Mr. Lovell was even worse. So I chattered on and on, and in so doing, failed to keep my attention on my companion.

"Wait," he said all of a sudden. I felt his hand on my arm, gripping it firmly and forcing me to a halt. I turned and realized he'd already stopped a few paces back.

"What's the matter?" I asked.

"I think—" Mr. Lovell's words faded as he paused as though to listen. Then he glanced back with a puzzled look. I followed his gaze, my heart pounding, but the path behind us was empty and cheerfully bathed with sunlight.

He chuckled, shaking his head, and turned back to regard me with a sheepish little smile. "Never mind," he said, and he released my arm. "I was just imagining things."

"The charm of our footpaths here," I joked though I didn't feel the same levity as before. "It's like walking in a spell sometimes."

"Yes—a most delightful one," he replied, his voice gentler now. I met his gaze and just as quickly looked away, a little abashed at the question that I thought I saw in his eyes.

We never ventured out to find Everleigh. Somehow we found ourselves standing on St. Catherine's Point, our faces to the sea and the sun, our horses (hired from a very trusting and obliging neighbor) idly grazing nearby.

Mr. Lovell talked to me about his travels, directed my attention to distant points in the horizon where he claimed France, Italy, and Switzerland lay. I listened and marveled, afraid to speak lest the moment—our moment—be tainted by my ignorance of the world. I led him to Smugglers Rock when he said that there ought to be a way for one to touch the sky. We climbed it and sat on its rough, cold surface, and I truly felt as though I could simply reach up and graze my fingers across the blue expanse above.

I couldn't think of a more glorious day.

Chapter 12

"Now why on earth would anyone wish to be a schoolmaster?" my uncle blurted out. He had me to himself in the oppressive elegance of his library a few days after Mr. Lovell's visit. In our interview, he asked me a good many questions about my ambitions, and like my parents, he wasn't at all pleased with the idea of a humble educator in the family.

I squirmed in my seat. "Because I see too many poor children running around with very little hope," I replied, feigning confidence. Truly, if a young person's dreams were to suffer a continuous barrage of indignant and embarrassed reactions from his elders, it's quite likely he'll lose his enthusiasm in proportion to the intensity of the disapproval he receives.

"I quite understand your meaning, Nathaniel, but England boasts a respectable number of schoolmasters and mistresses out there, and there'll be countless more to come. You do understand those who go to teaching college come from those very same families you're keen on helping."

Uncle Edward lit his pipe. Within seconds his nearly bald head was cloaked in thick smoke. I could barely see his spectacles, his white moustache and pointed beard though I still felt the weight of his eyes on me.

"Well," I began, hesitating, "for them to enter teaching college, should they not be apprenticed to schoolmasters and schoolmistresses first? I could be the one to teach them—"

"Yes, my dear boy, but you were never sent to such a school. Can't you see? Your father and mother thought to teach you themselves, not leave you in the care of a teacher as a monitor or an apprentice. You're fortunate. Those poor girls and boys who suffer through the miseries of a teaching college—they aren't."

He paused and leaned forward through the fog of smoke he continually puffed out, emerging from the swirling white curtain like an ominous shadow-figure. He stared through his wire spectacles and fixed me with a hard look.

"You're not poor, young man. You never were. Modest, perhaps, but never poor. Leave the less fortunate to the teaching colleges. If you truly wish to help them, step back and allow them to help themselves. No, Nathaniel, you're the

son of a respectable clergyman and a young man with very favorable connections. You deserve far better than the daily drudgery of the schoolroom."

I winced at my uncle's echoing of my parents' words. Modest but not
poor—I felt trapped in the modest privilege of my lot, and it irritated me.

"Uncle," I began after a moment's hesitation, "I don't mean to sound un-
grateful, but why are you doing this?"

"Because I can," he replied with an even voice and a hard stare. "And because I want to." Then he grinned at me as he sat back in his chair, looking quite
content even as he continued to blow smoke between us. "My dear boy, it's useless asking me such a question. I don't care to justify what I do. Be satisfied with
my assurance I'm concerned with your welfare, and that's all."

"Mama put you up to this, didn't she?" Had Papa been there, I'd be flogged
for my impertinence.

"I don't need to answer that, my boy," my uncle said, smiling complacently.
My anger simmered at his proud assurance. Images of Papa walking out of the
dining room, bent and defeated, swept over me and fueled my outrage.

I fought to keep my composure. "I'd like to go to Newport, Uncle, and
study the opportunities there."

"Newport! What! Why not London?"

"I don't wish to leave my parents."

He snorted. "I don't see why. They'd be beside themselves with joy at the
prospects that await you in London—far more promising than what an incon-
sequential town such as Newport can offer you."

"They wouldn't be so delighted if they knew I'd be unhappy," I returned,
now more affronted than ever. "I'm quite set on this, Uncle."

There was a good deal more smoke and a silent moment spent in derisive
head-shaking. My uncle conceded, however. "Very well," he said. "Go on and
explore Newport. Explore everywhere. Then write to me or come back, and we
shall make the necessary arrangements in getting you started in your profession."

"Thank you, Uncle. I'm certain I'll find something quite suitable for me."

Uncle Edward chuckled under his smoky cloak. "Considering your childish
fancies, I doubt it, but I like your spirit all the same."

"Give me time to explore my choices. This is all so sudden." I hated bargain-
ing with him, but I needed to. For Papa's sake, I needed to.

"Time, eh? How much time do you require?"

"A year."

He burst out in laughter—harsh, contemptuous, condescending laughter.

"By God, you really are your father's son! And—your mother's as well, I suppose. The way you look at me right now is very much the look Cecily gave our father the last time she dared to challenge his authority. It's quite uncanny."

He shook his head. "Very well, you young rascal."

Another cloud of smoke bloomed around him. I wondered how he managed to breathe, shrouded like that.

"Look around you. Consider your choices. Pray remember my bending to your request is done in good faith—that I expect you to return to me, well-informed and better prepared, and that you're not to fritter away your time in idle childish things."

"Once I turn eighteen, I hope to be much more experienced and wiser than I am now, Uncle."

"Indeed. For your sake, I hope to hold another interview with a young man, not a fanciful child, in a year's time." He held up his pipe in emphasis. "Mark that, boy. Mark that."

· · · ·

MY MOOD HAD TAKEN A turn for the worse by the time I stepped onto the road. I didn't care for the scheme my parents and my uncle had thought to weave while my back was turned.

No, I suppose I ought to specify. All anger and resentment that bubbled within me were directed at Mama and my uncle. They'd broken Papa, had worked together to further weaken his flagging will, taking full advantage of his kindness and fondness for me. They'd conspired against him. They'd undermined his authority—what little of it he had, it seemed—and emerged triumphant with their puppet-strings securely fastened to Papa's lifeless, wooden limbs.

While it pains me now, looking back at the resentment I felt toward my mother, my conscience wasn't at all touched at that moment. I blamed her and her desperate attempts at earning her family's favor once again. I even wondered if her claims of humbling herself at her brother's feet were really for my benefit alone.

Indignation and pity for Papa swirled in a maddening rush, and I fumed inside my uncle's carriage. We'd only reached the half-point between Downend and Blackwater when I called out to Renwick.

"Stop the carriage! I'm walking home!"

The horses slowed. "Begging your pardon, sir?" Renwick called back. "We're not quite there yet."

"I know. Gatcombe's not too far. I can walk the rest of the way, thank you."

Before he could raise further objections, I'd opened the door and leapt out, relieved. I never cared for coach rides, not so much for the discomfort of traveling in a vehicle that seemed to threaten complete collapse with every pebble it ran over, but for the cramped and dim interior.

The isolation when one traveled alone always seemed to intensify ten-fold, and staring at nothing but the shadowy walls and empty seat across from where I sat only served to plunge my spirits to lower depths.

Besides, my irritation played mercilessly with my imagination, and I was fancying staring at my uncle and aunt as they sat before me. Smug and secure in their wealth and their power over my family, their phantasms appeared. I could see them regarding me with smiles that were condescending in their pity.

I resolved then to do what I could to earn Papa's—not anyone else's—respect. Yes, let it all be at my uncle's expense. I laughed quietly at the thought, basking in the bitter thrill that could only come from a boy's limited sense of justice and honor.

"I'm much obliged, Renwick," I said with a nod as I stood at the side of the road and looked up at the coach driver's puzzled features. "Don't worry about me. I'll be quite safe. I doubt if I'll be crossing paths with footpads at any time."

"Footpads, sir?"

"Thieves—quite barbaric fellows, they were. Merciless and bloodthirsty."

"Ah." Renwick hesitated, looking doubtful and, I might add, faintly nervous.

"Renwick, I was merely teasing you."

He still looked puzzled, but was prudent enough not to pursue the conversation and touched his hat. "Very well, sir. Thank you, sir."

I chuckled as I stepped back and watched the confused fellow struggle to turn the carriage around. Before long, driver, horses, and vehicle were retracing their steps, and I was finally on my own. My anger had dissipated by then, but my mood remained quite dark.

Once I began my leisurely walk back to the vicarage, my thoughts again wandered to my earlier interview with my uncle.

I kept to the main road and simply walked along the side. I wasn't too interested in a more picturesque ramble down footpaths, and I wished to walk past cottages rather than an endless line of trees.

Before long I entered Blackwater and her small collection of cottages, all raising their weather-beaten heads from their beds of bramble, primroses, and violets. There was always comfort to be had at the sight of these plain and humble structures swaddled in faint afternoon haze, their chimneys belching thin plumes of smoke. Of soiled children playing. Of boys and girls moving about in service to their parents or employers.

I particularly liked the older folks—aging and weak, sometimes ill—peering out of rundown windows to watch me walk past or to wave bony hands at me in vague greeting.

Many of the people who lived in the area knew my family, and I was only too happy to be drawn into one brief conversation after another because it kept me from brooding too much.

I passed a church near the outskirts of Blackwater. An old structure, it called to mind every other church out there, but unlike many of its less fortunate counterparts, this one was never in want of worshippers. I remembered Papa talking about St. Anselm's church with much admiration. Though he'd always considered his own parish to be a little more blessed in its fortune. He thought the incumbent to be a dull yet jolly sort of fellow.

I'd passed the church several times before and had never given it much more than an indifferent glance. A stone wall surrounded the church—a low one, with a narrow iron gate breaking the weathered line of wall on the south side, where the church's entrance was.

A tiny gabled roof of dark wood protected the gate from above, and through the gate's thin bars, one could see the gravel path linking the main road to the church's entrance. Untrimmed grass and rows of discolored gravestones, crosses, and raised tombs flanked the path.

When I passed the gate and gave it a cursory look, however, I caught sight of none of those things because my vision was blocked.

A figure stood behind the gate and was peering out through the narrow bars.

"Is she trapped in the churchyard?" was my first thought. Then clarity bloomed, and I froze in my tracks to stare long and hard at the figure that watched me in silence.

It was that woman again—standing still, cloaked in black, her face a serene, white mask. Her eyes were shut just as they had been that time I saw her standing on the side of the road. With her appearing much closer than before, I felt the grotesqueness of the moment more keenly, and fear—genuine and unshakable—held me fast.

I knew then I was staring at a ghost, one that cared little for the hours because all of the hauntings had taken place in the day, not the evening as old tales often emphasized. I was convinced this woman—this thing—was responsible for the growing fear that had begun to dog my solitary walks. Unseen, it continued to shadow me, creep after me with inexplicable determination. Even Mr. Lovell felt its presence.

I swallowed as I stared at the ghastly thing. I held my tongue for a while and waited for it to do something.

Nothing. It merely stood there, framed by the iron bars, pale, still, and frightening. With its eyes closed, I felt as though I were staring at a corpse that someone had set upright, but as before, I could feel more coming from the apparition.

Behind the white eyelids came the distinct weight of a steady, watchful gaze. I took several steps up the road and turned. The specter remained as before, not once following my progress with a turn of its head or its body.

All the same, with the thing facing a different direction from where I now stood, I could still feel its eyes on me.

"What do you want?" I called out once I found my voice.

Only a slight breeze answered me. I was alone on the road, and nothing but a few stray leaves swirled past. I took a few more steps away from the church and glanced over my shoulder. This time, the specter had vanished. I ran the rest of the way home.

Chapter 13

Everyone mistook my agitation that day to be caused by my not-quite-successful interview with my uncle. No one could be further from the truth. Indeed, I nearly forgot the strained conversation I'd had with him.

What was the use in brooding over such a ridiculous trifle when I was faced with something far more inexplicable, horrifying, and clearly beyond my control?

I was exhausted, dusty, and disheveled by the time I reached the vicarage, much to Mama's amazement.

She peered out the window and saw no sign of my uncle's carriage, and her surprise doubled when I told her I'd walked half of the way home.

"Whatever on earth for?" she asked, and I was obliged to recount my conversation with Uncle Edward.

"Is that all, Natty?"

"Yes," I panted.

"Are you sure?" Papa prodded this time. He'd listened to me in grave silence all that time, while Mama periodically interrupted me with questions.

I regarded him warily and ran my fingers through my hair. I could barely imagine how I looked as I sat before my parents, soiled and unable to keep still. My backside rested nearly on the edge of the chair, and my knees knocked against each other. I could see the confusion on Mama's face deepening with every passing second.

"I'm sure, yes," I stammered, forcing a smile. "Why do you ask?"

Papa raised a brow. "Why do I ask? Why, indeed? You look about ready to flee the room."

"No, I'm just exhausted from the strain of running all the—"

"Run?"

I winced. "I didn't wish to lose time, Papa."

"Then you ought to have stayed in your uncle's carriage. I'm quite certain, Nathaniel, that horses can cover greater distances in shorter lengths of time than a boy on foot can."

"Quite right. I—I'm sorry."

Papa kept his gaze on me, his eyes narrowing slightly, almost imperceptibly. I knew, however, he wasn't at all convinced by any little lie I'd have the audacity to throw at him. Mama, on the other hand, sighed and rubbed her temples, once again looking paler and more drawn than I'd ever seen her before.

"Have Dorcas draw your bath. I can't have you come to the dinner-table looking no better than a ruffian."

"Yes, Mama." I stood up, relieved, and nearly ran out of the sitting room. I heard my parents speak just as I stepped out into the hallway.

"And this friend you speak of before we were interrupted—" Papa began.

"I told you, Frederick, we haven't seen each other since we were girls. She was the only good friend I had—"

"And she wants you to see her. Why can't she come here, herself, and meet the family?"

"Because she's an invalid, and she has no money. Haven't I told you that?"

The tone of their exchange alarmed me. A quarrel was brewing, and I expected it to be less civil than all their past ones. My heart sank as I widened the distance between us because I was growing more and more aware that these arguments had become too frequent lately. How could I prevent them from happening? I felt helpless.

Once I crossed the threshold of my room, however, my anxieties shifted. I was in such a muddle that, had there been a catastrophe, I'd have remained utterly oblivious to it. The fear—the cold, creeping iciness—the lingering sense of entrapment—I was completely overwhelmed. I suppose I ran from St. Anselm's church, and I hurried out of the sitting room in an effort to break away from this dreadful feeling of helplessness.

I would, if I could, have told my parents what happened on my way home, but any rational creature surely would have laughed me off, perhaps scolded me hard, at hearing about ghosts.

Besides, despite my earlier conviction that what I saw was something supernatural, the influence of the vicarage—the safety and security offered by familiar surroundings, made even more so by the presence of my parents—had managed to lessen the initial horror. By the time my bath was made ready, my mind was hard at work finding all kinds of logical reasons for my experiences.

In the end, I wished logic could be a much stronger talisman against the darker effects of superstition, but it failed me. I took an unusually long time in the bath, my exhaustion fading little by little as though I'd managed to soap it all away. My anxiety remained, however, and I emerged from my bath still unsettled but at least more comforted, knowing I was safely within protected walls.

I dressed and dared a look out my bedroom window, but I saw nothing amiss outside. The garden, the grassy expanse beyond our modest borders, all remained untouched by anything unnatural. If my initial suspicions were correct, I couldn't understand how I'd got myself into such a situation.

"What have I done?" I kept asking myself. Where had I crossed the line separating the living from the dead? I didn't know where to begin; indeed, I was so embarrassed at the mere thought I could be so shaken up by the encounter. Despite all evidence, I still couldn't help but question my own conclusions. Logic refused to be beaten down so easily, and it kept a tenacious and desperate hold on my mind.

I had never believed in all things supernatural. The stories from my childhood, while vivid and terrible, were still stories, all meant to frighten wayward children into proper behavior.

Even as a child I already knew that, for my parents had taken great care to instill in me a more objective view of the world. Imagination had its limits, I was always told, and while good exercise for the development of one's mind, its influence in day-to-day affairs ought to be curtailed after a certain point. Hetty and I might have enjoyed each other's stories, but we both knew—or at least I did—that nothing else came of them.

I stood before my looking-glass, staring long and hard at my reflection. Already I could feel the weight of such a secret eating away at me. Unless I found a trustworthy and sympathetic ear into which I could unburden myself, I was sure it wouldn't take long for me to go mad from the pressure.

"What's happening?" I asked, my gaze mapping out the pale, mystified boy who stood before me. I reached out to touch the surface of the looking-glass, the coldness and the hardness against my fingertips eliciting a tremor up and down my body. "Why me?"

My mind fumbled its way back in time as it searched for answers. When did all this begin?

It was in Liscombe, I realized, and I watched surprise register itself on my reflection. That day when I enjoyed a quiet and relaxing conversation with Mr. Lovell, both of us sitting atop one of Shepley Abbey's crumbling walls.

The woman's figure lingering in the distant trees—the one I first believed to be watching Mr. Lovell as though fascinated and infatuated with him—good God, that thing had been watching *me!* My skin crawled at the thought.

Already my steps were shadowed, even in Exmoor.

Even worse, it followed me back to Gatcombe. From the more distant past, familiar voices broke through the gathering fog in my mind.

They're not real!

Oh, but they are! My grandfather saw spirits wandering through an old churchyard when he was younger.

What for?

Why, they never knew that they were dead, of course! They moved around at night as they did when they were still alive!

But why wouldn't they know?

Because there are those who simply can't let go. They're attached too closely to something or someone, and they can't move on to the other side even after they die.

Someone? People are haunted, too?

They can be, yes.

I shook my head incredulously, adamant in my refusal to believe myself in such a situation. I saw the pale boy in the looking-glass shake his head as well, his blue eyes wide behind the soft fall of dark hair, his lips parted though no sound gusted past them. Our fingers continued to touch each other's though I could feel nothing but a cold and lifeless surface against mine.

"No," I finally blurted out in a voice that sounded rough as though it hadn't been used in years. "No, there's no such thing. This is absurd—utterly absurd."

The pale boy mimicked my soft outburst as we continued to stare at each other.

"I'm going to Newport in a year, and I'm going to find work," I continued. "There are no such things as ghosts, least of all haunted people. Imagination can be a horrible thing, and it causes nothing but harm if one were to allow fancy to overreach itself."

The apparition at Liscombe, the still figure at the side of the road outside Northwode Hall, the quiet watcher standing behind the iron gate of St.

Anselm's—something had caused me to hallucinate so strongly. I was convinced of it.

I was vulnerable to strange suggestions without knowing it. Yes, surely that was the reason behind these imaginings. Perhaps I was ill and yet not aware of it. It seemed to be a plausible reason.

I sighed and stepped away from the looking-glass, my hand dropping to my side. The pale boy appeared just as relieved. Something must be happening to me.

"Dr. Sharpton might help," I muttered, my confidence rising. Yes, the physician might help. He ought to. Only science had the power to set things right when clouds of superstition threatened one's steps.

· · · ·

THE PHYSICIAN REGARDED me with a puzzled little frown.

"You're far healthier than most of the people I've seen, young man," he declared as he sat back in his chair and stroked his bearded chin.

My face felt hot as I buttoned my waistcoat. "I don't understand. Surely something must be wrong."

"Why do you insist on it? You've admitted to not feeling ill. You gave me quite an impressive account of your eating habits. You're known to take long walks up and down the countryside. I've examined you myself, and I found nothing amiss."

"Perhaps it's something that runs deeper?" I couldn't hold back the note of desperate hope in my voice.

"Like what?"

"I don't know—something that might not make itself known at present, perhaps? But it will in time, once it worsens from neglect."

At this Dr. Sharpton laughed. He stood up and walked over to a basin sitting on a nearby table, rolling the sleeves of his faded coat and frayed shirt to his elbows. Then he proceeded to wash his hands.

"My dear Master Wakeman," he said with an amused glance over his shoulder, "you'll make a formidable doctor someday. But come now, I see no reason for you to worry about your health. I found absolutely nothing, and I'll continue to say that till I die."

I reluctantly reclaimed my coat and shrugged it on.

"What could cause strange visions, though?" I asked. "Surely I'm vulnerable to them because of something that isn't working as it ought to."

"Visions? Fleeting images, you mean? Being such a healthy young man, you ought to give your imagination proper credit."

"Imagination..."

"It's nothing more than a product of youth, my dear boy!" he said, wiping his hands dry. His face, already creased and browned by the elements, wrinkled further as he grinned. His gray eyes sparkled with energy. "I've never forgotten how much of a sensitive child you were. I wouldn't at all be surprised if you remained vulnerable to all kinds of influences—yes, even at seventeen."

I stood before him, glancing around his surgery—which was, really, a small sitting room in his tiny cottage that had been converted for his humble practice—to counter the doubt and disappointment that simmered in my breast. I took note of the old yet still functional accoutrements of his profession.

Nearly all items inherited from his physician father, I was told—carefully preserved and made full use of, strained in their purpose. Dr. Sharpton took pride in the fact he'd replaced his tools only when he'd broken them from so many years of use. I suspected that it was the physical connection he had with his dead father that encouraged him to save his instruments till they literally fell apart in his hands.

It's remarkable, I thought, *how long-gone fathers continue their hold on their children. Papa and his bitter isolation, Mama and her need to be called an Ailesbury once again, Dr. Sharpton and his battered instruments...*

After a moment of absorbing my dim, sterile environment, I felt a little calmer. The unpleasant scent of his surgery, of several years' worth of accumulated essences of disease and medicine, didn't unsettle me as it usually did.

His odd collection of bottles and powders, mismatched in size, color, and content levels, looked less like a cluster of ominous witches' concoctions that filled weathered shelves on every wall.

"I'd be obliged, sir, if you wouldn't tell my parents I came to see you," I said after a moment's pause, resting my gaze on him.

"You have my word." Dr. Sharpton nodded and smiled his sympathy, and when I inquired after the cost of my visit, he merely rested a hand on my shoulder and gave it a gentle squeeze.

Chapter 14

My duties around the parish never changed, and I dispensed them at Papa's side with the same energy as in the past. It was the journey, however, from vicarage to someone's cottage and back that changed, and not for the better.

I refused to travel alone and at first reasoned my solitary walks had grown rather dull, but Papa appeared not to be convinced.

"Natty, I need you to undertake small errands every now and then," he said with a heavy sigh, shaking his head in exhaustion. "And you've always done that on your own without trouble. How on earth have things turned so dull all of a sudden that you refuse to do something as simple as taking two loaves of bread to the widow Tuckett and her children? You know her cottage isn't more than half a mile from the vicarage."

My hands were damp, but I fought off the urge to wipe them against my trousers or jacket. "Can't I take the pony and trap? That will help in shortening the time for me to—"

"Absolutely not. The road will take you too far toward Chillerton. The quickest way to the widow's cottage is through the footpaths. Nathaniel, you know that."

"Just this once, Papa?"

"Stephen has the pony and trap. Your mother sent him off to Yarmouth."

"Papa, I—"

"Stop arguing, boy, and take the confounded loaves! Had you not wasted our time idling about and making all kinds of excuses, you'd have come back from your errand by now!" he roared, striking his writing-desk with his hands and making me jump. "Now go, for God's sake, go!"

I ran out of the room, my stomach turning. I'd sooner face Papa, endure any punishment that he might threaten, than come face-to-face with what surely awaited me on the footpaths.

Dorcas took Papa's side and scolded me while wrapping the widow's gifts in clean cloth. None of what she said fixed itself in my mind. I was much too afraid to pay her—or anyone, for that matter—much heed at that moment.

That familiar chill had already settled around me like a shroud, and it was all I could do to stand next to the fire, wiping my hands against my trousers and praying silently as I waited.

"It's not a terrible distance to cover on foot, Natty, especially for a strong, young boy like you," Dorcas said as I reluctantly claimed the wrapped loaves and moved toward the door. "If you think the walk's too dull, perhaps a quick run will help."

She grinned as she tapped the side of her head with her flour-dusted fingers.

"Something vigorous like that clears the cobwebs, and I'm sure you'll be feeling much more refreshed afterward. Just be sure not to drop your bundle."

"Dorcas," I said in a voice that was strained and thin, "are there special prayers for protection against supernatural things?"

"Supernatural things? Like the Devil, you mean? Why, you ought to know what prayers keep you safe from his influence. Don't you say them before bedtime?"

I merely nodded in defeated silence before stepping out the kitchen door. I was now alone, unaided, staring at the line of oaks some distance from the rear of the vicarage—the same oaks that shielded the intricate webbing of footpaths from view.

"Where's my Bible?" I murmured. I cradled my bundle against my chest, holding it as though it were a shield against forces I couldn't understand.

I ought to have whispered prayers as I ventured forth, but fear scattered my thoughts. I ran through the footpaths with my eyes wide and unblinking, my head turning left and right as I continuously searched my surroundings for telltale signs of the ghost.

I saw nothing, and neither did I feel an unseen presence like before. I could only blame my desperate running and its immediate physical effects for that, however. Once I reached the widow Tuckett's dilapidated cottage, my world had shrunk to nothing more than the furious rush of blood in my ears and the ragged gasps that burst out of my throat.

I leaned against the rotting door and looked back. The sun bathed many of the trails, the trees, and the surrounding shrubbery. All was bright and dazzling—a far, far cry from the more ominous shadows of death that followed me.

A small, thin child opened the door, and all thoughts of ghosts and hauntings vanished under the weight of pity.

"Good day, Miss Mary," I said, dropping to my knees before the tiny figure. "You look well today." Better than she usually looked, I might add, my heart breaking. Mary Tuckett was a mere shadow of a girl—unnaturally pale, terribly thin, her skin stretched almost too tightly over her bones because she barely had any meat on her illness-ravaged body. The faded rags she wore did nothing to counter her miserable state.

"I'm not doing poorly anymore," she replied with a shy smile.

"I'm happy to see that. I'll tell Papa you've recovered from your fever."

"Did you bring us a gift, sir?" She turned and led me inside the cottage when I inquired for her mother.

Murky rooms and spare, broken furniture welcomed me. The faint smell of rot and spoiled milk pervaded the air, but the more delightful aroma wafting from the kitchen helped soften it. I couldn't help but think back to my uncle's interview, and a little surge of anger rippled through me. I'd yet to accept his callousness, his disdain toward children like Mary Tuckett.

"There's time enough for that," I breathed, shaking off the irritation before stepping across the kitchen's dingy threshold. Mrs. Tuckett had called out for me when she heard my voice; she was, at that moment, too busy to greet me properly. I saluted the poor widow with a broad grin and presented her with the loaves.

"God bless you and your family, Master Wakeman," she said, clasping my hands tightly in hers while her three children gathered around the table to peer at the bread.

"Papa sends you and the children his blessings, and he promises to pay you a visit in the coming week—see for himself how Mary's health is coming along."

I picked up little Thomas under his thin arms and swung him around the room. All was going to be well with this family, I told myself though I failed to be convinced, while Thomas shrieked and laughed, and Mary and Constance capered around, begging to be the next ones to fly.

• • • •

I LEFT THE COTTAGE feeling a hundred times more cheerful and assured. My hands in my pockets, I whistled a lively and repetitive tune as I sauntered back to the vicarage.

"Life's too short to be afraid of shadows," I reminded myself even before I left the widow's company. My relaxed pace and happy whistling kept my spirits high, even defiant.

The daylight added to my confidence now, when before I didn't even notice it. Somewhere birds twittered as though in echo of my silly little songs, and my heart clung to the charming chorus, all the more buoyed by so much light music around me.

Sometime during my walk, I stepped on the dried shell of a snail. The crunch from underfoot wasn't at all loud, but it might as well have echoed through indeterminate distances.

The earlier spell had broken, and I stood in the middle of the footpath with my ears throbbing from the heavy curtain of silence that draped over the area. None of the birds chirped. I'd stopped my whistling. There was no breeze, no movement of leaves, branches, or small animals.

The icy prickling returned, trailing down the back of my neck and past my shoulders. My heart beat rapidly as I stared ahead. No one stood in my way. I turned to the side—left first, then right. Nothing. I swallowed, calmed myself, and slowly turned around.

The ghost stood there, several yards behind.

Just as it appeared to me in the churchyard, the figure merely stood still in the middle of the path. Silent. Watching me behind those closed, white eyelids. I took one step closer. It didn't respond. I took one step away. It did nothing.

"You don't frighten me," I said, though my voice betrayed me with a tremor. "You won't frighten me."

The thing remained unresponsive, mocking me with its silent presence. I couldn't remember how long I stood there, daring it to speak—to move—with a gaze. It seemed to welcome my challenge and simply remained where it was, still and watchful. Our confrontation turned into a macabre child's game, with both of us daring each other with a long, steady look, refusing to blink and turn away.

In the end, it was I who conceded. My eyes felt as though they were burnt, and I was forced to blink for relief and turn away. The thing remained standing. Exulting, I was sure, over its triumph.

I turned around and continued my walk, not at all knowing if it began to follow my progress with silent footsteps. I imagined it creeping or gliding along the footpath, maintaining the distance between us—a ghastly shadow of myself in the form of a dead woman.

I swallowed again and attempted to whistle. I floundered several times because my throat felt constricted, and my heart continued to beat furiously despite my efforts. I slid my hands back inside my pockets and affected the same careless stride as before. I hoped to rekindle my earlier defiance. My mind refused to remain calm, however.

I began to fancy something approaching me from behind. Something with footfalls that couldn't be heard, its burial dress dragging behind it in a whisper of rotting cloth. I could feel it reaching out to me with a cold, white hand. My neck felt the light grazing of dead fingers as it tried to touch me, stiff fingertips trailing down my back to my arm, closing around my elbow and...

"No!" I cried and broke into a full run. "No, no, no!"

I stumbled twice and fell on my face, but panic and terror pulled me back to my feet and pushed me forward.

In my blind hurry I turned into a narrow, unmarked passage through the trees.

It wasn't another footpath—only a bald patch of ground in which I'd foolishly got myself caught. Around me branches drooped, crisscrossing each other and forming a stiff, wooden web. They tangled with my hair and my clothes, and I was soon struggling against their hold.

Leaves fell here and there as I wildly flailed my arms and cried out.

In my half-mad state, I was convinced the thing was directly behind me, reaching out and moving forward, closing the distance with every second I fought against the branches that held me fast.

"Dear God, help me!"

I threw myself forward, blindly and violently, not at all caring where I'd fall. Branches snapped, my clothes tore, and my scalp ached.

"Stop! Stop it!" I cried out one more time, and I was tumbling headlong into space and down a short slope.

The world spun, my body throbbed in pain, and within moments I rolled to a stop and lay on my side, curled up and gasping. Nothing greeted my ears but the gentle whistling of the midday breeze and an occasional fluttering of birds' wings. With some effort I raised my head and looked around me with tear-blinded eyes. I'd fallen onto a road.

Once I recognized where I lay crumpled, I raised myself up, wincing from the pain that now wracked my body.

Scratches appeared on my hands, with tiny beads of blood forming on some. Leaves, cobwebs, and dirt peppered my clothes. I pulled a few twigs and leaves from my hair with trembling hands.

I glanced behind me and saw nothing standing among the trees from where I'd fallen. I was once again alone.

My legs shook as I stood up, and I was forced to lean against the sloping ground to steady myself. As I waited to calm down, I looked around once again and caught sight of something small and light lying on the grass, on the very spot where I'd fallen.

I picked it up with some effort and held it against the light.

It was the defaced miniature I'd found in the church of St. Bertram. Shock once again overtook me.

"This is impossible," I panted as I stared at the thing.

Hands trembling, I turned it around and inspected it. I ran my fingers over the violated surface and felt familiar scratches gouged into it. "No, no—this can't be. I left this in St. Bertram's. I saw it lying where I left it."

I shook my head in disbelief as I muttered again and again. I couldn't understand it. I swore that I left the miniature behind. I closed my eyes for a moment, and I could see—with such clarity—the pew where I set the object down, the position of the miniature itself on the dark, polished wood, the way the sunshine filtered through the church's windows and spilled over the area.

I could also see the interior of the church as I took my casual inventory of St. Bertram's religious paintings, walking from wall to wall, a good distance from the pews and the miniature.

I was certain—and I'd stake my life on it—I never took one step closer to that specific pew, and that I never pocketed the miniature after my brief and unsuccessful search of the solitary widow. I left Shepley Abbey empty-handed and returned empty-handed. I knew it. I was sure of it. The clothes I wore that day had been washed a few times since, and Dorcas never once brought anything unusual to my notice.

Yet there it was in my hands—disfigured, faded, and mocking. Like the ghost, it had followed me back to the Isle of Wight. Taking a deep, shuddering breath, I flung it into the shrubbery and limped as quickly as I could back to the vicarage.

"I'm not going mad," I whispered again and again. "I'm not."

A light knock on my bedroom door roused me from my thoughts. "Yes, who is it?" I called out.

"A visitor to see you, Natty," Dorcas' muffled voice said.

"Is Papa allowing the visit?"

"Your father isn't here as he's gone to see Mr. Kettle's poor sick wife. I don't think he's so angry that he'd keep you from seeing visitors, you dear boy." She sighed through the door. "You dear, stubborn boy," Dorcas added in a softer, sadder voice. Then I heard her walk away.

I stood up from where I'd been sitting for the last hour or so—at my small writing desk, the book of Keats' poetry lying open. In an old wooden bowl nearby, an assortment of odd objects was gathered—mostly things I'd picked up in my countless walks throughout the island.

Dried flowers and leaves, curiously-shaped stones—everything that marked the passage of time while stoking my interest and my imagination made up a small yet prized collection. If I had the defaced miniature with me—and had I acquired it under normal circumstances—I'd have added it to my treasure of curiosities, given its mysterious beginnings and strange possibilities.

Just a while before, I'd had another ugly quarrel with Papa. It came as no surprise, to be sure, for angry confrontations between us had become a common scene in the vicarage now.

Simply put, I refused to venture out alone and spoke the truth when asked for a reason. "I don't want to go out there without company," I said. "I won't."

"Why, for God's sake? You've never complained about this before!"

"Papa, I'm afraid." There. I continued to speak in the simplest, clearest manner I could though my voice quavered, and I couldn't bear to look him in the eye. "I'm haunted. I'm in danger."

Papa's expression defied—and continues to defy—words. "Afraid? Haunted? In danger?" he echoed, his voice rising with every word. "The devil you are! Who's been planting all this rubbish in your head, Nathaniel? Who?"

"No one! Something's out there, and I've seen it! I'm not lying! It's a ghost of a woman, and she appears to me when I'm alone, like that time when—"

"I'll have none of this," Papa interrupted in an even, menacing voice. He'd grown pale in his anger. "Did you hear me, boy? I won't hear another word of your nonsense—"

"But it isn't nonsense—"

Papa raised a hand in warning, silencing me. "One more word, Nathaniel. One more word. God help me, you're not too old for the switch."

He proceeded to rail against me in severest terms because what person in his right mind would believe that such things as ghosts existed? It was sinful to embrace superstition. It was un-Christian. It was a blot to my respectability as the well-educated son of a much-liked and much-revered man of God.

The threat of the switch was never repeated. My punishment then was to remain in my room without food till Papa decided that I'd had enough time to think things through and to pray for God's forgiveness.

This time, however, an unexpected reprieve helped lift my punishment much sooner than planned. I wasn't this fortunate before and had endured entire days when I went to bed without touching a single meal. Not once had I prayed for forgiveness, either because I was convinced I was in the right.

I gave myself a careless glance in the mirror. I'd long grown used to the pale, sullen, and drawn image that stared back at me. I went to the sitting room and nearly exclaimed in surprise and relief—above all, in delight.

Mr. Lovell rose from his seat as I stood at the door, momentarily frozen, and he held out his hand in familiar greeting. "Master Wakeman," he said with a broad, engaging smile. I hurried forward and grasped his hand in mine, shaking it vigorously. "Do forgive me for not warning you in writing, but I was in a bit of a hurry to travel and simply lost sight of propriety. It's a common fault of mine, I'm afraid."

"Please, it's no trouble at all," I replied, laughing. "You're always welcome, Mr. Lovell."

To say I was relieved to see him would be an error. I was much more than that. I was ecstatic. In fact, I couldn't speak for several moments, spending my time instead in looking him over, reacquainting myself with his person, his manners, his virtues.

As we hadn't seen each other in quite a while, I'd somehow forgotten how handsome and how superior he was in everything. It was all I could do to give his hand a final earnest squeeze before releasing it.

He was a much-needed distraction for me—for everyone in the vicarage, I was sure. After calling for refreshments, I sat down opposite him, relishing every second in his company as though we hadn't seen each other in years.

"It seems you approve of what you see," he noted with an arch smile.

"Oh—yes, I do! You look exceedingly well, sir."

"Well, that's a relief. You look no differently from before—"

"Ah," I stammered. No doubt disappointment or confusion must have etched itself on my face.

Mr. Lovell leaned forward and regarded me with a clear, brilliant stare. "That was meant as a compliment," he appended in a quieter voice.

"Ah," I stammered again, tapping my fingers against my knees. "Thank you, sir."

"You seem a bit sadder, though—and a little thinner."

"It's nothing. What brings you to this quiet corner of England again, Mr. Lovell?"

"A few things. Unexpected, for the most part, but perhaps necessary."

"Begging your pardon?"

He took a deep breath and sat back, clasping his hands and resting them on his lap. Mr. Lovell now appeared distracted. Rather than clarify himself, he instead glanced around the room, his eyes keen and restless as he swept his gaze around—eating, absorbing. Evading.

My bewilderment might not have been eased, but I didn't care. It was, I think, at that moment I grew aware of something in me. Something odd, alien, and well beyond my understanding.

It stirred as a sleeping child would stir, and it responded reluctantly and yet naturally to Mr. Lovell's presence. All I knew—all I could comprehend—was that curious movement in my belly, which was echoed in my breast, and all the while, my admiration of Mr. Lovell deepened.

"I adore the simple elegance of your home," he said, his voice calm and noncommittal.

"Mama takes pride in the house."

Mr. Lovell nodded, still looking around the room.

Dorcas appeared with a tray of tea and cakes, and while I thanked her, my guest seemed unaware of the modest bounty that sat before him, awaiting his pleasure.

His behavior mystified me, but I forced all questions out of my mind and began to pour the tea.

"You must try the cakes that—"

"Forgive me, Nathaniel," he said all of a sudden while meeting my gaze with a little smile, "but would you care for a walk?"

I blinked, frozen in mid-pour. "Walk? What—right now, sir?"

"Yes, if it pleases you. I feel the need for some exercise and fresh air at the moment. The journey here was rather constricting and difficult, and I'm afraid I still feel the need to recover from it." Mr. Lovell's tone sounded odd, though he spoke lightly. I could also sense his earlier relaxed, easy manner had vanished though he continued to smile pleasantly at me, and I couldn't understand why.

I set the teapot down and considered. Papa wasn't home, and neither was Mama, who'd gone out to visit her friend who lived in Ryde. She was given half-hearted permission to go, having suffered black, depressive moods when Papa at first forbade her to keep her friend company.

Simply put, he had no choice but to let her go. That day, she wasn't expected back till dinner-time. I was being punished for my obstinacy, but it didn't matter at all to me. No, not at that moment.

Not even my haunted walks disturbed my thoughts. I gathered myself, hoping I didn't appear too eager.

"Of course," I replied with affected ease. "I understand. Do you wish me to take you somewhere specific?"

"No—just an idle walk—very much like the one we had the last time I paid this charming house a visit."

I stood up. "It would be my pleasure, sir."

He stood up as well. He also muttered something in response, but whatever it was, I failed to catch it.

• • • •

I LED HIM THROUGH THE paths that took us to Bowcombe.

Our conversation turned out rather dull and strained, much to my disappointment. Mr. Lovell's distraction remained, for all my efforts at entertaining him. In time I succumbed to the mental exhaustion of forced levity. I fell silent, even more bewildered, but was convinced it would be best to let him take the conversation where he pleased. I certainly didn't seem capable of keeping his interest alive.

"I'm afraid I'm not very good company today," he said after a long moment of silence.

I glanced at him. Though unusually silent and pensive, he still carried on with the air of haughty ease I'd always admired. "One can't expect another man to be cheerful all the time."

He chuckled and tapped the ground with his stick. "No, I suppose not."

"Is something the matter, sir?"

He hesitated. "Quite a few things, really, but nothing for you to worry about."

"I can help, surely."

Another light chuckle greeted my words. "Perhaps. Shall we turn here?"

We'd reached a place where three paths intersected, and Mr. Lovell pointed at one that led us west. I didn't recognize the path, but I was confident in my ability to find our way back to the vicarage.

I led him onward. Eventually I felt equal to the task of discussing certain subjects that naturally dampened my spirits. It was only polite, after all. "I hope Miss Thornber is doing well."

"She is, thank you. Her family's in good health as well."

"I'm glad." No, I wasn't. I heartily disliked the thought of Mr. Lovell marrying Miss Thornber, regardless of anyone's family connections and wealth.

"Someday you'll find yourself in similar circumstances—"

"I haven't thought of marrying anyone," I cut in, sounding more resentful than perhaps I ought to. "All the girls I know are already attached—or they simply don't care about me." I shrugged. "Not that it worries me, mind you. I don't really think about them."

"You don't?" Mr. Lovell pursued, and I turned in time to meet a look of mild surprise. "But then, I suppose you're still very young. You've so many years ahead of you still—so much time for discovery."

I stared at the ground. "I've a year, actually. My uncle wishes to find me a proper occupation, and I told him to wait till I'm eighteen." I laughed in spite of myself. "I'm not even done with school yet. At least Papa isn't quite done with me."

He laughed along. "In many ways, Nathaniel, I envy your situation. During moments like this, I'd give all I have to walk in your place."

I looked at him again. It was my turn to be surprised, and it had nothing to do with his frequent use of my Christian name. "Begging your pardon, but are you unhappy, sir? Is that why you traveled here?"

"Yes and yes."

"I see. My cousin surely must have given—"

"Ailesbury doesn't know I'm here," he quickly said. "I never told him my intention to visit, and I'd be obliged if you didn't speak a word to him about it."

I regarded him, even more surprised. "I won't. You have my word, sir."

"Thank you. I shan't go further. My dear sir, you've nearly made me confess to something I never intended to share."

"Can't you treat me like a friend?" I prodded, feeling hurt by his evasions. "I might not be like Vincent—"

"For which I'm immensely grateful—"

"—and I might not be your equal, sir, but I can listen without judgment as well as any confidant. If you're unhappy, surely unburdening yourself to someone you can trust will help. I don't pretend to have all the answers, but I can at least try."

My words flowed out of me in a steady rush of confused ideas. When I'd done, I became aware of the heat that suffused my face, and I knew that I was blushing. It didn't matter to me, though. I'd said what was foremost in my mind, and there was nothing I could do to retract a single word.

Mr. Lovell met my gaze with a quiet, rueful smile. He reached out and rested a hand against the side of my face for a second before sliding it down my arm, lightly squeezing it. Then he shook his head, whispered, "Thank you," and moved on.

Chapter 16

We'd lost all thought of time. Judging from the sun's position, I guessed we returned to the vicarage in the mid-afternoon. I crossed the threshold first. Mr. Lovell lingered for a moment outside, for something had caught his attention just as I opened the door.

"What was that?" he asked as he looked off to one side. I stepped back outside and followed his gaze.

"I saw nothing," I replied, apprehension suddenly flaring alive.

"Wait—there it is again. Did you see it this time? Over there—between the trees."

I reluctantly obeyed but found nothing strange in the direction he indicated. "It must have been a bird," I offered, my heart racing. "We should go in."

Mr. Lovell appeared not to hear me. He continued to stare long and hard at the trees. Then he said, "I don't think it was a bird. Go on ahead, Nathaniel. I'll follow in a moment."

Without another word, he suddenly sprang away and hurried off, vanishing around the corner of the house. I stood by the doorway in mounting terror, unsure of what to do next.

"Where the Devil have you been?"

I turned around with a small gasp. Papa stood in the shadows of the hallway.

"I went out for a walk," I stammered, grateful for his presence despite his obvious fury. I swallowed to calm myself and stepped across the threshold.

"A walk! You went out for a walk, when I specifically told you to stay in your room! Good God, Nathaniel, your obstinacy has—"

Footsteps coming up behind me silenced him.

"I saw nothing," our guest announced a little breathlessly as he closed the door and approached me. "I followed the line around the vicarage and—oh, forgive me. Good day, Mr. Wakeman."

"Mr. Lovell," Papa said with a stiff nod of his head. "I didn't know you were here."

"It was my fault entirely, sir. My visit is unannounced, I'm afraid." He paused and glanced at me. "Forgive me, sir, for imposing. It was I who invited your son for a walk."

Papa's anger visibly eased. His shoulders sagged. He nodded, the tense lines in his face vanishing. "Thank you, Mr. Lovell. I was concerned. Natty simply slipped away without a word to the housekeeper."

"I'm sorry," I stammered. "I didn't think it would cause so much trouble."

"We'll have time enough for that," Papa replied, and he beckoned to us. "Come along. I'm pleased to see you here again, Mr. Lovell. Do stay for dinner."

"Thank you, I will."

"Where are you lodging?"

"Rookley, sir."

Papa stole a glance over his shoulder. "Rookley! Why not Havenstreet?"

"I prefer a small room in a quiet cottage."

Papa's eyes twinkled. "I see. You, sir, are an exile. Well, if you wish for advice from an old man, Mr. Lovell, I'm here to listen and offer something I hope will be of use to you."

"Thank you, sir." Mr. Lovell walked beside me as we followed Papa through the hallway toward the parlor. After their brief exchange, he nudged me gently with his elbow. "Your father suspects something amorous, I'm sure, about my being here."

"Does he?" I whispered back. "He said nothing."

"He knows, believe me."

I tried not to think about it. Instead I allowed my thoughts to alight on even more unpleasant matters.

"What did you see in the trees, Mr. Lovell?" I whispered again.

"I can't say for sure. It was a figure—something that was dark with a white face, I think. It stood among the trees at the edge of the grounds."

"Did you see it move?" My heart raced again.

"No, I can't say that I did. It just stood there, as if watching us."

"You saw it watching us?"

He hesitated. "No, but I felt that it did. I wish I could be more, uh, logical about that point, but all I can go by is a strong sense of being watched."

"It might have been an animal of some kind."

"Only if you think large dogs can stand on their hind legs for a long time without moving. No, it was too tall and too thin. I'm sure it was a person."

My hands were damp again. I wiped them against my trousers. "Did—did you feel threatened in any way?"

"I confess I was unsettled though I don't know why. It was—I don't know—a feeling I had, and it seemed to come from nowhere. I'm not a nervous sort, you know."

We'd reached the parlor by then. "But you saw nothing when you ran for the trees," I prodded.

He shook his head, his brows slightly creased. "Nothing," he replied. "I must confess I've never experienced anything like this. I don't have an overactive imagination, Nathaniel, and neither do I believe in superstitious nonsense. If I did, I'd say what I glimpsed was a specter of some kind." He chuckled and shook his head. "But that's damned ridiculous."

I said nothing in return. I did, however, feel some relief at the thought someone else—someone whom I not only trusted but also held in very high regard—had seen the ghost. While it didn't ease the fear and horror that had now become constants in my waking hours, it certainly assured me of one thing. I most definitely wasn't going mad.

· · · ·

MAMA ARRIVED JUST BEFORE dinner. She welcomed Mr. Lovell to our tiny circle less warmly than before, but she appeared tired from her journey to and from Ryde. She also didn't wish to talk about her friend, saying that out of respect for the lady's privacy, she couldn't share much more than the fact that Mama's friend was ill and perhaps may be dying.

"It's enough that we pray for her comfort and health," she added. No more words were said on the matter.

Over dinner, Mr. Lovell enjoyed the attention my parents heaped upon him. His spirits visibly rose, and his usual gaiety returned. His eyes brightened, the shadows that darkened his features vanished, and he looked handsomer than before.

Within moments, laughter and light conversation filled the dining room. Papa prodded our guest over his reasons for traveling to the island and not taking up a room at Northwode Hall.

"The secrecy of your journey and the modesty of your accommodations, sir, are quite telling. Let me guess—a lady's involved, am I correct?"

Mr. Lovell merely laughed, his cheeks coloring. It appeared Papa was correct, and I felt ill. "I've nothing to say to that, sir."

Thankfully my parents, though in a jovial mood, didn't press, but I knew how eager both of them were in finding out more. I'd yet to stir the calm waters in the vicarage with my own romantic adventures. For now, my parents had Mr. Lovell on whom to dote over matters of the heart.

I hated the subject they'd raised. I must confess I hated it. I added nothing to the conversation—merely listened and watched Mr. Lovell, torn between admiring him without compunction and resenting his presence.

I was mystified by the effect he had on me. If I could, I'd sit there and watch him, absorb every word he'd say, and think myself a far richer boy than I was before we crossed paths. At the same time, I was uncomfortable with the intensity of my admiration for him and the awful pangs of annoyance at the mention of a lady in his life. I found I had more questions than answers.

By the end of dinner, I wasn't quite sure I knew myself anymore.

Papa invited Mr. Lovell for more conversation and drink afterward. Mama retired for the evening, claiming a headache and exhaustion, but she nonetheless seconded Papa's invitation with a good deal of warmth.

"You may stay for the night, if you wish," she added with a smile. "I can have Dorcas prepare the spare bedroom for you."

"An excellent idea," Papa said. "If you came here on foot, Mr. Lovell, it wouldn't be wise to walk back to Rookley. We don't keep a carriage, as you know, and our Stephen is away at present and unavailable to take you back home by pony and trap."

"Thank you, Mr. Wakeman. I'm much obliged." Mr. Lovell then followed him to the parlor while Mama sent Dorcas upstairs before she herself ascended. I reluctantly shadowed the men if only to bid them goodnight as well.

"You're a coward, Nathaniel," I muttered to myself once I closed my bedroom door behind me. I leaned against it, scowling in the dimness of my sanctuary. Keats' poetry remained where I left it earlier, and its pages beckoned.

That was one comfort to be had, I thought, and I gladly sat down at my writing desk and lost myself in poetry.

• • • •

A DULL, THROBBING PAIN in my neck awoke me. I'd fallen asleep at my desk, my book serving as an uncomfortable pillow.

"Oh, Lord," I groaned, slowly raising myself up. Sharp pain stabbed at me now as strained muscles were forced back into movement. I grimaced and rubbed my neck and my shoulders. I also felt thirsty and decided to wander downstairs for something refreshing.

I didn't know what time it was—only that it was silent and dark everywhere. It had begun to rain as well. A gentle shower, I saw, my windows welcoming the light and rhythmic patter. It was a comforting sound.

Downstairs all was silence as well, with the only light coming from the parlor. I ignored it and went to the kitchen for my drink. On my way back upstairs, I stopped at the sight of light filtering out from under the parlor door.

Perhaps Papa was still awake. I suppose it was time for me to confront his anger at my bold escape.

"Better now than later." I sighed. He certainly wouldn't forget.

I knocked on the door and entered without waiting for an invitation.

"Oh," I stammered. "I didn't realize you were still awake, sir."

Mr. Lovell rose from his seat, setting a book aside.

"I've completely lost all thought of time, I'm afraid," he said with a rueful laugh. "I should retire. Your father was kind enough to allow me some time to myself. He said I needed it."

I leaned against the door and regarded him thoughtfully. "Were you able to confide in him about your, uh, troubles?"

"In a way, yes. He was very generous and patient with me. I owe him much." He paused, blinking, and ran his fingers through his hair. "I'm also a bit drunk, I'm afraid."

"As long as you're feeling a little more at ease, sir," I said. I tried not to be resentful like before, but it seemed I didn't try hard enough. I grew a little sullen at the thought he wouldn't trust me with his troubles despite my assurances and clear advantage as the keeper of his secrets.

In my childish way, I'd convinced myself having confided in Papa, Mr. Lovell was surely beyond my influence now. Another man had advised him, not a friend, and he was well on his way to being lost to me.

Surely, I thought, Papa would have told him to stop his dawdling and propose to Miss Thornber. I was sure one of the first things he'd do the moment he set foot on Liscombe was to hurry to the lady's side and beg for her hand. It was miserable.

Mr. Lovell's tired gaze strayed to the hearth. The fire had long died. "I wish I were at ease, Nathaniel," he said, his voice quiet. "I wish I were."

"Perhaps you didn't ask the right questions."

"The right questions, as you call them, aren't the best questions to ask."

I frowned at him. "I don't understand."

"I should go to bed now," he said with an impatient wave of a hand. "The longer I stay here, the more confounded things grow. I'm sorry I can't stay and speak with you longer."

Resentment turned to anger. "I'm sorry, too," I said. "I hope you enjoyed dinner. I know my parents enjoyed your company." I shrugged and turned around, taking the doorknob in hand.

"I appreciate your time, Nathaniel. I only wish I could have been a much better companion to you today."

He'd been using my Christian name throughout his visit. I found it extremely difficult not to cling to that fact, though it felt as though he broke my heart every time he said it. I paused at the door and looked back. "Then why did you come?"

"Because I had questions I needed answered." He hesitated. "Because I wished to test my strength."

"And? Do you find yourself strong, sir?"

"No, but I know where I ought to direct my steps."

"I'm sorry if your visit wasn't very pleasurable." I opened the door and stepped out into the hallway. "I'll show you to your room, Mr. Lovell."

Chapter 17

I didn't know what Mr. Lovell wished to accomplish by his sudden visit. I didn't know if he benefited from it at all. The only thing that kept a hold on me was the regret I felt when he left the following morning. My confusion, my irritation, all directed at him, manifested themselves in a cold and distant behavior toward Mr. Lovell throughout breakfast till the moment he left.

If he noticed anything amiss, he said nothing. He showed nothing. Then again I suppose it was inevitable, with my parents drawing him into their conversation the very minute he appeared in the dining room. It was all well and good, I told myself again and again, that the burden of entertaining him was never on my shoulders.

I was left alone to finish my meal in peace despite feeling the weight of his stare several times across the table.

I felt bereft when he left. It was far better for me to suffer the discomfort his presence caused than to feel alone.

I was polite in my farewell and hopefully didn't give him any reason to regret his visit, but the hollowness that followed the dying sound of his footsteps—he chose to walk back to Rookley despite the muddy paths—ate away at me.

Papa never forgot the threatened talk regarding my escape. Mr. Lovell had barely vanished from our midst when he called me into the sitting room.

"We need to discuss your sudden turn to rebellion, Natty," he declared as he took his place in his favorite easy chair.

I stood before my father, the picture of perfect repentance and grief with my head bowed and my hands clasped behind me. For all that, however, I said nothing. I heard nothing. My mind was elsewhere, and I refused to pull myself back to the present till my final five minutes in the sitting room.

I emerged from my gloomy distraction with my spirits low and listened to Papa's final words, which came to a serious warning against repeated displays of pig-headedness.

"And since you can't seem to stay put as ordered and appear to be so eager leaving the house at a moment's notice, I suppose it's best to take advantage of your amazing levels of energy and put them to good use," Papa said, and I felt my blood drain away from me at the implications. I couldn't argue, though, knowing it was pointless to pursue it.

I was once again punished, but instead of isolation in my room, I was ordered to take care of errands all over the parish, ghosts be damned.

Mama didn't say much about the incident when I approached her later and begged her to help me make Papa understand. She'd already been told about my ghostly encounters and had disregarded them the same way Papa did.

"Your father knows what's best for you," she observed without a glance up from her needlework. "Really, Natty, I can't see why you insist on challenging us at every turn. You've always been such a serious, disciplined boy—until now."

"But I'm not lying!" I protested. "You can ask Mr. Lovell, if you wish. He saw something out there, and he told me he's never experienced anything like that before."

She looked up at me, surprised. "Mr. Lovell? Are you involving your friend, Natty?"

"If you don't believe me, you're welcome to ask him."

"I think we're finished with this conversation."

I said too much, and I didn't care. I threw Mama a final, baleful look before turning around and moving to the door. Once I laid my hand on the door handle, however, I had to stop when a thought—coming from nowhere—suddenly crossed my mind.

"Mama," I said, turning to look at her. "Is anyone in our household ill?"

She stared at me, her brows furrowed. "What on earth are you talking about?"

"Is anyone here ill? I need to know."

"No one, of course. I've never seen a healthier household. What a strange question." She shook her head and terminated the conversation with a chuckle and a very emphatic shifting in her chair in order to turn away from me, her attention once again occupied by her sewing.

I wasn't aware of how long I observed her, but I now guess it must have been a brief moment—or at least long enough for me to catch something in her manner.

What was it? Confusion? Shock? Given my sudden question, I wouldn't be surprised to know that I'd just caught her off her guard.

I left her alone and flew out of the house, retracing my steps back to the area where I'd fallen that day I was sent out to see Mrs. Tuckett and her children. My mind raced as I hurried along the main road till I found it.

Bits of past conversations with Hetty came alive. It was a strange and frightening moment for me. I couldn't stop my thoughts as one quickly followed the other, every single one insisting on being the solution to the mystery of my ghost.

I searched through the shrubbery, the grass, the piles of dry leaves and broken twigs. I'd even fallen on my hands and knees and crawled back and forth, unmindful of the ridiculous picture I was sure I made to any passerby. Thankfully the road remained quiet.

"There!" I cried, snatching the soiled miniature from its bed of dirt and grass. With the recent rains, mud had caked it, and I hurried back to the vicarage, immediately washing it clean once I was indoors.

So many questions and possibilities—I didn't know where to begin.

• • • •

DORCAS MADE A FACE and shook her head. "I don't know, Natty," she said. "It's an old thing, yes. Quite likely children took to it like a toy and did this to it."

She ran a finger across the miniature's damaged surface. Then she gave it to Stephen, who frowned as he inspected it in his turn.

"It's strange, isn't it?" I asked, resting my chin on my crossed arms on the kitchen table. I watched Stephen turn it over in his hand, the miniature looking smaller and more delicate against his thick and callused fingers.

"It's strange," Stephen echoed thoughtfully. "I don't like how her face is all nothing, but you can still feel her looking at you."

"That's my feeling as well," Dorcas said with a nod.

"What does she remind you of?" I asked.

"A ghost, surely."

Stephen snorted. "A statue with no face. Ghost? Pah!" He set the miniature down on the table, in the middle, as we stared as if it were some odd relic. "I think some lady tore this thing up."

"Whatever for?" Dorcas asked, looking a bit stunned.

"Jealousy, no doubt. You women are always ready to tear each other's' throats out over a fellow."

"Oh, for heaven's sake! Men aren't angels, Stephen! I'm sure they've killed more men out of jealousy than women have destroyed other women's property for the same reason."

I stifled a grin, not offering a rebuttal. Instead I looked at Stephen and anticipated a response. What could I say? I was a mere child in comparison to their experiences and knowledge of matters such as jealousy and rivalry.

"Well, I'll never argue against that, of course." He coughed. Dorcas grinned in triumph. "But that's not to say that women are less likely to resort to violence when their security—emotional security, that is—is threatened by other women."

"Very well, very well, I'll agree to that. I know of two women from my childhood who were tangled in a rivalry of that kind. Dreadful story, it was, too. I remember Mama telling my aunt about it, when she thought none of the children was listening."

I looked at Dorcas with growing interest. "What happened?"

"It was a quarrel over a man, of course—some blacksmith who wasn't any good for either of them, really, but none of them saw it that way. He wooed each one, and when they found out about their rival, they turned quite savage." Dorcas shivered and sipped her tea as though to calm herself. "One killed the other, you know. Drove a knife into the woman's throat. When her lover rejected her after knowing what she did, she hanged herself before she could be taken away for her crime."

"That's dreadful," I breathed.

"It was a story that never died in Northchapel, Natty. I still remember hearing people from end to end talk about it for weeks after."

Northchapel was Dorcas' birthplace in Sussex, and she fled from it at the very first chance, when she was only fourteen. She rarely ever spoke of it unless prodded. Even then, much of what she said was quite sobering, but certainly nothing as dark as this story.

"So..." I paused and cleared my throat. "What happened to the blacksmith?"

She shrugged. "Nothing. He married some farmer's daughter, and that was it."

"You mean to say he wasn't blamed for what happened?"

"Oh, he was in many people's eyes, believe me, but he didn't kill anyone."

"But he drove someone to kill!"

Dorcas leveled me with a scolding frown. "The murderer made the choice. That was all, Natty. The man wasn't worth a drop of anyone's blood, but she made the choice."

Stephen shook his head and sighed. "Damned shame, it is. A waste of life."

I looked back at the defaced miniature. Straining my eyes further, I tried to take in the smaller, finer details of its tattered surface. The scratches, the slight gouges here and there—when observed from a certain angle, with the light striking the surface just so, it appeared to have a face of its own. Uneven features—crooked eyebrows, un-matched eyes, a broken nose, an oddly placed mouth—met my gaze.

I thought of it as a mockery of a face. I also saw a faint, faint shadow of a woman long dead, peering out from the shallow depths of an artist's painting against ivory. She didn't belong to the present, and it had nothing to do with her old-fashioned dress. There was something about her ruined likeness that spoke of distance not only in time but also of place.

My thoughts flitted back to the past and to the circumstances surrounding the discovery of this strange thing.

"Do you think that objects can be haunted?" I asked, breaking the momentary silence.

"Haunted?" Stephen chuckled. "Objects haunted? I don't believe in such things, Mr. Natty. That's all silly superstitious nonsense."

I pointed at the miniature, my words seemingly forming well before coherent thought. "This could be haunted." I didn't know where that idea came from, but I said it as though it were something that was natural and unarguable.

"What makes you say that?" Dorcas asked, pouring Stephen more tea. "It's just old and ruined, but that doesn't mean much."

"I don't know." I laughed, my face warming. "The words just came out of me. Then again, if any object were to be haunted, wouldn't something old and defaced like this be a good vessel for the dead to come back?"

"Well, perhaps."

I took a deep breath. "Messages from the dead," I prodded. "Can objects be haunted because they're used as a means for the dead to communicate with the living?"

Dorcas frowned deeply at me. "All this is nonsense. I hope your father doesn't hear it."

"Wait—a warning, maybe? We're being warned about a calamity in the future, and the dead can only do so through objects like this miniature." I paused to clear my mind and steady my heart. "I've heard of banshees before. Do you think our household has its own?"

"Why, have you seen one?"

I looked at Dorcas, hesitating, and then at Stephen. "I—I think I have," I replied in a smaller voice, my confidence wavering under such intense scrutiny from both.

"Oh, Natty, do stop. I really don't know where you get your ideas. This is dreadful—very improper for a bright, young Christian boy like you."

Stephen laughed before sipping his tea. "If I were Mr. Natty's age, Dorcas, I'd be fancying the same things. I've heard of something like banshees before, but that's always been superstitious rubbish. Besides, those creatures only haunt Irish families if I remember rightly."

The housekeeper made a sound of disapproval in her throat as she pushed her chair back and stood up.

"There's a pudding you're supposed to take to old Mrs. Winterton, Natty." She threw me a look of sympathy. "Your Papa specifically told me to make sure you don't dawdle like before."

I said nothing. Staring at the miniature with its phantom face was a far preferable alternative.

• • • •

THE SHEET OF PAPER seemed to mock me. It was blank, its white surface reminding me too much of a certain blank, white face. The rain's pattering offered me no comfort this time. I sat at my writing desk, my mind nothing but a mass of agonized thoughts, remembrances.

It had been several hours since my return to the vicarage. I was no longer shaking, but I was still terrified. The ghost appeared to me that afternoon—twice. It "came upon" me when I walked to Mrs. Winterton's cottage, and it "came upon" me when I walked back. I didn't take the footpaths that time, convinced the broader and busier roads would offer me some escape from the thing that dogged my steps.

There were carts. There were men on horses. There were stray wanderers. None of them did anything to keep the loathsome creature away.

Its first appearance was at the side of the road. It made itself seen just after a horse and cart rumbled past me. The way it suddenly materialized across the road from where I walked—so much closer than it was before—as though waiting for the intruding presence of horse and cart to pass, gave the sense of something that taunted me.

"I'm everywhere," it seemed to say. "Wherever you are, Nathaniel, you'll see me."

It appeared again as I walked back to the vicarage. As before, it materialized at the other side of the road and at a closer distance compared to when it first made itself known to me.

It was growing bolder. It crept forward every time, cutting down the distance between us. How long before I'd see it standing beside me? I was fortunate that the vile thing hadn't crossed the threshold of my home. Perhaps it couldn't, with Papa here. A man of God, I thought, surely would be an effective deterrent to supernatural forces. Or was I simply fooling myself? It could very well be a matter of time.

I returned home nearly sick from fear, the threat I sensed from the quiet figure growing more and more—like a rotting shadow that had taken root in my belly and begun to swell, eating away at everything in its path.

I ignored Papa on my return home, and I didn't care. He'd instructed me to go to him once I'd dispensed my task. Instead I ran upstairs and pulled a sheet of paper from my drawer. It sat, untouched, on my writing desk for a long time. In between surges of fear, panic, anger, and the overwhelming need to cry despite my embarrassment, I was momentarily crippled by shame.

Would he answer my letter? Would he even acknowledge it? Was he angry with me, given how I behaved toward him the last time we saw each other?

I refused dinner, claiming indisposition. No one thought to bother me with his or her presence. When the rain finally came, I'd finished my agitated pacing and had sat myself down.

"Do it, for God's sake," I hissed, wiping my eyes against my sleeve. I uncovered my ink-pot, pulled my chair closer to the desk, and began writing, pausing on occasion to dry my eyes because they now refused to hold back the tears.

Dear Mr. Lovell, I hope you'll forgive my boldness in writing to you, but I've no one else in whom I can trust...

Chapter 18

Mama's friend's condition worsened by the day, she told us. Every time she returned home from her journey to Ryde, she appeared more and more exhausted.

"I wish she'd see a physician," she said at dinner-time.

"Why won't she?" Papa asked. I thought his tone to be unnecessarily harsh whenever he talked about her friend.

"Lydia has no money, Frederick. Her husband left her with nothing after his ruin. I'm grateful she doesn't have children, or the poor creatures surely won't survive such destitution."

"She's given up then."

"She refuses to do anything more for herself."

Papa shook his head, glowering at his wine. "Pity for the poor widow. I'm sure she'd have found help somehow."

"Indeed." Mama spared him a brief, unreadable glance before dropping her gaze back to her soup. "A great pity."

"We can give her something, can't we, Mama?" I asked. She sighed and shook her head, swirling her spoon in her soup.

"It isn't necessary, Natty. I've tried, believe me. She refused. In fact, she threatened to keep me from seeing her if I resorted to charity."

I frowned at her. "I don't understand. Does she want to die?"

"She does. Please, let's talk about something more cheerful. I've had enough misery for the day," Mama replied with a faint smile. She met my glance and gently rubbed her temple with a slightly trembling hand.

"The best we can do is pray for her," Papa said.

Mama agreed with a lifeless "Amen," which Papa didn't seem to hear. He continued to eat, a dark cloud hovering above him. I didn't know why he appeared to dislike Mama's friend. He was always dismissive and curt whenever he spoke about Mrs. Lydia Stanton. One would think the poor sick widow had done him some grievous injury in the past, but from what I knew, they'd never even crossed paths.

Mama's visits grew more and more frequent. When she first discovered her friend's whereabouts, she ventured out once in a fortnight after Papa gave her leave, finally. Then her travels increased to twice in a fortnight.

As of late it was three times. Papa didn't seem to care much though I could sense the annoyance that crept into his speech and manner whenever Mama broached the subject of a coming visit she needed to make.

"Has this woman no other friends?" he demanded one time.

"As far as I know, she hasn't. Are you being unreasonable again, Frederick? The way you carry on about the poor creature, one would think she'd offended you in the worst way possible."

"Your visits, Cecily, are eating away at your duties around the house."

Mama regarded him coolly. She continued to embroider delicate patterns without a change in their rhythm and flow. From where I sat, she appeared both magnificent and unsettling.

"It's just as much my Christian duty to care for a sick and dying woman who's long given up on hope. Can you find it in yourself to deny her a few hours of comfort per week? Once she's gone, she won't trouble you with her needs. Perhaps you ought to look at her situation from that perspective."

She spoke with a cold bitterness that she didn't care to temper. The way she bit off her words, the way she looked at Papa with a gaze that flashed with contempt—this was a side of her I'd never seen before, and it startled me.

"Your charity remains unparalleled," Papa replied with equal bitterness. "Some people are unusually fortunate in their benefactors."

Mama fell silent. She carefully replaced her work in her sewing-basket and rose from her chair. Without another word, she swept out of the parlor in a heavy rustle of skirts.

When I sought her out afterward, I discovered she'd walked out with her bonnet and shawl. No one knew where she'd gone, but we all assumed she simply took a walk to clear her head and calm her mood. When she returned home after an hour, she appeared quite easy and even a touch cheerful as though nothing uncomfortable had just happened between her and Papa.

The subject of her frequent visits to Ryde wasn't raised for the remainder of the day. I was sure, however, it was never far from Papa's mind.

• • • •

THE RAINS PROVED TO be a blessing. Day after day, it had been nothing but one cloudburst after another. I was therefore unable to go out and be subjected to more hauntings. Within doors, I kept myself busy with my books and odd tasks Mama or Papa would assign me around the vicarage.

Through all these, I awaited Mr. Lovell's response to my letter. My anxiety and embarrassment rose with every day of hearing nothing.

"He must think me an idiot," I kept telling myself again and again as I paced around my room. Keats' poetry no longer offered the comfort of distraction. I'd spirited away another book of poetry from Papa's library, and it offered me even less.

It was all I could do to turn to prose for my diversion, and that appeared to help. I wish I could understand why novels proved to be more effective in easing my mind.

There was so much rawness of emotion in poetry. Perhaps because of that, I was unable to find peace at a time when so much doubt plagued me.

I grimaced as I looked at the weathered cover of my recent acquisition. "Oh, Lord," I muttered. "I used to mock books like this before. Now look at me."

It was a surprise, I also thought, seeing that book in Papa's library. I didn't know where it came from, for both my parents had expressed a good deal of disdain toward "sentimental claptrap." Mama, in particular, had always been partial to more "practical novels," as she'd call them—novels with little or no romance and plenty of Christian lessons.

It was a curious preference, I thought, for she'd always been much more of a romantic than she perhaps hoped the world to know. Indeed, who else would keep weathered and well-read copies of *Jane Eyre* and *Pamela,* all tucked away on dusky bookshelves groaning under the weight of philosophers and poets?

I'd pulled out Mrs. Burney's *Evelina*—undoubtedly one of Mama's favorites because it nearly fell to pieces in my hands, having been read so many times over—and read it at my leisure.

It didn't take me long to finish it, and I shelved the book feeling quite sheepish at the thought I actually enjoyed reading something so girlish and whimsical. Papa wouldn't have approved, I was sure, and I took care to ensure he wasn't home when I pulled out *The Mysteries of Udolpho* for my next literary indulgence.

And as though waiting for the perfect moment to come, Mr. Lovell's response arrived. I ran upstairs and kept to my room as before. This time, I did so without a shred of sullen misanthropy.

I sat beside my window and used the murky light filtering in from outside for illumination. The endless pattering of rain against the glass once again soothed my spirits. It was enjoyable pressing against the cold window, my ears a few inches away from the rhythmic and tuneless lullaby that carried on without a moment's pause for breath.

My dear Nathaniel, I must confess to being a little bewildered by your accounts, Mr. Lovell began. *I'm not a superstitious man, and I've never taken you for one. I've been, however, subject to a few odd imaginings here and there, and by and large, they've been nothing more than distorted perceptions caused by fatigue or emotional strain. I've had visions, but they were all fleeting at best, mostly furtive shadows and movements seen from the corner of my eyes.*

Yes, perhaps once or twice, I thought I sensed something else while walking by your side—a third presence or a pair of invisible eyes watching us from a distance. It all proved to be nonsense, however. There was no other person present, and if I correctly remember the paths we took, I know it's quite impossible for someone to hide himself so thoroughly in the immediate vicinity.

As for that shadow I saw among the trees on my last visit, I'm quite convinced it was nothing more than that: a shadow. When light filters through trees and branches at certain times of the day (and with just the right amount of cloud covering), it can play all kinds of tricks on one's eyes. I know I told you before I was sure it was a person, but distance involving time and place has allowed me a more objective perspective on the incident. I now feel foolish for causing you any anxiety with my conclusions. Believe me when I say giving you cause for alarm was the furthest thing in my mind.

I can only account for your visions as the product of an overheated imagination. Or dare I say an overburdened mind, heart, and, perhaps, spirit? You live a very sheltered life, Nathaniel. I know that you've no close friends to speak of, and you're at an age when certain things are magnified beyond reason, leaving you with more questions than answers. If I may be so bold, I'll add that you're carrying quite a burden on your shoulders, with no one in whom you can confide your troubles and your secrets.

I've not proven myself as good a friend as I hoped, though you offered your confidence a few times in the course of our still-young friendship. I'm quite aware I disappointed you in my last visit, and I'm heartily sorry for hurting you in such a way. I hope I haven't discredited myself so much that you won't believe me when I say that I simply couldn't confide in you then.

Perhaps in time the reason will be known, but for now, allow me my secrets. If it comforts you, what I told your father wasn't the complete truth. He'd guessed rightly enough that my current troubles involve a lady, but he never knew the real nature of my problems. He advised me as other gentlemen and ladies had before him—marry Miss Thornber, and all will come out for the best. We ended our conversation with me feeling no less burdened than before.

There. Even now, even with all these miles separating us, I still feel compelled to divulge more than I should.

I suppose, then, it's bad form for me to offer you myself if you're in need of a confidant. I'm sure it is, but I'll offer it all the same. Nathaniel, if there's anything I can do to help, please ask me. You'll not be denied anything. Believe me, I know how it is being alone—or at least living in the shadows of certain truths, which I've always thought to be the curse of men like ourselves.

I read Mr. Lovell's letter several times over. Something in me slowly stirred, shook off fragile layers. No, I still couldn't articulate what was happening to me, but somehow I understood. I knew what it was, that awareness being so deep and murky I continued to struggle in pulling it to the surface.

Seeing Miss Thornber's name mentioned caused another pang of resentment, and I knew then I was jealous of her. It was an ugly moment—and a frightening discovery. The confusion, the hurt, and the anger that all flared in my breast startled me.

I frowned at the letter on my lap. What would that say about my regard for Mr. Lovell, then? A sudden chill enveloped me when shadows of the truth took shape.

"That's not possible," I muttered. I shook my head as though to convince myself somehow I was horribly wrong in my conclusion. "No, that isn't right. It isn't."

My mind refused to be silenced, however, and fragments from the recent past swirled alive. I was soon drowning in memories of time spent in Mr. Lovell's company. Not only were these fleeting images of the gentleman in his most engaging, but they were also recollections of my responses to his presence, his conversation.

I realized I did more than admire the man. I adored him, worshipped him, without even knowing or understanding how or why.

I stared at the letter in shocked silence for a moment.

Then I looked out the window and at the rain-drenched garden below me as though compelled by a silent call.

The ghost stood near the farthest wall—a grotesque, ghastly statue surrounded by Papa's lush rosebushes. It faced my bedroom window though it didn't look up to subject me with a full view of its dead, stiff features. I could still see, however, that it watched me.

It watched, and it waited, even in the rain.

I hurried out of my room and down the stairs to the garden. I heard raised voices behind the closed door of the parlor, and I knew my parents were having another quarrel.

Bursting out the back door and throwing myself carelessly into the rain, I ran to the place where the ghost waited for me. It was gone, however, when I reached the spot. I turned around, my gaze sweeping the garden as the rain soaked me.

"Where are you?" I cried out. My voice sliced through the downpour's steady rhythm. "Show yourself!"

The ghost didn't appear. Damn the coward. I could feel traces of its presence in the garden, though, and I took those traces and fed myself with them, gorging on the icy fury the ghastly thing now roused in me.

"You don't frighten me! You don't threaten me or my family!" I shouted, turning around in a staggering little circle. I needed to fill the garden with my voice—and my defiance. "Can you hear me, you disgusting coward? You filth! You don't exist—not anymore! You're nothing! Nothing!"

I laughed, still turning around, throwing my head back to give full vent to my fury. The rain's chill did nothing to calm me. I shivered but not because of the incessant pelting of cold water. I was purging myself of so many things—shedding layer after layer of what I'd always believed to be, exposing what lay beneath. The relief that came with the sudden, angry release overwhelmed me.

I eventually stopped my outburst and staggered to a halt. The rain continued its assault, and I welcomed it, my head still thrown back, my face turned to the dark sky. I spread my arms out.

The ghost no longer frightened me. How could it? I'd just discovered who I was—what I was. I thought of Papa—the man of God—his lectures, his prayers, my obedience to God and His Word. I even thought of running to our little church for sanctuary and guidance, but even as I thought all these, I also felt none of them mattered where I was concerned. Unless my very soul was torn out of my body, I saw nothing my faith could do to save me. Somehow, that moment, I understood it was so, and nothing terrified me the way I terrified myself.

I loved—but not as prudently as Mama once hoped. I'd fallen in love with another man.

I opened my eyes to the rain, enduring the blinding discomfort.

"Miles," I murmured again and again. How I wished to speak his Christian name in his presence in that same quiet, gentle tone with which he always spoke mine.

Chapter 19

My cousin Edward was engaged, and a ball was held in his and his fiancée's honor not three days after my receipt of Mr. Lovell's letter. My family was invited. To my surprise, Papa agreed to go.

I thought not to ask the reason for his reversal, however, and simply prepared for it.

I didn't have much by way of fashionable things and simply chose to put on my least faded, least weathered suit. Dorcas cut my hair after a good deal of arguing against my refusal to admit I looked quite wild with my hair growing over my ears.

I was ready before my parents and so spent the time waiting for them in my bedroom. I couldn't read any of my books. My mind constantly wandered, and before long I'd pulled out Mr. Lovell's letter from my bureau and reread it for the hundredth time since my receipt. It had become a guilt-ridden pleasure of mine to do that.

I was painfully aware nothing could come out of my attraction to him—my love for him. I was certain he knew it. We weren't equals in any way. He had money, pedigree; I didn't. Even if what I felt for him were protected, supported, or justified by the Bible, the disparity of our ranks simply wouldn't allow such a foolhardy connection to happen.

Somewhere during my third perusal, my attention once again wandered. My gaze moved from the letter to rest on my wooden bowl and its collection of odd little treasures. The defaced miniature sat atop everything, and I picked it up without much thought, turning it over between my fingers as I'd done several times in the past.

"Such a strange thing you are," I murmured idly. "And what curious luck it was that sent me to St. Bertram's and—"

My words faded. I stared at the thing, this time turning thoughts over and over in my head. Little by little, like scattered bits of paper being collected and pasted back together, ideas began to form—ideas that followed a certain logic, a certain chain.

St. Bertram's church—the widow praying—the miniature found—ghostly presences. I looked back at the recent past and tried to remember when the first haunting took place.

There on the island, on one of the footpaths? No—it was back in Liscombe—at Shepley Abbey. I remembered now. It was the day Mr. Lovell and I spent a few idle hours walking through the abbey ruins. The ghost was there, standing among trees at a distance. I saw it, but he didn't.

The familiar sensation of my skin prickling and the hair on the back of my neck standing came over me again.

A lady. Over there. I think she knows you.

Oh? Is it Miss Thornber? Where is she?

In the trees over there.

Where?

She was there a moment ago. She must have hurried off when I caught her staring at you.

Was it Miss Thornber? Ah, never mind.

No. I don't think so.

She knows me?

It appeared so. She was looking at you when I saw her—must have been watching you for some time before I turned around, but she did nothing—just stood there.

I swept my tongue over my dry lips as I fumbled around for those incidents that took place on the island.

The ruined face stared back at me with desecrated eyes. Yes, I took that vile, ghastly thing home with me.

The mystery of the miniature's sudden appearance remained unsolved, and all I had to go by were fantastic suppositions—supernatural causes. I'd long grown tired of wading through the illogical web and learned to resign myself to the unknown.

What would the ghost's connection be, then? The painting's protector?

"That's absurd!" I breathed, frowning at the violated image. "What would be protected here? Unless the widow truly owned this thing, and—and—"

I grappled with words, with thoughts. Logic betrayed me again, and what at first seemed to be so rational suddenly dissolved in a flood of superstitious nonsense.

Things of ill-omen. Harbingers of misfortune. Hetty had talked about banshees once upon a time, and I'd managed to raise something close to a discussion with Dorcas and Stephen that one afternoon. Dear God, it was all rubbish, and yet...

No, there had to be an explanation. Surely, there'd be something out there that would make me understand.

Then again, perhaps things ought to be left alone. Perhaps there were laws that simply defied reason. Perhaps—perhaps—some things simply happened for their own sake.

What of coincidence?

What else had happened since the miniature—and the ghost— had followed me home? My parents' quarrels began because Papa had forbidden Mama from continuing her visits to Havenstreet. My mother also began her visits to her sick and dying friend, which, after a while, caused further friction between her and Papa. He'd already begun to voice his objections, at times forbidding her from visiting Mrs. Stanton. I'd also...

My face burned at the thought. "I'd also come to feel for Mr. Lovell," I said under my breath. For all my confusion, however, I still felt a surge of indignation. "No," I added, my voice steadying itself. "Why would I lower that to the level of superstition and ridiculous, nonsense things like ghosts?"

I took up Mr. Lovell's slightly crumpled letter and folded it before consigning it back to the shadows of my bureau. My pride refused to calm itself, and I continued to feel the sting of insult. My feelings weren't superstition. By God, they weren't! Neither were they objects of contempt among those whose feelings were marked for the opposite sex.

What I felt might be judged as wrong, but it was still real to me. I simply couldn't deny it. Why would God give me the desire and yet condemn me for feeling it?

Dr. Sharpton had long judged me a fit and healthy boy—absolutely sound in mind and body. Surely, I thought, a respectable physician such as he couldn't be wrong after all these years.

By that point in time, I'd also convinced myself the hauntings—the ghost and the miniature—followed a logic that was separate from the normal world. In brief, the hauntings had nothing to do with my mind or any threats to my sanity. I'd yet to understand what was happening, but I also knew I wasn't at fault.

A knock on my door broke through my thoughts.

"Natty, are you ready?" Dorcas called, her voice muffled. "Your mother and father are waiting for you downstairs."

"Yes, I'm coming!" I leapt up from my chair just as Dorcas slowly opened the door and peered in.

"Come along, dear. Your uncle sent his carriage for you, too. It's an impressive thing—looks quite new."

I hurried over to her, laughing off my earlier confusion. "And what a grand show we'll make of things, with Uncle's permission. What do you think, Dorcas? Am I genteel enough for his carriage, or do I deserve to walk to Havenstreet like the luckless peasant that I am?"

She chuckled and rolled her eyes as she stepped aside to let me pass. I forced encouraging thoughts to fill my head as I hurried to the stairs—fortified myself with reassurances that things, somehow, would work out in the end. That there was surely—as it often happened—a simple explanation for everything.

In the meantime, however, I ought to enjoy myself again—behave like an ordinary seventeen-year-old boy.

I'd hidden myself from the world and all its unpleasant surprises long enough. Hauntings or no, I couldn't—I shouldn't—be forced into hiding like a hunted criminal.

It was odd, but I felt somehow transformed by those few moments alone, struggling with questions that refused to be so easily answered. Faced by things that seemed to defy natural laws. My spirits had risen—even grown defiant.

I also felt some anger and a fierce desire to defend my territory—that is, my heart and my senses, their capabilities, regardless of their nature. If I was meant to love other men, I was sure it was for a good reason. Since I was a child, Papa had always taught me that God allowed things to happen in order to strengthen one's spirit, one's character, and to find ultimate fulfillment and happiness once he embraced his trials as hidden blessings from heaven.

Mama fussed over me when I joined her and Papa near the front door.

"You could have chosen something more proper," she said, sighing. Her hands flew up and down my body as she brushed off dust with her handkerchief. "Turn around."

"We'll have to send the boy to Newport," Papa said.

"The better tailors are in London."

"Newport, Cecily. Nothing farther."

Mama said nothing to that—simply fluttered her hands against me, tickling my nose with the sharp, swift movements of her handkerchief on my jacket. It took me all I had to keep myself from sneezing. I frowned at her.

She exuded so much nervous energy I wondered if she were ill. Indeed, I even wondered if her fussing over me was nothing more than an attempt to hide her restlessness and agitation. Eventually—though it felt like forever—she stopped. She gave me one final critical inspection before muttering her reluctant approval. When she drew her hands away, I saw they trembled most dreadfully.

I also realized her eyes were red-rimmed and slightly swollen. She turned away before I could say something about them, however. A glance in Papa's direction silenced me as well because he looked grim and distracted, not acknowledging Mama when she swept past him, his hands clenched at his sides.

They'd had another quarrel. I was sure of it. If not, perhaps one was about to happen.

We made a somewhat charming trio once inside my uncle's carriage. My parents sat side-by-side, but their attention was pointedly directed outside the window closest to each of them. I sat across from their seat, occupying my time with silly hopes of seeing Mr. Lovell at the ball.

My hands wandered over my jacket to smooth out the dull fabric, and I felt something hard and loose inside one of my pockets. I fumbled around and pulled it out. Anger and defiance flared in my breast again as I stared at the miniature in my hand. I couldn't remember slipping that horrible thing in my pocket when Dorcas came to my room, but I did somehow. It had found its way back to me again.

"Damn you," I hissed at it, and I meant every word.

Thank God for the carriage's noise, which drowned out my curse—no, my challenge.

I'd have flung it out of the window even in my parents' presence, but something held me back. I couldn't understand what it was, but I was compelled to listen to its silent, forceful voice.

. . . .

ALL WAS GLITTERING, golden, and garish at Northwode Hall. The size of the assembly amazed me because I never took the trouble of seeing—truly seeing—the circles in which my cousins moved. Each member of the family had his or her own list of guests, and each seemed determined to outdo the others in the extensiveness of their acquaintances.

When my family entered the great house, Papa hesitated by the door. His face paled as his gaze swept across the scene. His posture stiffened when Mama took him by the arm.

"It's only a ball, Frederick," she said with obviously forced gaiety. "You're not about to be eaten alive."

"Perhaps. My body might be safe, but God help my soul," he retorted. A small group of shrill, chattering young ladies swept past us, and he frowned at them.

"Oh, come now. Surely you'd enjoyed these fêtes as a young man."

"As a young man, and only as such," Papa said.

Mama laughed, her nervous energy intensifying. "Your occupation has soured you, my dear," she said. "Do be reasonable. I'm sure no sin attaches to you for living like an ordinary man who desires pleasure every so often."

I watched Papa, whose face had lost all emotion. I could swear he was made of granite.

One of the servants took to leading us to one of the sitting rooms, where my uncle and aunt wished to see us. Along the way a tall, handsome gentleman with dark whiskers accosted my parents with cheerful cries of "Frederick! Cecily! Good God!"

He appeared to be the same age as Mama and Papa, but to whose friendship he aligned himself, I couldn't say. He met them with equal expressions of familiarity and pleasure.

"Thank you, Harmon, I'll show the lady and the gentleman to their hosts, myself," he said, turning to the smartly uniformed servant who was sent by my aunt to escort us. The portly fellow took his duties quite seriously and seemed put off for being dismissed midway through his task. All the same, he bowed and walked off, his nose in the air.

"It's a delight to see you again, Sir Joseph," Mama declared with nervous pleasure, offering her hand. Papa echoed her sentiments with equal enthusiasm. It was not a comfortable scene by any means. Even with the bustle and the noise around us, I could feel an undercurrent of tension from all three adults.

It was an inconvenient place for a conversation as well because we all stood in the middle of a very busy hallway.

Guests whirled past us. At times they forced me out of their way with a quick nudge of an elbow or a sharp and forceful push of a hand. Some thought to look at me with clear disdain as they took in my clothes with a bored sweep of their gaze. Some smirked, and some raised their brows.

I stood behind my parents while they were engaged in conversation with the whiskered gentleman. It was all I could do to avoid being stepped on or pushed about, gazing around me like a misplaced urchin.

"So why did you stop your visits, Cecily?" Sir Joseph prodded.

"My duties at the vicarage," Mama stammered, a tight smile forming. She appeared dreadfully pale, while Papa's complexion turned red. "They were being neglected, I'm afraid."

Sir Joseph smiled in return, inclining his head as he listened. "Yes, of course. Shall we look for your brother?"

Mama nodded and looked away, a pained expression shadowing her features as she held Papa's arm.

Sir Joseph took his position beside her. I thought I saw him raise his arm as though to offer it to her, but it was such a quick and subtle gesture, I wasn't even sure if I saw things correctly from where I stood, hovering behind them. Indeed, I didn't even know if the defiant sneer that came with the gesture might have been a trick of the light because it was gone in half a second.

Sir Joseph lured my parents away from where they stood. They were so immersed in conversation—as well as the general hubbub of activity around them—they appeared not to notice me.

I didn't care, however. I was bored, and standing like an ill-dressed blockhead in the middle of a busy hallway annoyed me. I allowed them to drift away before turning around to follow the music, where I suspected the dancing was held.

Chapter 20

Once in the ballroom, I felt myself transported back to Somerset—to Huntley House in Dulverton. There was the door on one side that led people into a quieter room for rest.

The room assigned for card-games and other diversions wasn't connected to the ballroom, but I passed it on my way. Sedate and dignified, muted in light and conversation, it was the brief calm before the madness of dance and music two rooms away.

The orchestra this time was much larger, much grander. Men in bright and smart uniforms of some kind—I could think of no other word to refer to what they wore—coaxed lovely music from their instruments while looking quite imperious in their red, white, and gold finery.

The waltz again, I realized, because I'd learned to count beats in Huntley House. Besides, the dancers moving around in wide, wild circles up and down the room told me enough. This time, I didn't see anyone standing along the room's periphery who appeared offended by the scandalous intimacy of the dance.

Once I'd settled myself comfortably against one wall of the ballroom—a necessity to avoid being trampled underfoot by overenthusiastic dancers—I took to scouring the scene for familiar faces. One face, in truth, I hoped to find.

I caught sight of my cousins in all the confusion. All were kept appropriately busy, with Vincent and Marianne changing partners more than Edward. Of the two, Marianne changed partners the most, but it didn't at all surprise me.

Edward's bride-to-be appeared to be a handsome young lady. Tall, with a head of dark hair swept up in a high cluster of curls, she was dressed in a gown of pink silk and white lace that seemed to be an extension of her pale, flushed complexion.

From what I could see—which was nothing more than several fleeting glimpses whenever they swept past my wall—she impressed me with the haughty dignity with which she held on to my cousin as they waltzed. She appeared to be an earnest devotee of the dance because she looked quite serious whenever I saw her.

Even with her head held high despite her ceaseless turning to the music, she made me think of a scholar perfecting her lessons. Perhaps even a pedagogue demonstrating the most proper way of moving just so. As for Edward, he smiled, laughed, and talked, but his partner didn't seem to pay him much heed because her features remained unchanged.

Sometime later a red-faced gentleman pushed his way past the crowd toward the doors. He appeared to be muttering something as he escaped the room, but the noise prevented me from hearing him. I recognized him, however. He was one of Marianne's partners. I could only assume my cousin was once again up to her usual tricks and had pitted one suitor against another.

She could very well be laughing in contemptuous delight as she danced with someone new, but I'd no wish to see.

I didn't know how long it took me to find him, but I caught sight of Mr. Lovell eventually. He wasn't dancing, and I saw him only as he wove his way through the guests, smiling and excusing himself as he went. He didn't see me because I was quite hidden with all the dancing and moving around that carried on. At least he didn't at first.

I wondered if I ought to call out to him when he reached my general area. A sudden self-consciousness took hold of me, however, and, embarrassed, I watched him walk by and simply contented myself with admiring his tall figure and easy, negligent manner.

Perhaps he saw me and didn't recognize me at once.

Perhaps he felt himself steadily watched. Whatever the reason, he stopped before he reached the doors and spun around. He caught me staring in a second. It happened so quickly I didn't have time to look away.

He didn't hesitate at all. Mr. Lovell redirected his steps in my direction and was soon standing before me, shaking my hand.

"Don't you care to dance, Master Wakeman?" he asked with a broad grin. Somehow I felt bereft at not hearing my Christian name spoken in his usual way.

"I don't, no, and I don't care to learn," I stammered, braving a smile of my own. The ease I usually felt in his company had vanished. I suppose such was the price when one found himself in love. "You look very well, sir."

"My family spoils me, I'm afraid."

"It would be a shame if they didn't."

His smile softened a little. "If you're tired of watching people go round and round, perhaps you'd care for a walk. I must confess my head needs a few moments of silence, and my eyes ache for darkness."

"The garden?"

"That would be most pleasant."

My heart beating furiously, I moved away from my wall and led him outside. A thousand questions surged through my head, and I prayed for the strength and presence of mind to have them all satisfied before we returned to the house.

Indeed, I didn't know until we were outside that I'd taken his hand as I led him away from the light and the music. A sudden shock of fear and dismay overcame me at the realization people might have seen us move through the crowds with our hands clasped. That Mr. Lovell didn't think to pull himself free or to chide me for my audacity only compounded my fear—and stirred my elation.

· · · ·

"I USED TO PUT ALL THE blame on school," he said.

"Why?"

Mr. Lovell gave a light shrug. "Being in close quarters with other boys for so many months a year—day in, day out—the temptation was always there. No one would admit it, of course. Everyone was too frightened or bewildered by what we felt for each other."

I swallowed, not daring to look anywhere else but his face. In the moonlight, with his attention fixed steadily in front of him, his beauty never once diminished. "All of you felt it?"

"No, no—some of us, yes. Not all."

"Did anyone—well—act on it?"

My embarrassment, my confusion, and my horror rose to a painful level at the thought—at my own boldness for pursuing it. I realized, however, if I didn't ask, I'd never know. And how many other men in my life would share the same tendencies as I? Mr. Lovell could very well be the first and the last person in whom I could confide—and from whom I could learn.

He surely felt the same stab of mortification and anxiety at my bluntness. He didn't answer right away and instead glanced over his shoulder, perhaps to ensure we were alone in our discussion of outlaw feelings.

"I believe that one of us did, at least," he said, his voice dropping to a near whisper. "I can't be sure."

"It must have been terrible," I half-whispered back.

"Given the risks, Nathaniel, terrible would be the tamest way of describing it."

"Was anyone caught?"

"In the past, two pupils were. It was a scandal, as you may well know, but everyone did what he could to keep things quiet afterward. While I was there, no one was caught, but rumors were rife." He sighed and glanced at me. "I can only assume the guilty had learned to be careful with their dalliances, and we were all left with nothing but speculation. Perhaps—perhaps it was all for the best."

I hesitated. "You used to blame school. Now you don't anymore."

"I expected to return to a life of normalcy once I was out—that my experiences were nothing more than odd but dangerous trials that were unique to schoolboys in those circumstances. Even university didn't stir anything as frighteningly powerful as what I endured in my boyhood. For a time, I believed myself recovered—cured."

Our slow, idle stroll through my uncle's expansive garden led us to that familiar corner where, as a child, I was confined because of its remote location in reference to the great house. In the darkness, I recognized those places where Hetty and I used to play, while the household—even Mama—was kept safe from my presence.

"When did you think otherwise, sir?" I prodded. I suddenly realized my hands were damp with nervous sweat.

"When your cousin introduced us."

"You fell in love with me then?"

"I was attracted to you. You fascinated me, Nathaniel. I couldn't help myself."

I looked down to keep him from seeing—if one could see in the moonlight—my cheeks burn. I'd silence my heart if I could, but it kept its desperate pounding. I was afraid Mr. Lovell could hear its muffled drumming under my clothes.

"How can you be so sure of me?" I asked. "That you and I are alike in that way?"

He sighed. "The look on your face when you talk to me—or even watch me—says a good deal more than you probably think. You're very young and still unguarded in your manners, but my understanding of your nature goes deeper than this." He pressed two fingers against his temple. "Much of it comes from here and here." He moved his hand to his chest and then his stomach.

I stopped and regarded him in wonder. Embarrassment, self-consciousness, confusion—all had now merged into one sensation. I was now aware of solace. Of companionship, camaraderie. The relief I felt at the reassurance I wasn't alone—perhaps would never be alone even if Mr. Lovell were to vanish from my life the next day—overcame me. There were others out there like us.

Quietly hidden away, most likely, but still existing.

He stopped as well and faced me, his features perfectly schooled in showing nothing but calm expectation. I was sure he was simply waiting for me to say or ask more. He seemed to be no more than a teacher, doing what he could to help a younger, far more ignorant student.

My earlier reflections in my bedroom came alive.

Mr. Lovell might understand me, but he still didn't understand me. No, if I were to live with a preference that most people deemed to be immoral, I was condemned to do so without him by my side. He'd return to Liscombe, possibly marry Miss Thornber despite his doubts and his true nature, and respectability would remain undisturbed.

We were mismatched—not in affection, but in wealth and situation. His obligations paralyzed him.

Mr. Lovell ran the greatest risk because of that—disinheritance, scandal, perhaps prison or exile. I didn't know in full what the law could bring down upon us should we be compromised, but I understood it would be wrong for me to subject him to such danger.

"Thank you, sir," I said with a forced little smile. "Perhaps we should go indoors now. My parents must be furious at finding me missing from their side for this long."

We said nothing the rest of the time. We couldn't.

Scarcely a second had passed after I spoke before we pulled each other close. Mr. Lovell secured me with one arm around my waist, one hand against my cheek as we kissed. With his lips against mine, his scent and warmth sweeping over my senses, I thought myself touching infinity. The pain I felt was immense, unspeakable, and the tears flowed when we kissed.

He held me close for a moment, comforting me with whispered reassurances and gentle fingers stroking my hair while I cried softly on his shoulder.

The only mercy Fortune granted us that evening was that no one found us out.

• • • •

MR. LOVELL REMAINED with me when we stepped across the threshold, and we were once again swept up in a confusion of noise and activity. I wove through the crowds in the direction of the sitting room, where I believed my parents were being entertained.

My efforts were disappointed. Neither of my parents, my uncle and aunt, or even Sir Joseph could be found. I wandered from room to room, at one time pausing at the foot of the stairs and looking up, wondering if they were upstairs somewhere.

"Perhaps it would be better to stay in the ballroom," Mr. Lovell suggested. "Your parents surely expect you to be with the rest of the younger guests. They might be there right now, watching the dancers or searching for you."

"Yes, thank you," I said and walked closely behind him.

As I followed him back to the ballroom, I slowly became aware of a sense of dread that gnawed away at the pit of my stomach. It was, as I'd felt so many times in the recent past, an unsettling feeling of being watched by someone unseen.

That's impossible! I'm in my uncle's house, in the middle of a ball! I thought. I pressed a cold hand against my belly, however, stealing glances here and there as I usually did when walking along a footpath, knowing the thing was somewhere nearby.

I saw nothing. Only people I didn't know, walking, talking, laughing, all moving in a perpetual stream around me. My gaze swept over the area, and I found nothing out of the ordinary. No quiet, pale figure standing in a corner or by a window or by a door. I shook my head and chided myself.

No, it was my imagination at work again.

Before long we were back in the ballroom, and my imagination continued to toy with me. Perhaps it was nothing more than a desperate wish on my part for a sympathetic companion, but I thought Mr. Lovell felt the presence, too. I caught him dart a few puzzled glances left and right as he walked, but he said nothing. Neither did he show that anything was amiss.

Somehow I'd convinced myself he was merely searching the crowd for my parents, and that was all.

"Can you see them, Mr. Lovell?" I asked after a while.

"I can't say that I—"

A hand suddenly held my arm in a tight grip. I stopped and looked back to find Papa regarding me with a fierce expression. His complexion was dreadfully pale, and his eyes emoted painfully suppressed fury and hurt.

"Papa," I began, but he cut me short.

"We're going home, Nathaniel," he said. He bit off his words in such a manner as to make it nearly impossible for me to understand him. He barely spared Mr. Lovell a look.

"What—now?"

"Yes, now. Come, and don't argue." He turned around and pulled me along.

"But—"

"I said don't argue, and, for God's sake, keep up!"

I abandoned Mr. Lovell, who couldn't utter a single word in his surprise. I couldn't even look back to acknowledge him with a farewell. Papa's pace was too jarring and relentless, and I fought to stay with him.

He dragged me through hallways, past the main door, and eventually, into my uncle's carriage. He practically threw me inside before climbing in, pulling the door shut with a terrific bang and shouting at the driver to go.

Confused and shaken, I sat myself down and stared at him while he sank back into the shadows. My arm throbbed with a dull pain, but I dared not touch it for fear of infuriating him even more.

"Where—where's Mama?" I asked.

"Mama," he repeated, laughing bitterly. I could barely see his silhouette across the way. "As far as our family's concerned, Nathaniel, your mother died in childbirth."

Chapter 21

The days following our escape from Northwode Hall felt no different from a nightmare. The greatest difference was I couldn't expect to awaken from it.

None of the servants understood what had happened. I couldn't turn to them for answers. Papa refused to talk about it, even threatened to flog me if I vexed him with more questions about Mama.

He carried on with his duties as though nothing so dire had just happened. He visited the sick, laid the dead to rest, comforted the aging, joined young lovers in marriage—all without a sign of a troubled heart or mind. Indeed, he seemed to go about his days as though he truly were a widower, left alone to raise his son.

We continued our family prayers and my lessons. Through all those, I tried to observe him but couldn't read his mind—read his behavior. It felt as though Mama had never existed.

A week had gone without a single word from Havenstreet. I didn't even know if she was still there. I braved another threat of a flogging by approaching Papa afterward.

I tried to wait till he was in the garden, looking after his beloved plants. I'd hoped being in his private sanctuary would help my cause by soothing him into a state of peaceful openness.

"Papa, I think—perhaps I should go to Havenstreet," I said as calmly and as softly as I could.

"You think wrong. There's no reason for you to go there." He didn't once look at me as he continued to lose himself in garden work.

"But—I'd like to know if Mama's well."

He finally stopped and sat back on his heels, drawing an arm across his brow. When he looked up at me, none of his emotions—if he felt any—showed. He was flushed and slightly damp from perspiration, but his eyes didn't even exhibit strain from his exertions. Their flat calm terrified me.

"You're not to go to Havenstreet for any reason, Natty," he said. "You're not to write to your cousins or your uncle and aunt, and you're not to manipulate any of the servants into going there on your behalf."

"But, surely—"

"I trust that you'll not disappoint me in this."

He turned away without another word and moved on his knees to the next flowering shrub which he needed to tend.

• • • •

"YOUR FATHER EXPECTED you to go against his wishes when his back's turned. He warned me about you," Dorcas said, her tone disapproving.

My heart sank. "So you won't do it?"

"I won't, Natty. I'm very sorry. But I answer to your father, not to you, and if he wants his wishes carried out a certain way, I make sure they are."

My gaze dropped to the small packet I held. "I worked on my letter quite late last night," I protested.

"I can't take it, you dear boy. You worked hard for nothing, I'm afraid." Dorcas spared me a sad, sympathetic smile while brushing her fingers through my hair in that familiar gesture of comfort. "I know you understand my predicament."

I fell silent and watched her pour us more tea, pushing my cup and saucer across the table toward me. She was enjoying an afternoon of rest because Papa had gone to Mrs. Tuckett's cottage. The poor widow's oldest, Mary, was once again gravely ill, and the summons left me with no hope for the unfortunate girl.

Papa didn't expect to return till dinner-time, and from the look of hollow resignation on his face when he threw on his coat, he probably didn't expect to return home with happy news.

"But what can I do?" I asked, staring at my teacup. My letter—nicely folded and sealed—lay unwanted beside it. "I want to know where Mama is—or if she's at all well!"

"Your father forbids communication with Northwode Hall, and that's that. Now eat. See, I made you your favorite almond cakes."

I took a deep, exasperated breath. "Then I'm going there, myself!"

Dorcas sipped her tea, eyeing me above her cup. We dared each other in silence in such a manner. Duty and sympathy all at war, we questioned and challenged for several moments, and in the end, it was I who was forced to look away.

"I really am sorry, Natty," she said.

"I hope you are," I ground out. I stood up, took my letter, and left the kitchen.

I tried to post the letter, myself, but I hadn't the means—no money, no connections anywhere in Gatcombe to whom I could turn for a proper delivery. Dr. Sharpton was my greatest hope, but he never ventured as far as Havenstreet. Gatcombe, Chillerton, Blackwater, and Rookley were enough to keep him occupied, he said.

I suppose I couldn't expect the poor man to perform miracles and extend his reach well past our tiny cluster of villages. I burned my letter in the end.

Papa returned home about an hour before dinner. He seemed to have aged another decade. We said nothing to each other as I met him at the door, taking his coat and his hat from him—a task that used to be Mama's. The profound sadness in his eyes told me everything, however.

He rested a hand on one of my shoulders and gave it a comforting squeeze before walking off in the direction of the garden. I found him later sitting on one of the stone benches, gazing dully at the gathering clouds above him.

• • • •

ANOTHER WEEK PASSED, and still no word from Havenstreet. Papa's prohibitions remained, and I'd grown tired of arguing and begging. Mama could very well be ill or dead, and I'd never know.

He'd also taken care to keep me busy—fill my days with my lessons, errands, or all kinds of tasks around the vicarage—in an effort to keep me from pursuing schemes I might have regarding Mama, I was sure. He triumphed in the end because I'd be too exhausted to defy him.

I went with him to Mary Tuckett's burial and offered what comfort I could to the wretched little family. We escorted the fainting, heartbroken widow and her remaining children back to their cottage. Papa gave her solace with reassurances of her daughter's place at God's side, while I kept little Thomas and Constance occupied with stories as they held my hands tightly.

Along the way, I once again felt the ghost's presence. I gazed around me to find nothing, but the sensation was a great deal stronger than it had ever been. What surprised me, however, was my easy acceptance of the haunting.

It's dogged my steps for so long now, I've grown quite used to it, I couldn't help but think. I even managed a dry little smile at the absurdity of my situation. *Surely,* I added, *who else could boast of having such a unique traveling companion?*

Once Papa and I were back in the vicarage, however, I realized my ease must have had everything to do with the fact I had company with me. One person at my side—such as those times I enjoyed with Mr. Lovell—wouldn't have mattered. A larger group together seemed to have insulated me from the usual effects of the hauntings. There was courage in numbers, to be sure.

It even reminded me of the comfort I felt the evening of Edward's ball—after my private conversation with Mr. Lovell. The comfort of knowing there were other men out there such as us though they all might be scattered or hidden away. Had I believed myself to be alone in my preferences, I surely would have been terrified of my situation—perhaps done myself some harm.

I must also add that since the night of Edward's engagement ball, I kept the defaced miniature with me, safely hidden in one of my pockets. In its own macabre way, the miniature and its spectral protector—I continued to believe the ghost was, indeed, guarding the object—offered me the only constant during those times. The ghost appeared when and where I expected it to appear.

Your world might fall apart, it seemed to say, but never with me.

I continued dispensing my duties under Papa's guidance. I continued to feel terror at the sight of the horrid thing, regardless of its distance. I'd stopped, however, arguing with Papa about venturing out to the village with gifts from the kitchen. My former enthusiasm didn't return, but I no longer risked punishment at Papa's hands.

I took the basket or the bundle of food and sometimes drink and simply walked out the door, my gaze dully sweeping across the open area around me, searching.

There were two times when sudden defiance overcame me, and I stopped to pick up a sizable stone, which I hurled with great force at the silent figure that watched me several paces away.

"Go to the Devil, you monster!" I screamed before throwing the stone.

It did nothing, of course. The projectile simply flew right through the apparition though it retained its solid appearance. It seemed as though its body swallowed up the stone though I heard it strike the ground somewhere behind the figure. Again, the thing didn't move despite my physical attacks.

There were a few more times when I screamed at it again. If I couldn't vanquish it with stones or branches or other objects, I could at least give vent to my own contained poisons with all kinds of curses and execrations that would have caused me to be banished from Papa's house.

It simply took everything I had to throw objects and insults at it. Perhaps because of that, I walked away from the encounter with a heart that felt much more lightened than before though my body suffered some fatigue.

There was a time when I even burst out laughing at the absurd turn the hauntings seemed to have taken. Yes, I stood there, several yards from the apparition, laughing myself sick while it watched me.

In the end, all this spontaneous and violent purging seemed to help. The fear I still felt had grown more subdued—controlled, almost. I welcomed the change gladly.

In accepting the ghastly thing, I somehow found strength.

What a hideous, grotesque connection we had, but all the while, that creature—that thing—had taught me not just to check my fear of it, but also to overcome timidity and caution in favor of defiance—not be cowed by the consequences of challenging what seemed to be unbeatable.

All those were proven one day. I was on my way to see Mrs. Tuckett because I'd promised little Thomas and Constance more stories. I'd armed myself with two books from my childhood and a basket of bread and soup that Dorcas had especially made for them.

Unsurprisingly, the ghost appeared on the side of the footpath when I'd gone midway. If it tried to melt into the trees that lined the trail in order to fool me into complacency, it failed in its purpose. Against Nature in all her lush, earthy glory, the specter appeared quite stark with its unnatural shades and illogical existence.

I stopped for a moment and regarded its silent presence. Then I moved on. One foot followed the other, and before long, I was no more than twenty feet away. Then fifteen. Then ten.

I was close enough to reach out and touch it, test its solidity, discover its physical secrets. I ignored it, however, kept my gaze in the direction of the widow's cottage, and swept past it without a single glance in its direction.

It seemed to me to be no more than a tree standing near the path. The pervading sense of dread hung over me the entire time and that was something I couldn't shake off.

A heavy stillness blanketed the area. My footfalls couldn't be heard. Icy, creeping fingers lingered against my skin, and I shivered against their touch.

The debilitating, crippling fear that had once kept me in its grasp whenever a haunting took place was still there, but its effects were lessened. I don't know how far I walked past the specter, but I eventually stopped in my tracks and looked back. The area was once again deserted as before, but I felt something different. It was confidence—cautious, muted, but felt all the same.

I'd overcome something. I'd faced my walking nightmare without flinching, without turning around and running back in terror despite the steady hammering of my heart and the anxiety that reduced my breaths to shallow gasps. I didn't know how to rid myself of the thing, but I now knew I could dismiss it and reduce its power over me.

• • • •

"NO ONE IN GATCOMBE knows of what happened to your parents," Dorcas confided one afternoon.

We were once again in the kitchen. Papa and Stephen had gone off somewhere, leaving quite early in the morning and not giving Dorcas more information than that they expected to be back home by tea. I'd already seen to my tasks and couldn't sit still for two seconds together to read a book. My anxiety over Mama kept me distracted, and time didn't offer me much solace.

"Have you been talking to anyone in the village?"

She nodded, her brows slightly furrowed. She and Stephen shared my concern but were also held back by Papa's authority. "People all think your mother's gone to visit a dying relative."

"Papa told them that?" I gasped.

"They said so."

"He lied!"

"I don't think he had a choice."

Words failed me for some time. I finished my tea and was given more, and I still couldn't think of anything to say. Silence reigned for a long moment as we both drank our tea. It was a dreary repast, but I felt I needed to keep to my daily rituals in the face of my family's crisis, or I'd surely go mad.

"Natty, I—did wrong," Dorcas eventually said, her voice quavering.

I glanced up, meeting her gaze in surprise. "What is it?"

She was on the verge of tears as she stared at her teacup. "A letter from Northwode Hall arrived two days ago, and I didn't deliver it to the proper recipient."

I couldn't believe what I'd just heard. "Dorcas—why? Who's it from? Is it Mama?" I sputtered.

"Your cousin, Miss Ailesbury." Dorcas paused to dab her eyes with her apron. Refusing to look at me still, she turned to fumble around her skirts and pulled out a slightly creased letter.

"You should have given it to Papa! I don't care if he doesn't want to have anything to do with Northwode Hall! It's his letter, and he ought to have it!" I reached out and tried to snatch the letter from her.

"It's not for your father, dearest," she said, finally meeting my gaze, her eyes brimming with tears. "It's meant for you."

I stared at her both in shock and anger. "Why didn't you give it to me, then?" I cried. "You knew how desperate I've been for word from Havenstreet! How dare you? Give it here!"

She slid the letter across the table. I threw her one more look of outrage before tearing the envelope open, nearly destroying the letter in the process. I could barely read the contents. I was in such a rage and was impatient for anything other than simpering nonsense that I could only expect from Marianne. For the moment, it was all I could do to skim the letter for important details.

...vile strumpet of a mother...scandalous attachment to Sir Joseph Well- ham...hiding from good society and tainting our roof with her disgusting pres- ence...take her back to where she belongs...

Chapter 22

I knew nothing of the affair beyond what my cousin shared. Scattered bits of information were all I had, and without my Papa's help, I filled out the gaps on my own with weak guesses.

So enraptured was she by her own cleverness she thought herself above censure. Indeed, one wouldn't think, with her timidity, she'd be capable of such sordid behavior. How easily she'd managed to fool everyone—even you and your Papa, I'm sure—with such a cheap pretense to modesty.

Those were Marianne's words—a few among hundreds of angry, hateful, bitter ones that filled her letter.

Mama had been discovered at Edward's ball. Indeed, I could never forget her extreme nervousness that night. Perhaps she knew her lover was going to be present.

Lover. My stomach turned at the word.

It was Papa, Marianne claimed, who'd exposed the truth. In private company, he'd unleashed his fury, setting Mama and Sir Joseph Wellham against each other when it appeared he could no longer bear the insult of being in the same room as his wife's paramour—asking questions, leading them from one point to another till both were trapped, had no other choice but to fight their way out of the conversation.

What was Sir Joseph doing at such-and-such time? Where was he? What was Mama doing? Papa had drunk quite liberally, as had the other gentlemen that dreadful evening.

His purpose, however, had nothing to do with celebrating my cousin's upcoming nuptials. He'd meant to embarrass Mama and Sir Joseph and embarrass my aunt and uncle as well. I'd no doubt he blamed them for their complicity in the scandal.

She watches me, you know. She watches me while I'm in people's company. She watches Mr. Archer and Lord Southwell and Mr. Litton, and I've seen how greedily she devours the sight of those gentlemen whenever they engage my attention. She wishes to be me, to be young again. I suppose she wishes so pitifully to be desired the way she used to be desired, not resign herself to cold, aging remnants such as Sir Joseph.

I refused to believe my cousin's shocking accusations and disgusting slanders. Fine words, indeed, from someone who was more of a coquette and less of a lady! The hypocrisy of my cousin! I couldn't stop myself from reading her letter, however, for something—a tiny voice in my mind—urged me to continue because somewhere amid the rambling insults lay a scrap of truth.

She burst into tears—such charming fetches!—when Papa and Mama took it on themselves to intervene. Her life was wretched, she told them. She'd only made one mistake. What, did she expect to make more?

And which mistake was she referring to—Sir Joseph or your father? Her elopement as a young girl remains a blot to our family name, cousin. You don't know that, I'm sure. That she took to crawling back to Papa for forgiveness, waiting after Grandpapa died, says much about the audacity of such a person.

My family welcomed her back, and for what? So she could carry on with her vices, take advantage of my family's trust and good nature (again, how many dances and dinner-parties did she attend in the course of her reconciliation with Papa?), and begin an embarrassing flirtation with an old suitor?

She wished to die, she said—wished she were never born. What a lovely actress she'd make—a faded Ophelia, lamenting her Hamlet. But which gentleman is her true Hamlet, cousin?

The terrible confrontation took place in one of the smaller sitting rooms, with my aunt, uncle, Marianne, one of her suitors, Papa, and Sir Joseph present. They were, from what I could guess, gathered for a quiet retreat from the noise and activity. Marianne and her gentleman were to rejoin the guests once they'd sufficiently rested.

Instead of a relaxed and cheerful conversation among family and friends, they were dragged through several minutes of mortifying confessions.

Your mother claimed to have broken with Sir Joseph, very likely sometime before that evening. No one knows with any certainty, for that odious man refuses to speak about it. In fact, he denies being involved with her, but who would believe him?

He appeared to take perverse delight in adding to my family's embarrassments, insulting your father, leaving foul hints as to your mother's liberality despite his protestations of not being on intimate terms with her in the recent past. What else can we expect from such a barbarian, after all?

I never trusted the man even as a child. I blame my parents for insisting on keeping such a friendship alive because what had it brought them?

There, cousin. Have I given you enough reasons to persuade your father into taking this loathsome woman away from our hands?

I didn't know how long I sat on my bed, crying bitterly over Marianne's letter.

• • • •

PAPA RETURNED HOME for tea. I didn't wait for him to call me downstairs. I stood before my mirror, doing nothing to make myself more presentable. Seeing my reddened, swollen eyes and flushed complexion left me apathetic. I took the letter with me, however, and joined him in the parlor, where he'd taken his place in his favorite easy-chair, one of his books lying open on his lap.

He regarded me in surprise when I entered.

"What on earth happened to you?" he asked, and I gave him Marianne's letter.

The weight of the silence that followed was dreadful. After surrendering my cousin's letter, I poured myself some tea, claimed a slice of cake, and sat myself down across from Papa. I didn't spare him a glance—merely refreshed myself in silence, my gaze fixed on my food. I heard nothing from him for some time. Not even a shifting of his weight or the rustling of paper once he'd taken the letter from its envelope.

I simply waited for him to speak. He did, eventually.

"Your mother's friend, Mrs. Lydia Stanton, doesn't exist. Not anymore. Your mother confessed she died several years ago." I heard him fold the letter. "I didn't always suspect that. I'd have kept her from her travels to Ryde, Nathaniel, had I known. But when she began to insist so much on comforting her friend so frequently, I was forced to think—really think—of what might be truly happening. I trusted her, Natty. Enquiring after Mrs. Stanton behind her back was like poison to me, but I was compelled to do it. You can't imagine how I felt once I discovered the poor woman had long succumbed to her illness."

"He—Sir Joseph lives in Ryde?"

"No, he doesn't. He's not from the island, from what I was told. But, yes, they'd meet in Ryde."

I wiped my eyes against my sleeve. "You could have kept her here all the same."

"I did. You've seen it, yourself. Your mother left us for a walk after our quarrel, remember? She stopped her visits, yes, but things were never the same between us afterward."

I looked up to watch him slip the letter back in its envelope, which he set aside with frightening calm before taking another sip of his tea. "How long has she been doing this?" I listened to my words in disbelief.

Papa sighed as he set his cup in its saucer. He shook his head. "I don't know. I never thought her capable of behaving in such a way. I trusted her enough—loved her enough—to allow her those visits to Northwode Hall in the past. Remember? We'd always be invited to participate in balls and dinner-parties, but though my duties kept me behind, I'd still allow your mother every chance at enjoyment. I could see how much it meant to her to spend time with her brother and his family."

"You could have kept her home," I said, my voice breaking for all my efforts at control. "She could have understood what was really important if you tried."

He regarded me steadily. "Do you really believe that, Natty? Do you really think it would have made a difference had I intervened?"

"Yes, I do!"

"You're too young. You know nothing," he said. "I'm doing what I can right now to avoid scandal, and so are your aunt and uncle. This letter," he nodded at Marianne's missive, "undermines our efforts at discretion. Your cousin shouldn't have written. Had she stayed with us all that time, not run away before I was advised to leave, she wouldn't be tormenting you with unfounded judgments."

I blinked through my tears, tried to speak but couldn't. Papa didn't press.

"Marianne left with her gentleman before your uncle and aunt suggested I leave Cecily behind. A temporary separation was necessary, they said, and I agreed. After watching her mock our family—our marriage—by confessing to her affair with Sir Joseph—I wished for nothing but to take you as far away as I could. For us to start afresh somewhere—anywhere. But justice hardly happens, Nathaniel. Once things have settled a little, we'll have to take her back."

He watched me struggle against my emotions, our repast forgotten.

"I can't let her go, Natty. In many ways, I simply can't afford to divorce her."

"And then?"

He swallowed, his eyes deadened. "Live as we always have in the vicarage. What else is there for us to do? For now, I can only pretend I've no blood connections to anyone outside Gatcombe. It's all I can do to keep myself from going mad. It won't last, you know. Dreams and fantasies never do."

"Is it true she's broken with Sir Joseph?"

"She assures us of it. He left the house still denying anything had existed between them."

"When—when did she meet him?"

Papa moved his gaze to another point in the room. "He courted her when we were all much younger. He was a rival—one of many. After I married your mother, he found another woman and settled elsewhere."

"My aunt and uncle are to blame for this, I'm sure."

"They insist they never suspected anything amiss during her past visits to Havenstreet. I've learned to doubt them now—especially your aunt. She was your mother's constant companion all that time, and I think it impossible she never had a hand in things."

"I don't want to hear any more," I replied. My head throbbed, and I could barely breathe or see with my eyes and nose so swollen. "I'd like to finish my tea, please."

"Of course."

Nothing but thick, soul-draining silence followed. It felt like an eternity, but I finished my repast. I tried not to look at Papa when I stood up and excused myself. I didn't know how he appeared, to what extent my grief affected him. He said nothing and simply allowed me to escape. He didn't return Marianne's letter to me, but it didn't matter.

I wouldn't have wanted it back.

• • • •

DORCAS ROUSED ME FROM an unplanned but desperately needed sleep.

"It's time for dinner," she said, combing my hair from my eyes when I blinked them open. The look on her face shifted, but the shadows in my room prevented me from reading her. "You poor thing."

I raised myself up, quietly groaning from the effort. My skull felt swollen. I could barely breathe, and I was sure my eyes were half-shut. The only comfort I had was that I'd sufficiently vented when I returned to my room after tea. I was far too tired, my spirits far too depressed, for me to shed more tears again.

"I wish you left me alone," I mumbled, rubbing my eyes.

"You need to eat, dearest. Besides, your father needs to speak with you."

"I don't want to speak with him. Not at the moment, anyway."

Dorcas sighed as she brushed her skirts with her hands before walking to the door and waiting for me there. "He wants to speak with you, though. Now come along. You can have just one bowl, and I'm sure he'll allow you to leave the table afterward."

Papa waited for me in the dining room. After a quiet and awkward prayer, we began to eat, with silence pervading for some time. I could taste nothing of Dorcas' cooking. My senses were literally numbed by my earlier crying.

"Nathaniel, I think, perhaps, it would be good—considering the circumstances—for you to remove yourself from the vicarage," Papa said after a few moments. His voice was soft and gentle—quite loving, in fact. "For a few days, maybe a week or a fortnight if you're inclined."

"Where would I go? I—I don't want to go to my cousins.'"

"No, that would be unwise."

I blinked when the truth began to dawn upon me. "I can't impose on Mr. Lovell!"

"No, you can't, but—" Papa took a deep breath and tiredly added, "But he offered."

"I don't understand."

In answer, he pulled something from one of his pockets and unfolded it. It was a letter from Mr. Lovell himself, which Papa proceeded to read aloud to me.

In view of the sensitivity of your circumstances, sir, perhaps I can offer a retreat for both you and Nathaniel. A bit of distance in place and time, I think, will help. Liscombe's obscurity can provide you with much-needed space and soli-

tude—enough to inspire and encourage. Three days or a fortnight—time is of no essence.

"I can't abandon my duties in the parish, Natty. I can find someone who'll be willing to take over temporarily, yes, but that's not what I want. I prefer to keep my hours filled, but I'd like you to go. You need to be away for a little while for your sake," he said after he finished reading. He folded Mr. Lovell's letter and left it on the table beside his bowl.

"Did you write to him? Is that how he knew about Mama?" I asked, mortified. Dear God, how could I face him now?

In the dimness of our dining room, Papa looked far, far older than he was. Shrunken, wrinkled, dying inside—the only mark of his old spirit being the dull flickering of light in his eyes.

"No. I never did," he replied with a small, brittle smile.

Chapter 23

"You've Miss Ailesbury to thank, I'm afraid." Mr. Lovell's voice was gentle, yet I sensed his embarrassment. It fueled mine.

"I only hope she didn't tell everyone present that night," I said, unable to look elsewhere but at my hands on my lap. Shame was a painful, poisonous feeling. I felt as though I were being devoured alive, my insides rotting and falling away.

"If it reassures you in any way, it was to me and her brother—"

"Vincent?"

"Yes. We were in the gardens—that was nearly an hour after you left—and she came upon us there. Her spirits were agitated. She complained about your mother, which—I assumed—was her way of opening the subject. When Ailesbury asked her to stop speaking in riddles, she told us everything."

"If Vincent knows, it might be a matter of time before the rest of the Isle of Wight does," I said.

"Your cousin was too shocked and—forgive me—too embarrassed to continue the conversation. He refused to listen to any more of Miss Ailesbury's accounts."

I nodded, my face burning. "I appreciate—Papa and I appreciate your discretion, sir."

"I can assure you, Nathaniel, that proper measures have been taken to avoid a scandal. The family was forced to take me in their confidence once they discovered Miss Ailesbury's lapse in judgment." Mr. Lovell sighed tiredly. "I can't say the same regarding any gossip that might arise from this incident, but the least we can do is to prevent such talk from turning into something far more hideous than it really is."

How could he say that? My family had been shamed. Papa—a respectable man of God—turned into an object of mockery, insult, and heaven knew what else. Mama—a woman known for her piety and strength—now a blot to the family name. Once my parents recovered from the embarrassment and the pain?

We'd no choice but to live the rest of our lives as a lie before the world and before God, Papa had said. I, however, kept a tenuous hold on hope—reconciliation, forgiveness, a willingness to start over, our little family content and more devoted to each other than before. I loved Mama no more, no less, and I desperately missed her presence in the vicarage.

"Nothing can be more hideous than this, sir."

He hesitated before speaking. "Of course."

I braved a look in his direction, and he met my gaze with an uncomfortable little smile. The relief I felt being in his company again—this time alone, our connection shaped by something far more private than a mere holiday in Somerset—was difficult to describe.

I wished then I were older, that we'd crossed paths much sooner and so had developed a deeper, more sympathetic affection than what we now had. I even wished, however guiltily, I were born into privilege. Then I'd have enjoyed his friendship with greater assurance of a life spent devoted to each other.

"I'm sorry you have to be involved," I added. "Had I been you, sir, I'd have regretted my connection to the family."

"Thank heaven you aren't me, then. I regret nothing at all," he replied, his smile softening. "Especially my connection to your family."

My embarrassment took on an entirely new meaning, and my distress was temporarily forgotten. I forced myself to look out the window instead, forced my attention to the familiar discomfort of the carriage's rough progress through quiet roads that took me closer and closer to Shepley Abbey.

I also forced my attention back to the miniature I held on my lap—secure and protected from Mr. Lovell's view.

Against my damp palm and lifeless fingers it felt disconcertingly alive. I clung to it, grateful the journey to Somerset wasn't darkened by any unwanted presence.

Perhaps, I thought, the dead perceived the thoughts of the living. If I wasn't haunted throughout my journey back to Liscombe, it might be because the ghost—such a childish fancy!—somehow saw into my mind and knew my plans to return the miniature to the church where I'd first discovered it.

I'd long convinced myself simply throwing it away wouldn't have helped. I truly believed such an act would likely anger the dead, not appease it because its hauntings were attempts at making me understand that it wished to be returned to its proper place, where it shouldn't have been disturbed. I still couldn't fathom how it found its way to the island, but I did know that it remained with me for a reason I didn't understand.

I felt the gouged surface of the miniature against my fingertips. How odd, I thought, that an object with strong supernatural connections would offer me a measure of comfort and familiarity at a time of confusion and distress.

• • • •

THE FAMILY WELCOMED me to their circle with the warmth I could only expect from my superiors. Lady Lovell was indifferent, and the Hon. Richard Lovell and Miss Camilla Lovell were politely curious. Once I'd satisfied their inquiries regarding my age, Papa's occupation, and my place of residence, they thanked me and turned their attention elsewhere.

Lord Lovell, however, didn't forget me. He welcomed me back with his usual noise and bluster, shaking my hand and clapping a hand against my back with so much force that I coughed, much to his delight.

"A mere child!" he bellowed, his body shaking. "Well, you look like one. Yet here you are, alone, as though you're about to take on the world!"

"I'll be eighteen soon, my lord," I offered between coughing fits, my face burning.

"Yes, of course, you will be. I'd take you with me to my favorite lake, but the weather's been atrocious lately."

The gentleman indicated the window with a sweep of a broad hand. Outside the rain clouds gathered. Indeed, it had been gray and dreary throughout my journey, the chill winds reducing me to a shivering, blue-faced wretch despite my traveling-coat.

"I know no card games, I'm afraid."

"Card games?" he echoed with a derisive snort. "Who said anything about card games, pray? I've no interest in those! Young man, when the weather turns foul, it's always in one's best interest to read, read, read—not pass the time staring at bits of decorated hard paper!"

I stole a glance in Mr. Lovell's direction and found him busily scanning his father's shelves, running his fingers over weathered spines as he read their titles. Every so often, he'd pause and pull out a book, inspect the cover carefully, open the volume to the first few pages, and then return it to its shelf. I marveled—a good deal more than I perhaps ought to, given such an idle, mundane moment. I couldn't help myself, though.

"Yes, my lord," I said, turning my attention back to my host as he poured himself more drink. He sat back in his chair—a monstrous, puffed-up thing that looked like a giant, cushioned mouth that held Lord Lovell between its lips, ready to swallow him alive.

I took great delight in that it was only three of us in the warm, cheerful room—Lord Lovell's sanctuary. Everything seemed so far, far removed from my world that I clung to it with as much energy as I could. When Lord Lovell thought to embarrass me with blunt questions about my aspirations—both regarding work and marriage—I didn't care.

What did it matter, after all? He offered much more to me in a mere hour than the vicarage had in weeks. I took what I could get, selfishness or no.

"I wish to teach," I said in answer to his first set of questions. To his second, I replied, "I must confess to not giving it much thought. Not yet, at the very least. It's always been my desire to seek work first before considering marriage."

"Considering marriage," he chuckled, slapping a hand against his knee. "One might mistake you for choosing between occupations, young man. 'Considering marriage,' indeed."

"Papa, do stop your bullying," Mr. Lovell called from the other end of the room.

I suppressed a smile, but my host was quick to read my amusement, and he laughed despite his son's chiding.

"Well, I suppose such is the thing with young folks these days," Lord Lovell sighed, waving his free hand dismissively. "Choose, choose, choose—as though they had all the time in the world, with no thought to their obligations."

I surprised myself with my boldness that evening. "Perhaps, my lord, it would be a wise move for those who might not be in the best situation. Had I any brothers or sisters, I wouldn't be so cautious, knowing the family had other chances through them."

"And your father knows of your schemes?"

"Yes, my lord. He suggested I wait before making a decision."

"Did he now?" Lord Lovell's eyes widened, but he didn't seem offended or outraged. "A liberal gentleman, your father."

I nodded. "He is in his own way."

"You're always welcome to explore the countryside, of course," Mr. Lovell offered as he joined us, two books in hand. "I do believe an occasional walk—even in dreary weather—suits your nature far more than endless hours with your nose between the pages of a book."

"And I suppose it also suits the boy to catch something incurable out there," his father snorted before swallowing his drink in two great gulps. He proceeded to pour himself more wine.

Mr. Lovell laughed and took his place beside me. "I don't believe in such nonsense, Papa. Fresh air, however cold it is, will serve him much better than confinement."

He looked at me with a broad smile, and I couldn't help but return it.

"Should the boy take ill and die, Miles, it will be on your head."

"I'll take the blame, only because I know it will never happen."

"I'd like to see St. Bertram's church tomorrow, actually," I said. Lord Lovell blinked, looking bewildered.

"Tomorrow?" he echoed. "Good God, boy, do you wish to succumb this soon?"

"Peace of mind, my lord. That's all I've ever wanted."

Lord Lovell looked askance at me. "And you believe a walk to that pitiful pile of stones will give you that?"

"Yes, I do."

He now turned to give his son the same doubtful look.

"Miles, you really ought to choose much more promising sights for our guests. Never in my life had I expected St. Bertram's church to be referred to as a cause for someone's peace of mind."

Mr. Lovell, as always, apologized to me as he led me to my bedroom. As always, I didn't mind and tried to convince him his father gave me a much-needed respite from my current troubles.

He looked unsure at first. Then he nodded, running a hand through his hair. "You're either brave or foolish."

"I'm one more than the other," I replied, turning to face him as I stepped inside. He regarded me in silence for a moment.

"I suspect we disagree on which one it is. Good night, Nathaniel."

Chapter 24

It was strange, going back to St. Bertram's the following morning. Everything was so different now. So many things had changed in that small span of time between visits. The day was much more dismal than when I first ventured out on my own, with nothing but Mr. Lovell's instructions and untainted curiosity guiding my steps.

I also enjoyed the benefit of Mr. Lovell's company this time. Dreadful weather didn't threaten my spirits despite my strange purpose for returning to the church.

As we walked along the same footpaths I'd taken that fateful day, once upon a time, I told Mr. Lovell my reason for going back to the church. He listened patiently, his head bowed for a moment. Once I'd done, he looked at me in surprise—perhaps even worry.

"Nathaniel, do you really know what you're doing?" he asked. He might have sounded incredulous, but I sensed no judgment in his manner.

"I do, yes." I looked away and shrugged. "I don't expect you to believe me. I never have. I just—you understand me. Far more than even my parents do, perhaps—perhaps far more than they ever can. I trust you because of that."

"That's too much of an honor you give me."

"That's all I could hope for, really—to be able to confide in you, and no more." I avoided his gaze and kept mine fixed ahead. I could feel his eyes on me still. The subject had undergone a shift to one that left us both on very uncomfortable ground.

"You mean to tell me you're willing to risk so much—for us."

"I don't see how confiding in you becomes a risk—"

His voice softened. "You're exposing yourself to me—rendering yourself vulnerable to my judgments. Your secrets, your thoughts, your feelings—England doesn't want these from her children, you know. By law, our nature's an aberration."

I felt my cheeks warm. "I understand the dangers, sir. It's mad to risk my reputation and my freedom—"

"Over such a trifle."

"It isn't a trifle! You're not, and neither am I!" I retorted, turning to him and stopping in my tracks. "Perhaps to you, yes, but you can't presume to know my mind!"

He stopped as well and faced me. "Or your heart," he added, his voice dropping again. "No, I can't presume to know. I'm sorry."

"There," I said, feeling much more reckless now. "Do you still not regret knowing me?"

"You give me too many reasons not to," he replied, a sheepish little smile forming. "You've disarmed me easily enough to use your Christian name on our first meeting. I've been so liberal with it since then, and yet you never checked me for my impertinence."

"That's because I never cared." I almost added, in embarrassing detail, the pleasure I took in hearing him say my name. I opened my mouth, stopped myself, and merely dismissed everything with a rueful rubbing of a hand against the back of my neck. "We ought to move along."

"Is that it, then?"

"I don't understand."

His confidence had wavered, and he looked as though he'd shed a few years from his age with his sudden doubt. I was speaking with another boy not a day older than I—and just as confused with our situation.

"Is this all we can say about us?"

I shook my head. "I don't know what else to say."

"Do you think we could have been happy together?" he prodded gently, his complexion flushed.

"I do," I replied without a moment's hesitation and looked at him in challenge.

He nodded. "So do I."

I expected as much. I knew, however, nothing else could come of this despite our confessions, and I was right. In another moment, Mr. Lovell was once again twenty-two—a gentleman well above me in rank, experience, and knowledge, set to claim the hand of a young lady who was quite likely his best match. I simply had no place in his life of wealth and obligation.

He leaned closer and kissed me—a light pressing of mouths this time, followed by a gentle brushing of his lips against my cheek. He didn't look at me when he pulled away. He simply walked onward, and I nearly stumbled to keep abreast of him, my mind frozen in grief.

• • • •

NO ONE WAS PRESENT in the church. I didn't see the widow, but then I never expected her to be there. Something told me she never existed at all, and I shook off that wordless voice despite my inclination to believe it.

Mr. Lovell stood by the door and waited. I walked along the aisle, wondering if it mattered where I left the miniature. It was back within St. Bertram's weathered stone walls. That ought to be enough.

I chose a pew a little past the midpoint and set the miniature on the floor. I regarded it for a moment before uttering a silent prayer for the dead. I asked for peace—both for the deceased and for me. Then I hurried to rejoin my companion, who idly scanned the church's interior before taking me by my arm and leading me out.

We spoke very little on our way back to Shepley Abbey. Neither of us said a word about the ghost, but it didn't matter to me.

It's finally over, I kept thinking.

The winds had picked up. I pulled my coat more tightly around myself, and Mr. Lovell urged me to walk faster.

We hurried through the bluebell forests, the river Barle serving as our crystalline guide till we reached the Tarr Steps. Mr. Lovell walked ahead of me while I fell back a little, my attention momentarily taken hostage by the waters that flowed beneath our feet.

I stopped, contemplating the river. "Mr. Lovell, I was wondering if—" I looked up to find my companion standing still near the middle of the rocky bridge as though frozen. "Sir?" I moved forward and reached him. "Mr. Lovell, are—" My words died.

The ghost stood near the end of the Tarr Steps, blocking our way. It appeared as it had before. Silent and unmoving, this time ensuring Mr. Lovell was another witness to its ghastly existence.

"We should go back," I said, my voice shaking.

"What on earth is that thing?" he asked. Then he blinked and turned to me, wide-eyed. "Is this—"

I nodded, my spirits withering in disbelief. I couldn't be rid of it.

I couldn't be rid of it.

Surrender. That was the first thing—no, the only thing—that came to mind. I was defeated in a battle of wills for reasons I still didn't know. It was a battle of wills into which I was forced without even understanding when, how, or why it had to be so.

"You see it, too," I whispered, not once taking my eyes off it.

"I do."

I felt Mr. Lovell take my hand and envelope it in warmth, giving it a gentle, reassuring squeeze. My terror wavered, and I returned his touch. "Let's go home," I said and stepped forward, my teeth clenching. "This way."

The battle of wills continued even as we walked closer and closer to the apparition. It refused to vanish, and neither did we choose to turn back. *No,* I told myself despite my heart's desperate, wild thumping. *No, you can't win. You're dead. Gone. You belong nowhere else but the past.*

I was vaguely aware of Mr. Lovell's hand slipping off my hold. I was just as vaguely aware of my pace increasing the closer I came to the end of the ancient stone bridge. Before long, I was lightly running toward the apparition—determined, angry, and defiant. Reckless. I could lose my footing and tumble into the river, but I allowed the vile figure to direct my steps down a safe line.

I saw its face from a frighteningly close distance. I fancied I saw the eyelashes that lined its shut lids. The narrow bridge of its nose. The faint—very faint—Cupid's bow of its lips. For a brief, mad moment, I thought I recognized the dead, white face.

I pushed on and ran through it, forcing my eyes open the whole time. There was a dreadful iciness that wrapped around me as I ran onward—the remnants of a dead woman's presence. It nearly tore me apart with its painful sting, but I knew, even then, only the present mattered, not the past.

Only the living and the real, not the departed and the forgotten. I stumbled onto safe, solid ground again, nearly falling over on my knees but managing to stay upright.

I was shivering violently, my breaths coming and going in deep, wrenching gasps.

"Nathaniel, it's gone," Mr. Lovell panted, and I felt an arm wrap around my shoulders. He turned me around.

"My God. You're cold." He held my face between his hands and forced me to look at him. He was pale despite his exertions, his eyes wide as he observed me. "Here, wear this." He released me and removed his coat, throwing it around my shoulders. "Let's hurry."

Leaning against him, I half-ran, half-stumbled all the way back to his home. Somewhere along the way, I nearly broke out in hysterical laughter.

I won, I crowed silently. *I won.*

• • • •

A BLAZING FIRE AND a hot dinner were all I needed. Mr. Lovell's fears remained unrealized, thank God, and despite his anxious watch, I showed no signs of illness or emotional shock. He said nothing to his family on our return back—only that I nearly fell ill.

"I warned you, didn't I?" Lord Lovell sniffed. "But youngsters nowadays don't care to listen. Go call the doctor if the boy needs him, Miles. I daresay the fellow knows how to give obstinate sorts a good talking-to."

Mr. Lovell didn't need to call the doctor. I showed him nothing but good health and a full recovery from my earlier terror. In fact, I tried to engage him in quiet conversation about it despite his reluctance to agitate my spirits.

After dinner, he and I confined ourselves in the drawing room, where we talked till well into the night. He insisted I sit as close to the fire as possible without burning up, and I indulged him. For the most part, I engaged him with my accounts of the hauntings—from start to end. He listened, speechless with amazement and worry.

"I must confess, I find all these too difficult to believe," he said once I'd done. "Had it not been for what I saw—"

I waited for him to continue, but he seemed to be at a loss and merely shook his head in disbelief. So I prodded, "You sensed its presence—a few times, I think, while you were with me."

"I did," he echoed weakly, frowning at the fire. "Yes, yes—I remember. On the island—on one of the footpaths, I felt as though someone were following us."

"Or watching."

He nodded, still staring at the fire. "The figure in the trees—I dismissed it in my letter, didn't I? My God."

"At my cousin's ball? You felt something, didn't you?"

"Did I?" he turned a dazed glance in my direction. I briefly described the moment because it was still deeply etched in my mind. Mr. Lovell showed no signs of recognition.

"I—don't remember. I'm sorry, Nathaniel. There were too many people, too much happening around me—the only things I do remember are my talk with you and with your cousins."

I shook my head and tried to reassure him with a wan smile. "It doesn't matter. We won. We showed how little it mattered." I watched him look at me, still dazed, before nodding in vague agreement. "We conquered it," I added.

We conquered it. Those words sounded so sweet to my ears. I relished them, repeated them in my mind over and over. Something in me had awakened. Something unexpected, different—perhaps another self, hopefully one that was stronger and wiser than the one that was slowly loosening its childish hold after so many years.

We fell silent after a while, lost in our thoughts as we absorbed the remarkable events of the day.

Outside, the rains began. Every so often thunder rolled.

I stood up to stretch my limbs and then, filled with burning curiosity, walked over to the window. My body felt quite relaxed—loose. All those hours following our harrowing confrontation had drained me of tension from head to toe. The warmth and comfort of the drawing room, Mr. Lovell's company, and the onset of heavy rain outside threw me further into a state of delightful lethargy.

The windows in the drawing room faced the church ruins. I thought to take advantage of the wild weather to observe the picturesque collection of decaying stones.

Flashes of lightning ought to provide the area some dramatic illumination, I thought.

I walked up to one of the windows and took hold of the curtains. I drew them apart.

Outside the window, besieged by rain and outlined by a flash of lightning, the ghost stood about a foot away from the glass, facing me. I recognized the dead face again.

Chapter 25

"You fell back and struck your head against a chair," Mr. Lovell's voice gently pierced through the fog in my head. "Lie still and rest, Nathaniel."

My eyes fluttered open, and just as my vision cleared, the throbbing ache in my skull sharpened. I recognized the ceiling of the guest bedroom and turned to find Mr. Lovell sitting at my bedside, lines of worry marring his features. He looked as though he hadn't slept in days.

"What time is it?" I murmured. Speaking proved to be even more painful.

"It's near noon—"

"I'm sorry—"

Mr. Lovell's brows creased. "Whatever for? You stumbled backwards and hurt your head. It was an accident."

His gaze moved from my face to my hand, which lay on the coverlet. He immediately moved to cover it with his own, his thumb idly stroking my knuckles. "You were startled," he added, his voice dropping. "I heard you cry out and looked in time to see you fall. What happened, Nathaniel?"

"It was there. That—thing. I didn't win against it, Mr. Lovell. I thought I did, but—I couldn't. It won't leave me in peace. It just stood there, outside the window, looking at me through the glass."

He shook his head. "No—enough. Let's not speak of it anymore. This is agitating you unnecessarily. Be still and rest, Nathaniel. The physician's seen you and says there's nothing to be concerned about."

"What's going to happen to me?" I asked, my vision blurring with hopeless, angry tears. "I'm not going mad, sir. I'm not."

"I know. I've seen the thing myself. But that isn't a proper subject to discuss right now—not with you in this state. I desperately want to help you, but I don't know how. I—" he faltered and shrugged, a light of helplessness in his eyes. "Not while I myself can't understand everything. My own beliefs have been shaken. It's disconcerting, not having confidence in—in what I'd always held to be true. I'm sorry I can't do much more." His words withered in his throat, and he ended our conversation with a gentle squeezing of my hand.

"Thank you," I said. "You've done far more for me than you can ever imagine."

"No. No, I haven't," he replied, his manner defeated.

For a second or two, I sensed it wasn't the ghost that occupied his mind. I stared at the ceiling, wishing I had never left the vicarage.

When Mr. Lovell finally abandoned my side, I worked my battered mind into forming a proper farewell speech for my host. I resolved to return to the Isle of Wight as soon as I was able, and I was determined not to listen to Mr. Lovell's attempts at persuasion.

• • • •

TIME DRONED ON. THE minutes turned capriciously sluggish when one was incapacitated, and I was no exception. I only needed to remain in bed for a day, but it felt like ten. The weather outside improved by only a little. Mr. Lovell and an occasional servant broke the tiresome monotony of my hours, but those tended to be too brief.

In time I declared myself fit enough to venture out of the bedroom. My bath was drawn, and I washed myself thoroughly. Perhaps, I thought, being cleansed would bolster my spirits, strengthen my resolve and my confidence—an act of rebirth, almost, both physically and mentally.

The family had broken up that day because Mr. Lovell's brother and sister were expected to dine at a neighboring friend's estate. Lord Lovell hid himself from the world as he always did, and Lady Lovell took to her own sanctuary in the music room.

Mr. Lovell met me in the drawing room, and there we spent our time in quiet conversation. Nothing about the ghost was discussed though I sensed the subject hovered above us, haunted our awareness even as we lost ourselves in idle, objective chatter.

Objective, yes. Just as unwanted subjects involving the supernatural were kept at bay, so were those subjects that were, very briefly, touched upon the day before. His kiss remained with me though he might appear not to be moved by it. I should have expected no more from him.

Mr. Lovell was all politeness and good humor, but he was a little more distant in his manners. Aloof, guarded, perhaps even self-conscious—I couldn't rightly tell. It might very well be he sensed the finality of our time together. His reserve could be his way of easing both of us in the direction of what was clearly inevitable.

Had I been older—had I more experience—more wisdom—more control—I could have met his generous, considerate efforts equally. As it happened, I reverted to awkward silences more often than I wished, my heart breaking again and again despite all attempts at fortitude.

Perhaps in time, I kept telling myself, my good fortune in meeting and earning the friendship of Miles Lovell would teach me something about myself beyond what I'd already discovered. I also hoped, in time, to honor his unlooked-for companionship and affection with my struggles and even triumphs—if, indeed, triumphs were allowed men of "our kind."

When I finally found the courage to tell him what I'd carefully rehearsed in my mind during my brief convalescence, he nodded and smiled.

"I was afraid you'd resolve to leave sooner than planned," he said. "I saw it in your eyes when you first awakened. That determination of yours—I can't fight it."

I couldn't help but tease him a little. "Do you wish to fight it, though?"

He smiled, coloring a little. "No, never."

"Then there's hope for me yet."

"You'll make another gentleman very happy, Nathaniel," he said. "Someday, I'm sure of it. And it will be a very good match."

"A dangerous one, too..."

"Which makes it more worthwhile to keep, don't you agree? I can easily see you fighting for what you want—for what you deserve—and you deserve far better than the unhappiness you feel now." He gently touched my cheek with the back of his hand. "I'll never forget you, Nathaniel Wakeman."

It was with great effort I offered my hand to him.

The look on his face when he shook it in his was indecipherable. Perhaps it was best to leave it unread. I only hoped mine was painfully calm.

• • • •

I DIDN'T WRITE TO PAPA and merely traveled home without any expectations. I brought very few clothes with me, which made my solitary journey much easier to bear.

Papa had given me some money as well, and I still had enough left for a fairly comfortable ride home.

Throughout my journey, when I wasn't occupied with Mr. Lovell, I thought of the ghost. The threat hovered above my head, and I was convinced I was meant to see it again—perhaps indefinitely. None of my childhood stories offered me a solution or even comfort. None of the prayers I learned did anything for my peace of mind.

All that was left for me was time.

The vicarage was empty on my return. Papa, Stephen, and Dorcas appeared to have gone somewhere together. Seeing as how everything was clean and in its proper place, I concluded they didn't leave in a hurry.

Perhaps they were coming back later that day. With that in mind, I went upstairs and shut myself in my room and, awash in the comfort of familiarity, tumbled right into bed and slept off my exhaustion and melancholy.

Papa's voice roused me later on.

"Natty, I didn't know you were coming home so soon."

I shifted to face him and opened my eyes to a room sunk in twilight gloom. "I didn't have time to send word. I just wanted to be home."

Papa bent over me at first, but then he sighed, rubbed his temple, and sat himself down on my bed. He turned to face me despite the growing murkiness in my room. I could barely see his features.

"I—you didn't give me much time," he said, his voice heavy with exhaustion. "No, I suppose that isn't true. No one had much time. No one."

I frowned and blinked away the remnants of sleep.

"Papa, what's wrong?" I paused and glanced around the room. "Mama—has something happened to her? Why was no one here when I arrived?"

"Dorcas is in Havenstreet, yes. Stephen's downstairs. He took me back here because I needed to collect a few things before returning to Northwode Hall."

"Why?"

Papa hesitated for what felt like an eternity.

"Your mother's dead, Natty." He paused, waiting for me to respond, but I could only stare at him, stunned speechless. "She—she went to St. Agnes' church in Havenstreet and—" A slight hesitation. "She used a knife."

I still couldn't speak. I tried, but nothing came out—not even an expulsion of breath. For a moment, it seemed as though I myself had died.

"Your uncle said it happened yesterday morning. She'd fallen ill after the night of the ball and had been isolated for some time. Two or three days ago, she appeared to have recovered, everyone claimed. She behaved normally—took walks around the garden, talked, read her books though she seemed much sadder than before. No one suspected anything."

Papa's head drooped. "Then yesterday she said she wished to walk to the church and pray. No one thought anything of it, and she wasn't kept back. When she didn't return for lunch, a servant was dispatched, and she was found lying in one of the pews."

He took in a deep, tremulous breath. "She left a note, Natty—for us. She bade us farewell." With that he pulled out a crumpled piece of paper from his jacket pocket and unfolded it with trembling fingers. "I can't free us all in any other way. My poor boy, how he must despise me now," he read.

"But I don't! I never did!" I cried.

"It was my fault, Natty. I wasn't strong enough for her. I gave her reason to—"

I sat up, and he pulled me close for a tight embrace. We held each other desperately in the dark. Within seconds low, hysterical sobbing rent the calm of my bedroom.

Nothing I murmured could calm Papa. Nothing.

• • • •

THE INEVITABLE WHISPERS came, spread throughout the parish and, I was sure, beyond. Papa was regarded with a great degree of pity, Mama with darker thoughts. We bore the forced embarrassment and the taint of a suicide with as much dignity and restraint as we possibly could, our hopes fixed on the healing powers of time.

I did everything in my power to ease Papa's spirits because he continued to blame himself in so many ways. He refused to talk about my mother during those difficult times, but I often caught him speaking to her when he believed himself alone. In the garden, in the library, he'd talk to her in tones that were gentle and wistful—as though he and Mama were reliving happier moments from their distant past.

During prayers, he carried himself very well—his voice softened, having been told by Mama several times before of his tendency to pray as though he were still at the pulpit. I believed he took his strength from those prayers just as I continued to fumble with them because they never showed me the road I ought to take. Neither did they answer any of my questions, and in time, I stopped expecting so much from them.

It would take several months before I could attempt to understand Mama's heart. It would take several more before I could fully accept, forgive, and ask for forgiveness in turn.

The ghost never returned.

There was no need to, I thought because it took physical form the day we laid Mama out in her coffin, clad in her favorite dress from her younger years—a white, simple, but elegant gown—and safely cloaked in black, her hair covered. It was Papa's idea to dress her as though she were setting off to travel, for such was Death, he'd said. She used to wear the cloak when outdoors in bleak weather.

Mama had used a knife on herself—a fatal strike to her heart. I saw her only after she was washed and prepared for burial, but I couldn't keep my past and my present from merging together in her coffin. I imagined her white dress stained with blood, the red spots turning brown in time. And for a moment I believed she was about to be buried in that awful wedding-dress that Edward and Vincent had forced me to wear several years before.

What a symbol it was to me now, after everything that had happened. What a reminder!

I made myself turn away with a suppressed sob, clear my head, and resume mastery of my emotions before honoring my dead parent properly again. Through the mist of unshed tears, I looked at Mama's peaceful form one last time. Her dress was once more white—unspotted, youthful, simple. Her face was pale, her eyelids as bloodless as her lips.

"I recognize you," I whispered to the body. "You've shown yourself to me so many times."

That day at the Tarr Steps, when I challenged the specter, and for an alarming moment, I believed I recognized its face—it came back to me as I looked at her. That moment of recognition returned when I saw it outside the window of Shepley Abbey's drawing room.

Yes, there it was, all flesh and blood, lying peacefully. The memory of the widow in black who walked past me inside St. Bertram's church—yes, she looked like Mama.

She *was* my mother, dressed in mourning, both physically and literally—reaching through time to touch me with an event that had yet to happen.

The miniature? I didn't know its purpose. Perhaps it never had one; it was nothing more than an old, discarded thing in a church that somehow came into my hands with strange coincidences marking its existence. It could very well be so, but I couldn't help but think it meant something more than that.

Was the apparition a premonition? A warning? A glimpse into an inevitable tragedy? I didn't know. I never understood it, and I still don't. What wisdom and guidance could all those fireside tales of my childhood offer me now? I knew little, if not nothing, of the world outside Gatcombe. What could I have done to prevent Mama's death? I was only a boy. I'd no power to change anything. I hardly understood myself as it was. The regrets, however, nearly destroyed me.

Seeing the ghost lying in state stirred something in me because it was finally given a name and a former life. For the first time since it began haunting my steps, I pitied it—truly pitied it.

Hetty's words came back to me as though they were spoken only yesterday: *To be sure, Master Natty, I can't say where the specter comes from. Does it appear as a warning? Does it appear because the person marked for death wishes to die so badly?*

Or does it appear because whoever sees it wishes for someone else to die so badly? Sometimes desperation—if you feel it so deeply—like it's tightly wrapped around your core—turns into something quite unexpected.

I never wished Mama dead. I could come to only one conclusion, then, if Hetty's wild claims were, indeed, true.

Does it appear because the person marked for death wishes to die so badly?

Was the ghost, then, her conscience? Was I the cause of such desperate guilt since I was the only one in my family to see the specter? There were too many questions, too many uncertainties.

"All will be well, Mama. I promise you," I whispered again, and I blessed my ghost with a silent prayer, leaning close to kiss a cold forehead.

Chapter 26

Time had been kind to us. We coped, comforted each other, and eventually moved forward. Mama's absence was the only change that took place in the vicarage. Otherwise, everything was as it always had been. Stephen and Dorcas refused to leave our side, and for that I'd always be grateful. Upon them Papa and I leaned, like prodigal children just returning home, weathered and humbled. It was their loyalty—simple, modest, shaped by love—that held us together, helped sustain life in the vicarage.

Papa's alteration happened in a brief span of time.

Once the limits had been reached—or, rather, once his conscience had pieced itself together and mustered enough strength to look forward, not back—he turned into a gentler, more forgiving man.

White streaks appeared in his hair despite his relatively young age, and lines of care marked his features, giving him a sadder, more pensive appearance. His powerful frame suffered a bit of weathering as well, and he was forced to counteract his drooping posture by pushing his shoulders back and raising his chin whenever he was outside.

People often remarked about his tall, imposing manner, for he looked much prouder and statelier than everyone perhaps expected to see from a man who'd just suffered such a cruel loss.

How little they knew this regal bearing they so admired vanished once Papa was within doors. In his favorite chair, at the dinner-table, in his room—I'd catch his back and shoulders bent as though an unbearable weight continued to push down on him. Though not as often as before, he continued to speak to Mama—his tone soft, reassuring, loving—when he believed himself to be alone.

I tried, whenever I could, to approach him during these moments. "Perhaps we ought to spend time traveling somewhere," I offered. "Even if only for a week, a holiday in Brighton will do us some good."

"I'll have to consider it, Natty. For now I need to keep to my duties around the parish and here."

In time I learned to take his evasive answers to mean, "No, never."

Papa's duties around the parish never varied. Neither did mine. My education enjoyed a rebirth, in a way. For some time following Mama's death, I turned to my lessons as a means of easing the pain of her loss.

I welcomed the distraction offered by science and mathematics, literature and art. I was sure Papa was equally glad to have one more occupation to help him through difficult and dark times. In our mutual search for solace in knowledge, our energies redoubled, and I devoured my lessons as I never had before. Every so often, I'd go to Newport to search for new books for me to take home.

Sometimes Papa read them, sometimes not, but not once did he forbid me from expanding my reach. In fact, he'd grown quite liberal where my reading was concerned and always kept a respectful distance while I absorbed book after book.

My education went past my eighteenth year.

When I turned nineteen, I secured a position as a tutor to the only son of a gentleman who'd recently moved to Everleigh House—because my grandparents' estate continued to be let out—from London. It was a most desirable position for me since the distance between Gatcombe and Everleigh was practically nothing.

It would be easy for me to spend time at the vicarage and with Papa. Visits that required me to make elaborate plans for transportation and other things would never be a problem. Indeed, I could, with my employer's leave, have tea with Papa every day, if not remain at the vicarage and simply walk to Everleigh for my daily lessons.

In the end, however, I moved into my employer's great house with Papa's blessing. It was as though I'd come to reclaim my heritage even in a menial position.

"Your uncle won't like your decision," Papa warned me with a sly little grin as he sipped his drink. He'd set down my new employer's letter of offer beside his plate after reading it over dinner.

"I don't think he wishes to dissuade me," I replied with equal good humor. "Not after the letter I sent him last year. I promised him, remember, to tell him my plans when I turned eighteen?"

"I do, yes. What did you tell him?"

"That I'm resolved to follow my heart in these matters. He didn't insist as I was afraid he would, Papa. He wrote back to me and assured me if I were to change my mind, his offer of help will still be mine."

Papa nodded, wiping his mouth with his napkin as he sat back. "I'm pleased to hear that, Natty."

"It might as well end this way. I think he prefers to sever ties with us. I can't help but wonder if his offer of help was largely because of Mama and not because of any real concern for my welfare." I glanced up cautiously.

Papa watched me with a calm and thoughtful look. He said nothing in return, but I somehow suspected he agreed with me.

The last communication I received from Havenstreet was a letter from Vincent, accompanied by a small, wrapped package.

'Tis a damnable situation, cousin, and I'm sorry for it. Such is the misery that's caused by imprudence and, yes, family, for even I am feeling the suffocating weight of the marriage vow.

With the recent wretched affair that affected our families, Papa and Mama are now doubly determined to ensure a safe and happy haven for Edward, Marianne, and me. Approval from the highest levels of both parties is a requirement.

Can you believe that? I might as well go back to university and live out my days there! If I'm forced to bow and scrape and mold my preferences to the image of someone else's, I'd sooner associate the ordeal with Oxford and its moss-eaten stone carcasses than the preposterous simpering flattery of Northwode Hall.

I don't expect us to be traveling partners again. I don't even know why I thought of writing to you, given our situations and the scandal that now taints our family name.

I suppose somehow I feel I can trust you more than anyone I live with. You're not so bad for all your deficiencies, cousin. Not at all. Sometimes I wondered how things would have turned out had we changed places, and I lived in the obscurity of a murky little cottage instead.

Then again, my prejudices are too strong for me to stretch my imagination that far.

I'm enclosing a small token that I've spirited away from your mother's old bedroom. I doubt if anyone will notice its absence. Better for you to keep it safe, I thought, than allow it to languish, ignored and despised, by those she'd injured. By God, I'd make a good Christian yet.

The package contained a small portrait of my Mama.

"Miss Cecily Ailesbury, age 16," the inscription said. It was a miniature of a confident, sweetly smiling girl. Dark hair gathered in a crown of curls, pale complexion softened by a rosy blush, she met my gaze with a proud lift of her chin, poised to take on the fashionable world on her coming-out. Vincent didn't even think to take the painting out of its elegant gilt frame. I thought of writing him a letter of thanks, but his missive left me no doubt as to the finality of our severance.

As I held it in my hand, I realized the miniature—St. Bertram's miniature—had found its way back to me one final time. I understood then its other-worldly purpose, and for the second time since Mama's death, I welcomed my ghost with a kiss.

My guesses were eventually proven correct. All of my cousins married—one after another—and no one in the vicarage was told. We never received so much as a hastily scrawled note from Northwode Hall, and handed-down scraps of information were all we had—bits passed on from acquaintances who traveled between Havenstreet and Gatcombe.

The connection between us was too painful, too tainted, regardless of where the fault lay, I assumed. Papa didn't give this any further thought. In fact, he seemed to welcome it with an air of relief.

The breakup of our family was complete.

• • • •

MR. PHILLIP GOLDWYN hailed from Sheffield and was a widower and a father at twenty-five. He rose from humble but respectable beginnings and married the daughter of his late father's friend. Mrs. Goldwyn was a delicate creature who, according to her grieving husband, refused to listen to reason and insisted on having a child.

"Give me half a moment of happiness," she'd pled. "A husband and a child are all I've ever wanted." Mrs. Goldwyn died in childbirth, and her family never forgave Mr. Goldwyn for granting her wish despite knowing the risks. He was isolated, cut off. Like Papa. Like Mama.

Like my family now.

"I regret nothing, Master Wakeman," he said in that sad, gentle manner that roused a spirit of protectiveness in my breast—one that was as intense and surprising as it was sudden.

He'd inherited substantial property from his only other relative, an uncle from London whom he never knew existed. As it was, Mr. Goldwyn found the noise and filth of the city to be terrible for his son, who was born weak and sickly. He didn't care to return to Yorkshire once his new home was sold. He instead welcomed the move to Everleigh House with enthusiasm and relief.

"I'm afraid he inherited his poor mother's constitution," he said while we both watched little Phillip play with some paper boats I'd made for him. He was a small boy—underdeveloped and pale, reminding me so much of little Mary Tuckett.

"I'm very sorry for your loss, sir," I replied, meeting Mr. Goldwyn's gaze with equal self-consciousness. "But you've done quite well bringing up your son on your own."

"Yes, I suppose I have. I've grown skilled at choosing the right nurses for him. You've yet to meet Amelia, I believe. She's a good woman. Pip's long regarded her as his second mother." He paused and laughed lightly, blue eyes sparkling. "He's even asked me twice if I planned on marrying her despite our age difference of twenty years. She's older than I, you know, but never too old for Pip."

"Perhaps you'll consider marrying again, sir."

"Yes, perhaps. Perhaps."

I watched his laughter subside and took in his figure. His manners. His mind. He wasn't as worldly or as wealthy as Mr. Lovell, but in all other ways, they were equals. I wondered if those tiny sparks of hope I felt throughout the interview—fleeting glimpses of comfort and companionship whenever our eyes met—were nothing more than desperate attempts on my part to fill up that still-yawning hole left by Mr. Lovell.

Reading Mr. Goldwyn was at first confusing. His natural shyness and reserve masked far too many things, I thought, but once I was hired, small bits began to fall away, one after another. In time, doubts faded, to be replaced by cautious assurance.

Our roles served as our shields. We hid behind them whenever fear or anxiety stirred. I hoped—perhaps foolishly—those roles would someday lose their power, and we'd have nothing left for an excuse.

He'd always engage me in long conversations whenever he felt the courage, I think, and I'd gladly stay with him, no matter how tired I was, until he let me go.

Little by little, our exchanges would involve the shrinking of our physical proximity. Our growing closeness was so subtle, in fact, I'd never even noticed it till we stood, walked, or sat within touching distance, and I'd catch Mr. Goldwyn's gaze dropping to which hand of mine happened to rest closest to him with a palpable air of doubt and nervousness.

It was never one-sided, either. He'd caught me a few times staring at him too long, and I'd turn away with an awkward little sound in my throat, my face burning.

Little Phillip, at five years of age, proved to be a bright pupil though his fragile health at times hampered his progress. We both persevered, however, with Mr. Goldwyn urging us on from a discreet distance—a distance that dissolved once school hours had passed, and I was free to spend time with him when he wished for my company.

I often thought of Mr. Lovell during my hours of rest and solitude. At times I'd reread his most recent letter to me, finding much to be cheerful about whenever he shared stories of his growing family. He married Miss Thornber a few months after Mama's burial, and the lady was now big with their second child. The news didn't surprise me at all.

· · · ·

TODAY, AFTER SCHOOL, I received another letter from Mr. Lovell, and I read it in the privacy of my bedroom.

I believe there's only one true happiness, Nathaniel, but several different roads a man can take to reach it.

You might agree with me, or you might not. I think—no, I'm convinced—the happiness and contentment I feel with Roxana might be defined differently from the happiness and contentment I felt with you, but in intensity and completion, neither surpasses the other. I don't regret my choice though I do regret not knowing you sooner.

At times I wonder if things would have turned out quite differently had we met well before. Perhaps they would have, and I know I'd have gladly risked my family's affection for you. I might have proven myself a survivor, restless and wandering the world, with you by my side.

As it stands, however, Fortune has thought it a far better thing for me to glimpse what could have been mine in order to appreciate more what's inevitably laid at my feet. Perhaps it's an odd philosophy, but it's all I can manage, with my spirit torn in two and yet brimming with joy.

Someday, perhaps, I'd feel equal to the task of seeing him again as a father and husband, not an ounce of sadness edging my memories of him.

"Yes, someday," I murmured, folding the letter and hiding it in my bureau drawer.

Just outside my window, directly below it, Everleigh's garden lay spread in all directions—lush and vibrant, full of life and color. It was far humbler than the gardens at Northwode Hall, but its simple beauty and its promise of quiet comfort far exceeded my uncle's ostentatious sanctuary. Through the garden two figures strolled, enjoying a quiet, private moment together.

Mr. Goldwyn led his son by the hand and answered little Phillip's questions about anything that caught his attention. Little Phillip—or, rather, Pip—exuded so much vibrant energy despite his meager appearance. I could feel it even at a distance, even with the glass adding one more layer to my separation from them. Pip's voice was light and musical, his questions at times broken by giggles or exclamations of surprise.

The child had so long been used to the dreary, smoky confinement of London. His removal to the Isle of Wight must have come as a bit of a shock to him, and he was absorbing his new environment with a great deal of delighted wonder.

After some time, perhaps I'd be able to convince my master into an occasional ramble through the footpaths that had long become an inextricable part of my life. Yes, Pip—and Mr. Goldwyn—would adore them.

As he spoke, Mr. Goldwyn glanced up to catch me boldly staring, and he smiled. It was a familiar expression—boyishly uncertain but rich with meaning he seemed to ensure only I could understand. And, yes, I did understand. Very clearly, in fact.

I answered with my own, and from the way his shoulders sagged and his smile broadened in pleasure, I knew he'd read me correctly. We were growing used to our silent language even as we edged closer together, inch by patient, cautious inch. It was only a matter of time before the distance between us would be no more.

Pip noticed his father's distraction and looked up as well. He laughed and beckoned for me to join them.

"With pleasure," I said as I waved back though I knew the child didn't hear me. When I hurried out of my room, I paused before my mirror to inspect my clothes and my hair. The young man in the glass who returned my gaze gave me hope. I saw optimism in his eyes—optimism, determination, and strength.

Love prudently, he said, his words soundless yet loudly heard. I flicked stray hair from my face and then half-walked, half-ran in the direction of the garden.

Pip had wandered off by the time I reached Mr. Goldwyn's side, and we could hear his light voice laughing and shrieking in delight somewhere among the trees. It hardly mattered; Mr. Goldwyn waited for me in the shade, hidden and patient as always.

That familiar self-conscious little smile of his broadened to an unaffected grin when I reached him, panting. "Where are you off to?" I asked, and he shook his head.

"Nowhere," he said, his eyes fixed on mine, a soft light in them.

"I'll have to do something about that."

Mr. Goldwyn's grin eased, his gaze dropping to my hands in that familiar doubtful glance. It looked as though he took a moment to decide on something because he stared at my hands in thoughtful silence. I was about to speak when he took a quick, deep breath and reached out to take one of my hands in his.

He raised his eyes to meet mine again. I must have smiled or said something in encouragement—I can't remember now—because the look of nervousness I'd long grown used to wasn't there anymore. I saw relief and quiet, exultant joy. I moved my hand, feeling bold now, and laced our fingers together, my heart thundering in a wave of exhilaration and disbelief.

"Yes," he said quietly after another moment of silence. "You've already done something—Nathaniel—more than I'd ever hoped." He seemed almost in tears. I refused to have it, told him I'd see him smile more often, and kissed him.

Epilogue

I am now twenty-five. I continue to live in Everleigh House and continue to see Papa, who has soldiered on and flourished despite the weight of tragedy in his heart. He's never married again, but he's become a much-loved figure among the locals. Even more so than before, I believe. I tease him about being utterly spoilt by the entire island, and while he rolls his eyes and waves me off, I can see him smiling a little when he believes I'm not looking.

He still misses Mama. He'll forever miss Mama. Just as I will.

Life has long settled into quiet contentment for me and for Phillip. Young Pip's nurse has retired, sadly because of ill-health, and I've offered to look after the child in addition to being his tutor. It's proven not to be a hardship on the whole, for Pip and I've forged a strong and tight bond, and he's already met Papa. Phillip has, as well.

Papa adores them both, especially little Pip, who's become a regular visitor to the vicarage and continues to ensure that Papa stays quite fit by taking him out for longish walks.

Much to Papa's delight, of course. Pip's companionship allows him another chance at being a father again, I suppose—or perhaps a grandfather in a way. I do know little Pip often comes back to me grinning and endlessly talking about new fanciful stories about the island Papa's just shared with him.

As for me and Phillip and Papa, well...

I don't think Papa suspects a thing as Phillip and I have been extremely discreet—not to mention retiring. I suppose it helps that the rest of the community hereabouts knows about the gentleman's situation, and they've been quite respectful of his need for solitude and quiet. I've also taken great care in keeping busybodies out of his business, and I suppose it helps that they respect me and Papa far too much to push and have accepted Phillip as their resident "heartbroken gentleman widower".

People do love a tragedy, don't they? Particularly a romantic one.

Pip might never be fully healthy, but he's vastly improved as well and has displayed a surprising turn for the artistic. Heaven knows how many old books he's ruined with childish drawings along the margins. His poor father's been obliged to spend a good deal of money on drawing books and pencils for the boy before Pip completely destroys the library.

"Nobody from either of his parents' side has a drop of artistic blood in them," Phillip once said to me as we lay in bed, naked and holding each other close.

"Then we must take care to nurture it in him," I replied, smiling against his damp skin while he gently ran his fingers through my tousled hair.

And we have. We continue to do so.

The three of us have now become fixtures in the sprawling woodlands, with Pip dictating where he wishes to settle himself for an hour or so spent in drawing or painting. Phillip and I always bring a basket of food as well as books, and in the soft shadows of the canopies above and surrounded by glorious springtime colors, we sit and indulge.

We turn into creatures of two worlds, of mortals and their incongruous experiences and of the less understood and shadow-laced world of magic and superstition.

Indeed, on one such beautiful day, Phillip and I exchanged whispered vows to each other, including lockets containing our hair tied together as one. Our union might never be avowed by man or any religion, but before Nature and infinity, it was blessed a thousand times over. And that was enough for us.

Surrounded by glorious springtime colors, we now live and love in hushed companionship. For all the silence and the obscurity of our world, however, we become greater than Gatcombe. Greater than the Isle of Wight. Greater than England and her wretched, suffocating laws. Our love transcends the limits of ordinary mortals, easily shifts into magic and all that's beyond.

And we become fairies of the flowers and the wood.

Don't miss out!

Visit the website below and you can sign up to receive emails whenever Hayden Thorne publishes a new book. There's no charge and no obligation.

https://books2read.com/r/B-A-LFQC-KBSX

BOOKS 2 READ

Connecting independent readers to independent writers.

About the Author

I've lived most of my life in the San Francisco Bay Area though I wasn't born there (or, indeed, the USA). I'm married with no kids and three cats.

I started off as a writer of gay young adult fiction, specializing in contemporary fantasy, historical fantasy, and historical genres. My books ranged from a superhero fantasy series to reworked and original folktales to Victorian ghost fiction.

I've since expanded to gay New Adult fiction, which reflects similar themes as my YA books and varies considerably in terms of romantic and sexual content.

While I've published with a small press in the past, I now self-publish my books. Please visit my site for exclusive sales and publishing updates.

Read more at https://haydenthorne.com.